This is just one of my Fathers books. He took great pride writing them. I hope you Like Westerns. I wish he was here to Sign it, But you will have to settle for his daughter.

Leanna Gay Wingfield

The Tarnished Texan

by
Don Wingfield

1663 Liberty Drive, Suite 200
Bloomington, Indiana 47403
(800) 839-8640
www.AuthorHouse.com

First published by AuthorHouse 03/16/05

ISBN: 1-4208-3603-X (sc)

Printed in the United States of America
Bloomington, Indiana

This book is printed on acid-free paper.

Chapter 1

Sara and Thomas Durham were standing in the lobby of their new bank admiring the huge building that replaced a small wood framed structure that left them no room for growth and was slowly becoming an eye sore.

It was one of the first brick banks west of the Mississippi River and Thomas Durham was very proud of it. It had the most modern safe ever built. It was shipped all the way from Boston. They placed it on the lower floor of the two-story building, along with the teller's cages and other banking facilities.

On the second floor they had built four office spaces that they rented out before the new bank was even completed. There was a lawyer's office, a medical doctor's office, a dental office and an apothecary shop. They all represented the future and would contribute to the growth of the town.

The apothecary shop was located between the lawyer's office and the doctor's office. Their drugs were as up to date with the latest formulas as there could be in the mist of the nineteenth century.

Most people seemed to fall back on the old remedies like starve a cold, and feed a fever or vice-versa. These remedies seemed to stay with the older people who had little knowledge of the medical field and really didn't care that much on how far technology had advanced.

Doctor Robert Dewberry, who was very young for his profession, had come all the way from Boston, Massachusetts to accept the position of medical doctor for the town. He opened his office over the bank because of its central location and the fact that the bank gave him a lot of unpaid advertisement.

His work kept him from going to the church socials, or town meetings, or any type functions where the people gathered to spread the local gossip, so Doctor Dewberry had to rely on his patients to keep him informed of the odd things going on in his community.

He had noticed that his landlord had a very pretty daughter named Hannah. She was in her last year of high school and she spent most of her time working in the bank. Robert took a liking to the banker's daughter right away, he was hoping to be officially introduced to her in the near future. He wished she would show some interest in the medical field because he could use a pretty nurse to aid him with all the office work that he had to put up with on a day by day basis.

Then there was Frank Spencer who rented an office on the second floor of the bank to set up his law practice. He was one of two lawyers that practiced in Abilene. The rush for legal advice hadn't reached Frank's office yet, so he wasn't overwhelmed with any legal problems at the moment. He and his father needed to reduce the cost of their overhead, so they shared one office together. Frank Spencer, the lawyer, was also known as a gambler. Some say he could bluff a losing hand into a winning hand just by convincing other players how good his hand was before he ever drew another card. Then, he always improved on his hand after the draw if you believed everything he said. The other poker players had never figured out when Frank was bluffing or when he really had the winning hand. It was not unusual for Frank to win more money at the poker table every month than he made at his legal work.

The doctor and the lawyer had such different personalities. The doctor was shy and well mannered, while the lawyer was debonair and very friendly with the women. They both seemed to have noticed that the banker's daughter was growing into a beautiful young lady.

The town of Abilene had one of the largest ranger stations in west Texas. It was built next to the Durham

National Bank and Thomas Durham looked at the ranger station as added security for his bank.

Thomas Durham always welcomed the head of the rangers, Captain Keith Benson, into his bank for a cup of coffee, or anything else for that matter. Thomas Durham wanted the customers to see the ranger walking around in the bank. It helped to make the investors feel their money was much safer.

Hannah Durham had always had a crush on Brady Wells, a half-breed boy whose mother had been kidnapped and raped by an Apache warrior over nineteen years ago. Marge Wells, Brady's mother, had given birth to him after she was forced to marry an Apache warrior who went by the name of Nomi.

The Apaches treated Marge Wells like a slave until she became pregnant with her half-breed child. After the Apache Nomi was killed in a raid on a wagon train the women of the tribe would have nothing to do with the white woman and her half-breed son.

A year after Marge Wells gave birth to her child, the army raided the Apache village and rescued all the white captives. After Marge Wells was rescued she managed to get her hands on a doctor's scalpel and committed suicide by cutting her wrist.

The Fifth Cavalry chose to keep the male child as a military dependent. He became a child that was raised by anyone assigned to Fort Abilene. He grew up to be a six foot three teenager that could compete with any grown man.

Every year on St. Patrick's day, they held a contest in town to determine the best all around wrangler. Everyone was invited to participate or watch the competition. In order to win, a cowboy had to be the best at riding, shooting and roping. Participants paid to compete in these events and the winner took all the entrance money in each event. During these activities, the women held a pie-eating contest for all the men in town, the money went to benefit the women's movement. The last two years Brady Wells had won every event in the contest except for the pie-eating contest and Billy Ray Baxter always won that competition. This year had been no different.

Sara and Thomas Durham noticed how their daughter looked at Brady Wells during all the events. She acted as if he was crowned the king of Texas and not just the winner of the local contest. This worried Thomas Durham because he wanted the best for his daughter and he felt that Brady Wells would never make anything of himself. Thomas Durham wanted his daughter to grow up as a society woman, and to marry a man that was from a high society family that could keep her in the life style that was worthy of a banker's daughter.

Seemed like every time Hannah got close to Brady Wells, she became a cow-eyed schoolgirl that had no sense.

Thomas Durham knew he had to get his daughter in a girl's school back east before she did something stupid like fall in love with this half-breed who had no family ties at all.

The soldiers at the fort felt that Brady had the makings of a ranger and as soon as he was old enough, he would join up with the rangers and ride the lawman's trail. But around that same time Brady's thoughts turned to horses.

No one ever understood why Brady liked working at the blacksmith shop. He had learned to shoe a horse faster than the smithy himself. He knew more about horses than any man at the fort and for those reasons some thought Brady might become a Veterinarian.

Hannah ran up to her parents and bragged about the events that Brady had won. She was so proud that she asked her parents if she could invite Brady home for supper.

"Hannah," her father said. "We need to sit down and have a talk about you and Brady. There are things you don't understand."

"Birds and the bee stuff, right Dad?" Hannah said jokingly, as she ran in the direction of the big stage that the soldiers had built for the dance later in the day.

Brady was standing on the stage along with Billy Ray and the judges. The band was sitting in chairs placed next to the stage and they gave out a loud blast of sound as the judge called out for silence.

The judge praised Billy Ray Baxter for his ability to eat more pie than any kid in town and handed him two dollars of the prize money.

Then the judge called Brady Wells over and praised him for a job well done. He explained that for the first time the prize money totaled over fifty dollars. "What are you going to do with all this money?" the judge asked.

"Don't rightly know at this moment," Brady said. "Got so many things that need to be done that I just don't know where I'm going to start."

The crowd clapped and waited for Brady to leave the stage before they returned to their activities. Hannah came running up to Brady and gave him a hug. "You're the greatest," Hannah said. "No one can come close to you in any kind of competition."

Brady felt his chest swell because he had always liked Hannah. He felt that one day they would get married and raise a bunch of kids. He liked being around her, talking to her and she gave him goose bumps every time she touched him for any reason.

"Hey Brady," a voice said from behind him. "You sure were something out there today. You ride like the wind and can shoot the eye out of a buzzard flying in the sky. Reminds me of my younger days."

"Hello Graven," Brady said as he recognized the old bearded man that had walked up leading his mule. "Where've you been lately? We don't get to see much of you any more."

"I've been in Colorado searching for gold," Graven said. "Ran out of money and no one would back me in my diggings so I had to shut down and come back and try to find me another backer."

"Did you find any signs of gold while you were gone?" Brady asked.

"You bet we did," Graven said. "I was about to hit the mother lode when my food and water gave out. Flossy, my mule, could smell the gold and she didn't want to leave neither. But we couldn't stay and take a chance on starving to death."

"That's a shame," Brady said. "Maybe you might get the chance to go back and strike it rich one day."

"I will if I can find me a backer," Graven said. "I feel if a person would take a chance on me I could make him a rich man one day."

"How much money would this backer have to have?" Brady asked.

"I could get back to my diggings and go to work for about fifteen dollars of that money you won today," Graven said. "That much money could last me long enough to find the mother lode."

Brady laughed and counted out the fifteen dollars and handed it to the old timer. "You take this money and get back to those diggings."

Graven grabbed the money and shoved it into his britches pocket. "You won't regret this I promise you. No sir, I'm going to make you a rich man one day." Graven was still muttering as he led his mule off toward the main street of Abilene.

"You're one gullible guy Brady," Hannah said. "That old man's a drunk and he's headed for the first saloon he can find."

"That old man is a dreamer and he needs that dream to keep him going," Brady said. "I won that money and if it'll help that old man find some happiness, then so be it."

"I believe that's why I like you so much," Hannah said, as she took Brady's hand and led him over to the stage where the dancing was getting ready to take place.

Amazingly the St Patrick's Day celebration went without any problems between the army and the civilians. The two elements seemed to mix very well even though the civilian men felt that the army was moving in on their hometown girls.

By midnight, the streets of Abilene were empty and the soldiers were headed back to Fort Abilene. Brady was among the soldiers and he was asked if he would like to come back to town the next morning. The soldiers were to picked up the mail along with the army payroll and escort it back to the fort. Brady was always ready to come to town where he might get to see Hannah again.

The next morning found Lieutenant Josh Davis and Sergeant Patrick McKinley waiting in front of the main gate for Brady to arrive. "Sergeant McKinley," the lieutenant yelled. "Brady was informed of the time we were leaving?"

"Yes, sir," Sergeant McKinley answered. "I believe he's coming now, sir.

"This mail run is to start for town in ten minutes with or without Brady Wells," the lieutenant said.

They watched the mess hall door open and someone come running out. He mounted his horse and rode toward the two soldiers. The fort's mail wagon was standing by waiting orders.

"Hi, gentlemen," Brady said. "I'm not late am I?"

The lieutenant just shook his head and turned his horse toward the open gate. Sergeant McKinley and Brady followed along behind the mail wagon talking about yesterday's celebration.

The ride to town was a pleasant one and Sergeant McKinley made Brady promise that he wouldn't get into any trouble in town. Brady promised he would be on his best behavior.

Hannah would be in school so Brady would go to Hank's Saloon to get one of his cool drinks. Old Hank had a way of keeping his drinks cool for the cowboys that came in hot off the range.

The saloon was small and handled mostly hometown traffic. So when Brady entered the saloon he walked to the far end of the bar and ordered a sarsaparilla. The bartender recognized Brady and pulled a sarsaparilla out from under the bar.

This caught the attention of a drunken loudmouth cowboy that was standing at the other end of the bar with another hard case. They both looked like they had just come off a month long cattle drive except for the way they wore their gun belts. Their guns were hanging low on their hips and the scabbards were tied down to their leg.

The silent one had a scar on his face that ran from his left ear lobe to his chin. He had a void in his eyes that carried the look of death.

The loudmouth cowboy took a big swig of his whiskey and washed it down with a glass of beer. "Hey boy, are you old enough to be drinking with us men?"

"We don't need any trouble in here," the bartender said. "Let the boy have his drink and he'll be on his way. He didn't come in here looking for trouble."

"Are you his mama?" the loudmouth cowboy asked, as he slammed his drink down on the bar and told the bartender to give him another.

The scar-faced cowboy smiled showing broken yellow teeth and said in a joking manner, "Reckon you can handle this big, old ruffian? He looks like he might wet his pants if you scare him bad enough." Then he slung his head back and let out a loud burst of laughter.

"He's wearing a gun just like the big boys," the loudmouth said, as he took his partners lead and started laughing also.

The loudmouth cowboy didn't see the fist coming. It landed squarely on his nose, breaking gristle and spraying blood in every direction. As the loudmouth cowboy grabbed for his nose he was slammed with a one-two punch in the mid-section doubling him in half. Then a right upper cut lifted the loudmouth off the floor and hurled him back across a table where his weight caused the table to smash into small pieces leaving the cowboy laying on the floor in a state of unconsciousness.

"You handle yourself pretty good with your fist sonny-boy," the scar-face cowboy said, as he stood away from the bar in a fast draw stance. His arms and legs were bent and ready for action, "Now you have ten seconds to say your prayers before you meet your maker."

Brady watched the deadly eyes of the scar-face cowboy waiting for him to make his move and when he did reach for his gun, like magic, Brady's gun jumped into his hand.

The dead look in the scar-faced cowboy's eyes had turned to fear. He hadn't even cleared leather when he was looking down the barrel of a Star-Double Action Army .44 already cocked and ready to fire.

You could hear the silence in the saloon as everyone held their breath waiting for the young cowboy's gun to erupt. But much to their surprise, the young cowboy smiled and said in a loud voice, “Bang! You’re dead.”

The scar-faced cowboy froze against the bar, eyes wide open, fear showing all over his body when a dark spot formed on the cowboy’s pants between his legs. The dark spot spread down his pants legs.

Brady laughed as he pointed to the wet spot on the scar-faced cowboy’s pants. Then Brady walked to the bar and finished his sarsaparilla, thanked the bartender, holstered his gun and walked out of the saloon.

He saw the lieutenant and the sergeant leading the mail wagon in his direction, so Brady mounted his horse and rode out into the street to meet them.

Lieutenant Davis looked at Brady and said, “I hope you stayed out of trouble today.”

Brady answered in a low soft voice; “There’s no way a fellow could get in trouble drinking a sarsaparilla in Hank’s Saloon in the middle of the day.”

The men rode slowly out of town with the sergeant asking Brady if he was interested in the offer Captain Benson had made about him joining the rangers.

“I’m thinking about it,” Brady said. “Right now I need to get my education finished just in case I might want to become something other than a ranger.”

The sun was setting when the men reached the fort. Brady left the soldiers in front of the headquarters building and went to the mess hall to fill his empty stomach.

There were some stragglers left in the mess hall but most of the tables were empty, Brady went through the chow line picking up a large steak with mashed potatoes and red beans. Then he went to a table to eat.

Captain William Moss walked over and sat down at the table with him. He had a cup of coffee in his hand and he seemed to be worried about something.

"Hello Brady," Captain Moss said. "A wagon train pulled in today. They had trouble at Mead's Crossing along the Rio Grande River. They lost some horses and two men were killed. They figured it was a small band of Apache warriors that attacked their wagon train."

"Sounds like Naiche," Brady said, as he took another bite of his steak. "There's going to be many more raids if Naiche can get his hands on a few more horses and weapons."

"I've been ordered to track down Naiche and his band of raiders," Captain Moss said. "The general wants to put a stop to his raiding along the Mexican border."

"That's a tall order," Brady said "The Apache have so many places to hide and strike from around that area, especially along the Rio Grande."

"Sergeant McKinley says that you've tracked down Naiche before. He said you did it when the scouts were teaching you to read sign. Is that true?" the captain asked.

"Tracking Naiche is like tracking a squirrel across the forest," Brady said. "You might find a sign or you might even see him from a distance but to actually catch him would take a lot of luck.

"Would you be willing to try and track him down again?" the captain asked.

"Most people refer to my talents as the half-breed tendencies," Brady said. "Anything I do can be related to my Indian father or my white mother."

"I certainly didn't mean to give you that impression," the captain said. "I just feel like I'll be moving blindly around the desert. I'll need some good eyes and as young as you are you're still the best tracker in camp."

Brady pushed away his tin tray and leaned back in his chair. "Captain Moss, you have a duty to your soldiers, your country and to yourself," Brady said. "That duty is to serve this country as best as you can and if I can help you do that, then I'll become an army scout."

"Thanks, Brady. I'll still have to talk it over with the commander," Captain Moss said. "I don't think he'll be comfortable with a young civilian placing his life in danger for the sake of the army."

"Old Iron Pants ain't going to stop at a chance of getting Naiche for any reason," Brady said, as he stood up and walked out of the mess hall with the captain.

As they entered the headquarters' building the sergeant at the desk stood and saluted the captain. Captain Moss returned the salute and asked for an audience with the general. The sergeant went to the door of General Oliver Hamilton's office and knocked.

"Door's open," the voice from within said.

The sergeant held the door open as Captain Moss and Brady entered the general's office.

"Sir," Captain Moss said, as he saluted the general. "Requesting an audience, sir."

The general returned the salute and looked over at Brady. "What're you doing in my office at this time of the night? Are you in trouble again?"

"Sir, Brady is here at my request," Captain Moss explained. "I was hoping to get permission to take him with us to help track down Naiche and his warriors."

"You're asking for permission to take a boy out on patrol?" The general said, as he stood up and walked to the front of his desk picking up his corncob pipe and stuffing it with tobacco.

"Sir, if you'll look again you'll find a nineteen year old man that stands six foot three and weighs over two hundred pounds," the captain said. "He's the best shot on post and the best scout too. Every soldier on the post has had a hand in training him. He's familiar with military tactics and I'll personally see to his safety."

"You've grown up right under my eyes and I've been blind about it," the general said. "What's your feelings about all this Brady?"

"I would like to give it a try," Brady said. "I would like to see if I'm ready to take on my grown up responsibilities."

"This mission, if successful, will help keep the border of Mexico and Texas safe for those that will be moving west for the gold strikes," the general said. "I have a feeling that you're ready for any assigned responsibilities. I'm going to okay the request for your enlistment as an army scout just for this mission."

Captain Moss stood at attention and saluted the general. "Thank you sir. I'll see that Brady gets a lot of help and the Fifth Cavalry will make sure his safety is a priority."

"You do that captain," the general said, as he returned the salute.

Captain Moss and Brady left the orderly room and headed for the officers' barracks. Brady had a room there even though he had never joined the military. Captain Moss had a room next to Brady and the two had become good friends even though Captain Moss was more like a brother to Brady.

"Check out what you need from the supply room and make sure you check your equipment yourself," Captain Moss said. "We'll leave the first thing Monday morning."

"That gives me two days to say my good-byes," Brady said, as he walked into his room shutting the door behind him.

Brady had always been a loner, but tonight he felt more alone than usual. He had no one to turn to when he felt this way. He had never minded being alone before, but tonight he wished he could go to someone and talk about his feelings. He had always wondered which half of him was in control when he felt this way. The Indian or the white man. Neither seemed to get along very well in side of his body.

Sleep came late that night as Brady let his feelings control his mind until exhaustion took over and forced him to sleep.

The bugle sounded before the sun had shone its face and Brady was still struggling with his sleep. He could hear all the solders scurrying around and he knew if he didn't get up soon, he would miss his breakfast and he couldn't do that because it was his favorite meal.

Climbing out of bed, Brady looked into the mirror that was hanging on the wall and he looked just like he felt, weak from the lack of sleep. He washed his face and combed his hair as fast as he could so he could make it to the mess hall before Sergeant Burke closed and locked the doors.

His tray could hardly hold all the food he had stacked on it. Pancakes, grits, eggs, sausage, and anything else he could pile on. He buried all this under hot maple syrup and washed it down with black coffee.

The fort was showing signs of anxiety as "Baker Troop" was preparing for their scouting trip into Apache territory.

They would be tracking down Mescalero Apache using some volunteer Apaches as scouts. Captain Moss had no confidence in these untested Apache Indian scouts. He had been ordered to attack whatever hostile Indians they might find and to get Naiche at any cost. These Apache scouts had once lived and fought with Naiche and when it came to battle who would they fight for?

There was a commotion at the gate and Brady ran to see what was going on. A stagecoach was approaching fast. There was a band of Mescaleros close behind them.

The fort's gate was opened as the Indians started slowing down their chase and soon stopped to watch the stagecoach disappear behind the fort's huge gate.

The stagecoach had a half-dead cowboy at the reigns. He had knelt down in the front of the driver's seat to protect himself from the warriors' bullets as he guided the stagecoach to the fort. Some of the local soldiers grabbed the lead horses and pulled the stagecoach to a halt.

Inside were five dead passengers and up in the drivers seat next to the cowboy, they found the dead stagecoach driver. The cowboy who drove the stagecoach into the fort was loosing a lot of blood as the soldiers lifted him down from the stagecoach and rushed him to the post doctor.

There was only two people left alive inside the stagecoach, Lieutenant Walter Stewart and Corporal Benjamin Black, both of "Charlie Troop", who had been expected back at the fort over a week ago.

The parade ground was filling up with soldiers and their families all wanting to know what had happened to the rest of "Charlie Troop".

The general stood on the headquarters porch observing everything that was going on outside. He asked the orderly to bring the soldiers to him as soon as they were examined and determined to be okay.

The white settlers were never able to let their guard down while renegade Apaches were known to strike with increasing frequency. Some of the problems were Indian agents who permitted Apaches to leave their reservations to murder and steal then return to the reservation for food and water or medical care if they needed it.

It was up to the soldiers to smoke out the bad Indian agents and to get rid of them before a larger uprising could take place.

Along the Texas and Mexican border the army didn't want to depend entirely on Apache scouts so they turned to an extraordinary unit known as the Seminole-Negroes. They were descendents of run away slaves and were forced west by the U.S. Government. Some of these Negroes had become scouts for the army.

Brady had already grown friendly with Alvin Simpson who had attached himself to Fort Abilene over a year ago. He had proved himself as one of the best scouts and Indian interpreters in all of Texas. He was scheduled to go on the hunt for Naiche and his warriors along with the Apache scouts. Brady felt this to be a strange development unless the general felt the Apache scouts might remain faithful to Naiche and his outlaw band of warriors if a show down did occur.

After talking to the survivors the general found out that "Charlie Troop" had been ambushed along the Mexican border and all the soldiers were killed except for Lieutenant Stewart and Sergeant Black.

The renegades had attacked some ranches and left their sign so they could be followed by the army troops. It was their way of sitting up more ambushes to kill as many soldiers as they could. They needed their horses, rifles and ammunition. Their trick had worked against "Charlie Troop."

General Oliver Hamilton passed the story on to Captain Moss and his troops so they would be aware of the tactics the Apache renegades were using.

The weekend seemed to have passed by quickly when a bugle wakened Brady long before the sun was ready to make its appearance. The army post came alive with activity and men getting ready for the long ride to the Mexican border.

Breakfast was eaten, horses watered and saddled, and wagons for carrying provisions for twenty-five troopers over a month's period of time were hitched and ready for the long march into Indian Territory.

Brady found himself caught up in the excitement of the time as he saddled his horse and made himself ready for the hunt.

The soldiers gathered on the parade field and Brady found himself side by side with Alvin Simpson, the best Indian scout Brady had ever known. Brady got most of his scouting information from this black man because he knew so much about the Apache Indian.

Captain Moss was in charge of this mission as he rode among the troops checking to see if all was ready for the march. A pair of mules pulled a small howitzer, followed by the ammunition wagon and mess wagon.

Everything seemed to be in place as the captain yelled out the order to march. He sat on his horse watching the column move out of the fort into the barren land of southwest Texas hoping that these men weren't marching to their deaths.

Chapter 2

Alvin Simpson pointed out the plants that grew in this vast arid land. Plants that served the apache with their basic needs of water, food and medicine and kept them alive when they had nothing else to survive on.

This part of the country was known as the most rugged, untamed territory in the United States. There was nothing that the white man could exist on but the apaches had learned to survive and even flourish in this land.

The scouts rode ahead serving as the eyes of the soldiers while the troops followed far behind. The movement of the troops was slow because the country was rough-hewn, unleveled and the horses had to climb up and down steep rocks that covered this rough terrain.

Rivers that flowed through this area thousands of years ago were now filled with giant saguaro cacti that were growing in the depth of the canyons.

Alvin Simpson showed Brady the Mescal plants that the apache used for food and liquor. The nomadic apache had neither property nor permanent settlements of any kind.

They roamed about the country like coyotes and found shelter whenever there was a need for it.

The apache knew every foot of this territory and could endure without food or water for long periods of time. The fruit of the Cholla Cactus was a source of moisture and seemed to give the apache more energy. The fruit of the Spanish Bayonet Yucca was also a major food source for the apache and helped to keep him alive for long periods of time.

Brady was taking in everything Alvin was pointing out. He also skirted the surrounding area with his eyes looking for any movement in the rocky terrain. The army had been moving for three days now and there had been no sign of any Indians, let alone stray apaches.

Alvin Simpson pulled his horse to a stand still and pointed toward a gust of smoke that was winding itself upward toward the sky. It was a small, almost unseen streak in the sky that blended in with the hazy overcast. Only someone with a good eye could've spotted it. "That smoke spells trouble for someone," Alvin said, as he strained his eyes to guess the distance to the smoke. "It's at least a days ride from here."

Brady turned his horse around and rode back to the column of soldiers. He pointed out the stream of smoke to Captain Moss.

"Old man Reed's place," the captain said. "He has a wife and two boys that stay to themselves, never bothered anyone."

"It's their stock that the Apaches are after," Brady said. "They'll move the stock back across the Rio Grande to their Mexican quarters to feed their people for as long as the cattle will last."

"Nothing we can do about that, is there?" Captain Moss asked.

"Depends on how hard you want to push your soldiers," Brady said. "The Rio Grande must be flowing very hard right now. The snow was heavy in the mountains this winter and the run off is keeping the river flowing pretty fast."

"Do you have an idea?" Captain Moss asked.

"I can talk it over with Alvin and get his opinion," Brady said. "But I feel we can get to the first crossing in the river before the Apaches can. We may not get Naiche but we can slow down the Apache food supply."

The captain shook his head in the affirmative and Brady kicked his horse into motion and rode back to where Alvin Simpson was standing watch.

The two men talked of the advantages and disadvantages of this kind of ambush and decided they would take the chance of getting to the river crossing before the Apaches.

The troopers rode the rest of the day and through the night stopping only for the horses to get a breather and to rinse their mouths with what little water they had left in their canteens. When the sun came up Alvin and Brady could see the winding river in front of them.

Alvin rode ahead to find a safe place to hide the troopers while they waited for the Apaches to arrive with the stolen cattle. The army wagons would remain out of sight and away from the river.

Brady rode back to the column to tell them they had sighted the river and the best place for a crossing. They had to make their plans because no one knew how much time they had before the Apaches would arrive.

"There could be as many as fifteen Apache or as little as five, depending on what ranches were left for the Apaches to raid." Brady explained all this to the captain. "We need to prepare for the worst."

Captain Moss split up his troop into two groups. He sent half of his troop across the Rio Grande to hide among the poplar trees that grew along the riverbank. He put Lieutenant Josh Davis in charge of that group and gave orders not to fire until they had the Indians in the water where they had less of a chance to escape.

Captain Moss hid the second group behind the tall boulders that lay along the northern side of the river. Then he rode along the riverbank to make sure the soldiers were completely out of sight. Alvin and Brady rode up the trail to see if they could find out from what direction that the Apaches would be arriving.

The sun was starting to get hot and the soldiers appreciated the shade of the poplar trees and the shadow of the boulders to keep the sun from bearing directly down on them. The sun had moved farther to the west when Captain Moss saw his two scouts returning from the north.

"They're coming from the northeast," Alvin Simpson said. "Looks like about fifty head of cattle with five Apaches driving them."

Captain Moss signaled his men across the river to get ready. Then he spread his soldiers on the north side of the river to a position that would allow a clear shot at the Apaches when they crossed the river.

Then the rebellious sound of the cattle filled the air. The herd was getting closer and the Indians could be seen swinging their ropes over their heads while directing the cattle toward the shallowest part of the river. The dust was blinding and the soldiers wondered if the dust would hide the Apaches from their sights.

One of the Indians rode up to the shallow spot just in front of the hidden soldiers. He looked around and let out a screeching yell that caused goose bumps to run up and down the soldier's spine.

The soldiers lay still and didn't make any movement. They knew any form of motion could give away their position and let the Apaches escape.

Then the Indians made their move and started the cattle across the river. One Indian took the lead and rode across the river first to show the rivers depth and to lead the herd as the rest of the Indians drove the herd across. When the last cow had entered the river, the other Indians rode into the water and that was the signal for the troopers to open fire.

Alvin Simpson had his eyes on the one Indian that had already crossed the river. When the shooting started Alvin pulled the trigger of his Henry .44 rifle and the lone Indian fell from his horse. The firing of weapons seemed to have just started before the captain gave the signal to cease-fire.

The gunshots caused some of the cattle to stampede across the river into Mexico. Captain Moss felt the cattle needed to be rounded up and brought back to the Texas side.

He assigned some troopers to hunt down the strays while the rest of the troopers buried the dead Apaches.

The troopers camped on the Texas side of the Rio Grande that night and the following morning they headed back toward central Texas. The cattle slowed them down a lot, but they had no particular direction to follow until one of the scouts could pick up a trail of Naiche's warriors and that came early on the morning of the fourteenth day.

Alvin Simpson had pulled his horse to a halt and had climbed down to pick up a cedar stick and drag it through a pile of horse droppings.

Brady rode over and waited for Alvin to give his conclusions. This was the first sign of anyone crossing the trail of the Apaches since they left the fort.

"Indian pony," Alvin said as he looked toward the horizon for any movement. "They passed by this spot earlier this morning. They can't be more than two hours ahead of us."

"There's more than twelve of them," Brady said. They're traveling in a straight line because they don't want to give away their numbers."

"Can you make out where they might be headed?" Alvin asked, as he kept looking around for any other signs. "They may know we're on to them."

"The Camden Ranch is just over the next ridge," Brady said. "They have a horse ranch that provides the cavalry with some good horse flesh."

"Maybe that's what the Apaches' are after," Alvin said. "They may be after their horses. If they are, we need to warn the ranch of the Apaches' presence."

"That ranch has more wranglers working on it than the Indians have in their raiding party," Brady said. "That's not what the Apache need at this time. The only other thing I can think of is Gobi Springs Reservation. It's one of the few reservations that still welcome the Apache.

The two scouts returned to the column of soldiers to explain their findings. They told the captain what they thought the Apaches were up to.

"I'm open for suggestions," the captain said. "Do you think we could pick out the Indians that's causing us all this trouble?"

"Alvin and I have seen Naiche and we can recognize him," Brady said. "The problem is if we arrest him on the reservation it could cause us more trouble with the other Indians. That might be a bigger problem than we can handle right now."

"We could ride into the reservation with the cattle and make them think we're bringing them provisions," Alvin said. "That could give us a reason to look around for Naiche and his warriors."

"The stop could give our troopers time to freshen up and restock themselves with fresh supplies too," Captain Moss said. "Let's take the chance. Keep your eyes open for Naiche and his warriors. If any are spotted, we'll get together and try to figure out a way to capture them with the least amount of trouble."

The reservation had a cabin made of cedar wood that housed the Indian agent and his family. There was a corral and barn located at the back of the house between the Indian agent's home and to the west of the trading post. "There could be over two hundred Indian families living on this reservation." Alvin said.

The army was to supply the Indians with provisions until they learned to farm. They were to receive some guns and ammunition so they could hunt for their food until the crops started growing. Now, less then a year later the army has broken all of those promises. The army was already talking about moving the Indians again. This time they were to be sent to the Oklahoma territory, better known as no man's land.

The attentive eyes of the Indians were observing the troops as they drove the cattle into the corral behind the Indian agent's home.

The soldiers and their cattle were a welcoming sight to the agent at this time and he assigned the soldiers a bivouac area where they could pitch their tents. There was plenty of feed and water for their mounts and the Indian trustees were already taking care of the animals. The agent had given orders to slaughter enough steers to feed the soldiers.

Alvin and Brady went to unsaddle their horses, as they did, they looked around the barn and corral to see any sign of the apaches that they were chasing. Several apaches were in the area but only one, a short squatted Indian, looked out of place.

He wore a headband that showed signs of sweat and dirt, and was half-naked with only a loincloth covering him. The other Indians were wearing clean headbands and army issue pants and plaid shirts.

Brady pointed out the Indian to Alvin and then walked into the crowd of Indians that had gathered to see the cattle. The Indian agent had more steers butchered, the meat was to be split evenly among the Indians.

The cooking fires were burning bright all over the reservation that afternoon and the mescal alcohol was flowing freely.

The young maidens were gathering so they could do their dance around the campfire in hopes that the young bucks could get a good look at them. There wasn't much time for any social life among the Indians since the arrival of the white man.

Brady had followed the half-dressed Indian back to one of the teepees. The Indian met with one of the local Indians. Then he left the teepee and headed for the outskirts of the reservation. Brady followed until he came to an area where the light of a campfire was hidden by the surrounding rock formation that also concealed the Apaches from the soldiers.

Naiche was sitting next to the fire smoking a corncob pipe. The men around him were looking into the fire humming a strange tune as they rocked back and forth on their haunches. There seemed to be an aura around the area of death and destruction. Brady watched for a long time before he made the decision to return to camp and explain what he had seen.

Brady was very quiet as he left the Apache camp to return to the area of dancing and drinking. The Indians were putting on a show that held the attention of all the soldiers.

It was Alvin that found Brady. The two men walked to the outskirts of where the dancing maidens were performing.

. "We've got to get the men away from the festivities without causing a disturbance." Brady said. "I found the Apache camp."

"I'll take the right side of the circle and warn the soldiers to leave in an orderly manner while you take the left side. We'll meet in front of the corral," Brady said. "Remember, don't disturbed the festivities."

The troops gathered in front of the corral and Brady explained the situation to Captain Moss. The captain made the decision to surround the boulder formation and see if they couldn't take the Apaches alive.

Lieutenant Josh Davis took half the soldiers to the north of the boulders and spread his men out in a way that made it hard for anything to get past him or his men. Captain Moss surrounded the other section of the boulders with his men. The trap was set.

Alvin Simpson stepped into the campsite of the Apaches with his rifle held above his head in a sign that he wanted to talk.

"Naiche," Alvin said in fluent Apache. "We need to talk about you and your warriors raiding along the border."

"You no talk about raids," Naiche said. "You come to kill Apache and we fear no white man's guns." Then he and his men suddenly flattened out on the ground and rolled toward the surrounding boulders cocking and firing their weapons rapidly.

Alvin fell to the ground as the soldiers returned fire on the rolling Indians. The small area became filled with smoke hiding any movement in the area. Then the captain called for a cease-fire to let the smoke clear.

Alvin had crawled behind a small boulder to protect himself from any more sporadic fire. The smoke had cleared enough so he could see that a number of Apaches were dead or wounded. Alvin wasn't sure all the Apaches were dead. He stayed in his place long enough for the captain to send someone into the area to check for survivors.

It was Brady that made his way into the small campsite. He was crawling on his belly with his rifle cradled in his arms.

He reached Alvin first. "You okay?" Brady asked. "They didn't give you much time to get out of the way of the line of gunfire."

"I think I got hit twice," Alvin said. "My shoulder feels like a sledge hammer hit it and there's blood running down my leg."

"Lay still until I make sure all's clear," Brady said as he continued to crawl across the small opening to the first Indian. He was dead. He had taken several bullets in the body.

Brady continued to check each Indian until he stood up and motioned for the captain to come on into the campsite.

Naiche had chosen death for himself and his men, a sign of honor. He went to his death apache style. It was believed among the apaches that, if he died fighting his enemies, he would ride the heavens on his favorite horse for an eternity.

The Indian agent heard the army's side of the gunfight on how it started and ended. He would allowed the apaches to handle their dead in their own fashion There were prayers sung by the apaches and the death dance was carried on for hours.

Captain Moss felt it was time for the solders to leave. The Indians were mourning their dead but when the mourning was over, there was no way he could judge what the Indians might do.

The soldiers packed their gear and moved out in the middle of the night. Alvin was placed in the chuck wagon and the acting medical attendant kept Alvin's bandages clean in order to prevent any infection.

The trip back to Fort Abilene was filled with the anticipation of being back among friends and relatives again. The troopers were feeling good because they had completed their assignment without loosing one soldier.

The gate to the fort was standing open as "Baker Troop" rode in with their heads held high. Captain Moss made his report to the general while the rest of the troops dispersed to their living quarters.

The talk of the fort was the experience that the solders had picked up while under the orders of Captain Moss whom the general promoted to major as soon as he got the orders back from headquarters. Seems everyone got a promotion except for the scouts. They had to be satisfied with just a job well done.

Brady had become a close friend with Alvin Simpson while on the mission. He heard how Alvin was born of a white plantation owner and a young black slave girl. Alvin explained that he too was of a mixed union and that he had married a Seminole Indian.

Over a week passed before Alvin was sent home to recuperate. It was another week before Brady found time to ride to town. Hannah would be out of school by now and Brady was looking forward to seeing her again.

When Brady entered the bank he saw Captain Keith Benson talking with Thomas Durham. They didn't seem to be caring on business so Brady walked up to the two men and greeted them with a smile and a tip of his hat. "Mr. Durham," Brady said. "I was looking for Hannah. I guess I missed her on the street."

"No, Brady, you didn't miss her," Thomas Durham said. "She's gone back east with her mother. She's going to a girl's school in Boston. We felt she would need some brushing up on her womanly manners if she was ever going to find a man to marry that would fit into her social standings."

"What is it that you don't like about me Mr. Durham?" Brady asked. "What have I done to make you dislike me so much?"

"You've done nothing that I would take a personal disliking to," Thomas Durham said. "I've just been telling Ranger Benson how good I felt about you joining the Texas Rangers and he assured me that when you were ready he would be glad to swear you in."

"Would a Texas Ranger be good enough for your daughter?" Brady asked. "Is there some kind of standard that I have to meet in order to ask for your daughter's hand in marriage?"

"Could you excuse us for a minute, Ranger Benson?" Mr. Durham asked, as he guided Brady toward his office, by pulling on his right arm.

The office was huge and held large furniture with a big desk that seemed to cover a large portion of the east wall. Mr. Durham walked behind the desk and asked Brady to sit in a big over stuffed chair that sat across from his desk.

Mr. Durham picked up a box of Havana Cigars and offered Brady one. Brady turned down the offer and sat down to wait for Mr. Durham's next move.

"Brady those are dollar cigars," Mr. Durham said. "They cost more than a wrangler makes putting in a days work."

"Is this part of the reason that you don't want me to associate with your daughter?" Brady asked. "I'm not rich?"

"That and the fact that you're a half-breed with no ties to your past," Mr. Durham said. "You could never afford to keep my daughter the way she should be kept. With you she could never move up in the world's chain of society."

"One day I'll make you eat those words," Brady said. "You'll find that money can't buy true love. Hannah once told me that you and Mrs. Durham started your marriage with a hope and a prayer and not much more." Brady stood up, opened the door to the office and walked out.

Captain Benson saw Brady leaving the office and he saw the look of despair on Brady's face. He wondered if he should start a conversation with him at this time. Brady walked straight for the front door of the bank not looking around at anyone or anything.

Captain Benson strolled to the door and walked out just after Brady. "Hey, Brady," Captain Benson yelled. "Wait up a minute. I want to talk to you."

Brady didn't break stride and never answered the captain. He just kept walking down the street with that blank look on his face.

Captain Benson finally caught up with Brady and placed his hand on Brady's shoulder. "Hey, partner, what's your hurry?" Captain Benson asked.

Brady stopped walking and shook his head as if he was coming out from under a trance. "Sorry, captain, my mind was elsewhere," Brady said. "What do you want?"

"Well I wished there was something I could do for you," Captain Benson answered. "I got word from headquarters in

Dallas last week that I could hire me another ranger. Pays good, forty five dollars a month, expenses paid while on duty."

"That's good pay," Brady said. "Much better then a cow puncher or a wrangler gets. Maybe I could save up for a ranch of my own in a few years?"

"Remember the Reed's place that was raided by the apaches while you were on your scouting mission?" Captain Benson asked.

"Sure, it was a bad experience for everyone," Brady said. "They didn't need to die like that."

Mr. Durham holds the note to that ranch and from what he has been telling me, he could sure use a buyer for it," Captain Benson explained.

"I don't have that kind of money," Brady said. "Besides I don't feel like handing him my business right now."

"Pay off on that ranch is less then eight hundred dollars," Captain Benson said. " There's no horses left on the ranch and all the cattle has been driven off, so you're only paying for the land and buildings that are left. I'll give you that much as a bonus, if you'll sign up for a couple of years with the rangers."

"Can I let you know later?" Brady asked.

"Sure take your time," Captain Benson said.

Brady shook the captain's hand and then walked across the street to the blacksmith's shop. Brady could hear the banging of the blacksmith's hammer as he walked up to the huge barn.

Brady pulled up a keg of shoeing nails and sat down on it. He was watching Bernie Greenwood banging some hot iron strips into shape for shoeing a horse that was tied just inside the barn. The big black man was wiping sweat from his brow when he noticed Brady setting on the keg. "Want to finish this job for me?" Bernie asked.

Brady smiled, stood up, pulled down an apron from the wall and placed it over his clothing. He walked over to the bellows and pumped some air into the hot coals. The coals turned red as they heated the iron strip. Brady grabbed the hot iron with the metal tongs, placed it on the anvil and started banging the iron into shape.

"What have you got on your mind?" Bernie asked as he watched Brady turn the iron strip into a horseshoe.

"As a young boy, I thought they called you the blacksmith because you were black," Brady said. "As I grew up I found out that blacksmith described your job and I was to embarrassed to ever tell you."

"What's that got to do with your problem?" Bernie asked.

"What makes you think I have a problem?" Brady said, as he pushed the iron strip back into the hot coals and waited for it to turn red so he could continue to shape it.

"Remember, I've known you just as long as you've known me," Bernie said. "You can't fool me. There's something on your mind."

"I was told today that I wasn't good enough for the banker's daughter because I'm a half-breed," Brady said. "I'll never have enough money to keep her in the style that her father wants."

"Through the eyes of some people I'm a black man," Bernie said. "Through the eyes of others, I'm a nigger. Through the eyes of my friends like you, I'm just another man making my way through life and that's what really counts."

"The captain has offered me a chance to buy the Reed Ranch," Brady explained. "He's offered to give me a bonus large enough to buy the ranch if I'll join the rangers for two years.

The long strip of iron was shaping up well as Brady stuck the hot iron into a barrel of water. He then walked over to the horse and lifted its right hind foot and held the horseshoe up to it's hoof for a measurement.

"Looks good," Bernie said, as he watched the work of the young man. "What's your problem with buying the ranch?"

"I'll have to be away a lot and I'll need someone to oversee the ranch while I'm gone," Brady said. "Then I'll need wranglers to help out and I don't have the money to pay them."

"How well do you know Alvin Simpson?" Bernie asked.

"We rode together on a scouting mission for several months," Brady said. "I got to know that I could trust him with my life," Brady said.

"So you did get to know him?" Bernie asked. "Did you know he was married?" Bernie pulled another strip of iron from the barrel that sat next to the Anvil.

"Yep," Brady said. "What's this got to do with me needing someone to help me run a ranch?"

"On that last scouting trip they put two bullets into his body. His wife doesn't want him to scout any more," Bernie said. "Alvin Simpson is one of the best wranglers in Texas and he would rather work a ranch than to track any apache."

"What makes you think he would work for me?" Brady asked. "Then again, there is the problem of wages."

"Alvin is married to a beautiful Shoshone princess," Bernie said. "He lives with her and her family over in Forge, Texas. I bet if you promised him a third of your ranch for his wages, he would bring his whole family over and turn your ranch into a profitable working ranch in no time."

Brady stopped his work, snapped his fingers, took off his apron and turned to Bernie. "Great idea," Brady said, as he shook Bernie's hand. "Don't let anyone tell you that you're not a good blacksmith,"

Brady left the blacksmith shop and headed for the livery. Bernie smiled, as he watched the young half-breed leave his shop. Bernie felt the boy was on his way to Forge, Texas.

Forge was a days ride from Abilene. Brady was in a hurry to talk with Alvin about the proposition he had to offer. The thought of him being a part of a working ranch was keeping his blood flowing at a very fast rate.

The long ride seemed to go by fast. Then Brady came to the small town called Forge, Texas.

There was a crowd gathered outside the livery when Brady rode in. He slowed down and watched the crowd spread out as two men stood holding the arms of a black man that looked a lot like his friend Alvin Simpson.

"This nigger has been asking for this for a long time," a big man said, as he took off his coat and started rolling up his sleeves. He held a buggy whip in his hand.

The crowd stood back and offered no help to the man that was being held. Another man came over and ripped the shirt off Alvin's back.

Brady stopped his horse and swung down to the ground. He tied the horse to a hitching rail and walked over to the crowd.

"Hello Alvin," Brady said, as he walked up to the two men holding Alvin's arms. "Seems these people don't like the way you're dressed."

"Keep out of this cowboy," the big man said. "This nigger has walked around here shooting off his mouth about his family needing a doctor and he knows there ain't a doctor that'll fix up a black or Indian in these parts."

"Is there a white doctor in the crowed?" Brady asked. "I believe that my friend asked for a doctor and I don't believe he made a reference to his color."

"We don't doctor any niggers, Indians or half-breeds like yourself," the man repeated.

Brady pulled his gun faster than the eye could follow and brought the barrel down across the head of one of the men holding Alvin's arms. This caused the man to lose his grip on Alvin and forced him to the ground.

Alvin wasted no time in bending at the waist and throwing the second man over his shoulder, then dropping a knee in his midsection knocking the wind out of him.

The man with the whip reached for his gun when Brady heard a shot from behind him. The man with the whip stopped his movement toward his gun, as Brady's head turned to watch a man fall from the roof of the building across the street.

"Feel free to continue your draw, Mr. Nigger Hater," a girl's voice said from the outskirts of the crowd. "I've got a feeling that you've met your match in a half-breed that's faster than you."

"This ain't fair," the man said, as he threw his gun to the ground, "I'm unarmed and you can't shoot an unarmed man."

"He wouldn't be shooting an unarmed man," the girl said. "He'd be shooting an unarmed skunk."

Alvin stood up and walked over to the man and removed the whip from his hand throwing it to the ground. Then he picked up the man's gun, wiping it clean of dirt and stuck it in his own belt. "You and your men have ten minutes to get to your horses and ride out of town or I'll see that you're buried on cemetery hill."

Chapter 3

The crowd watched as the loud-mouthed ruffian helped his friends up off the ground. They dusted themselves off with their hats and walked toward the livery. They had pushed their luck too far by bulling the town's people throughout the Civil War and then through reconstruction.

The people started to applaud the way Alvin forced the bullies to leave town. One man even walked up and shook Alvin's hand asking him if he would hang around and run the rest of the trash out of town just like he did this bunch.

Alvin turned to Brady with a grin on his lips and said, "You can put that gun away now old scout. You have saved my life and I'm indebted to you." Then, Alvin Simpson opened his arms and wrapped them around the young man that rode with him when they hunted down Naiche and his band of warriors.

"You know better than to hug me in front of all these people," Brady said. "Who was that girl that shot that hombre off the roof?"

Alvin laughed and started walking toward the prettiest little girl Brady had ever set eyes on. She had a dark complexion, raven black, curly hair and the bluest eyes Brady had ever seen. She couldn't have been much over five feet two inches tall and she stood there looking like an angel holding a Henry .44 Rifle. She wore a buckskin shirt and a pair of men's britches. Her boots were made of deerskin same as the pair Alvin had on when they were on their scouting mission.

"Brady, I want you to meet my stepdaughter, Abigail Simpson. We call her Abbey" Alvin said, as he placed his arm around the girl's shoulders. "She thinks she's a man and she acts like one at times."

Brady pulled his hat off his head and placed it over his heart as if he was getting ready to say the pledge of allegiance. Alvin had to laugh.

"I'm glad to meet you Miss Abbey," Brady said. "I want to thank you for protecting my back during this little ruckus."

"You were helping Alvin, weren't you?" Abbey said. "So I believe we're even on all counts."

An older man stepped up holding a little black bag. "You folks were in need of a doctor?" he said. He went on to introduced himself as Doctor Gillian.

"It's my wife, doctor" Alvin said, as he pulled the doctor toward a buckboard that was located outside the livery.

"Hurry, doctor. She's been running a fever for some time now."

Abbey and Brady mounted up and followed the buckboard as the doctor and Alvin rode out of town.

The ride to Alvin's place wasn't as far as Brady had expected. He lived in a settlement of tents and fallen down shacks that stood just outside of town. There wasn't access to water and their living quarters weren't fit for sheltering animals, let alone humans.

Alvin pulled the wagon to a halt in front of one of the tents. He jumped from the buckboard and ran to the other side to help the doctor down.

Abbey swung down from her horse and ran to the tent, she held back the flap so the doctor could enter. The only light in the tent came from the flap opening. The doctor knelt down next to an animal hide bed to check the woman for a pulse. Her body had started turning cold even with the warmth from the animal hides.

Alvin waited patiently for the doctor to give him some sort of a sign as to the condition of his wife.

The doctor looked up and said, "There's no pulse. This woman's already dead. She's been dead for a while."

Abbey ran out of the tent so no one could witness her grief. Alvin just knelt beside his wife holding her lifeless hand in his. The doctor and Brady walked outside to give Alvin some privacy.

"I'll drive you back to town," Brady said, as he helped the doctor back onto the buckboard. Then Brady tied his horse to the rear of the buckboard and climbed up in the driver's seat. The two men rode silently back to town.

After returning the buggy to Alvin, Brady rode back to town and took a room at the local hotel. It wasn't much to brag about but the sheets seemed to be clean and the hotel served a good meal. Brady needed a good night's sleep before he could ride back out to Alvin's place to try and talk business.

Brady had no memory of loosing a loved one. He had lost his family before he could remember what they even looked like. The thought of what Alvin and his stepdaughter were going through touched Brady's heart but he still couldn't feel the hurt the two were feeling.

Brady's first sight of Abbey Simpson lingered in his mind that night. He couldn't push it aside no matter what subject he tried to concentrate on. The young girl was his best friend's stepdaughter and it wasn't right for him to have feelings for her.

Brady was looking forward to seeing Alvin and his stepdaughter the next morning. He just hoped they wouldn't be so upset that they couldn't talk business.

After a good night's sleep Brady woke up and went for a morning walk to the livery. He became more familiar with his surroundings and he seemed to have picked up an appetite on his way.

The stable boy had heard that the wind was going to blow in some much-needed rain for the farmers and he relayed that information on to Brady as he tossed hay into the nearest stall.

Brady asked the boy if he could have his horse ready to ride by sun up?

"You can count on me mister," the stable boy said.

Brady left the livery and walked to the hotel restaurant. It was empty of customers when Brady walked in. He chose a table by the window and sat down.

The lady that waited on him was a very pretty Mexican girl that spoke better English than Brady could speak Spanish. The young waitress talked of the events that happened the day before and she was very happy that those men were forced to leave town.

Brady told her he had business in town and when it was over he was going back to Abilene where he had a ranch.

Why he liked talking to this young girl he didn't know, but before he left she had his life's story and a two-bit piece that he used to pay for his breakfast.

The smell of pending rain filled the air and made the surroundings smell fresh and clean when Brady walked back to the livery. His horse was saddled and ready for the ride back to the settlement. The clouds kept the sun covered all morning and this made for a cool and refreshing ride.

Before Brady arrived at the settlement he had to put his rain slicker on. He pulled his hat low over his head to prevent the drizzling rain from running down his collar.

Brady rode to the same tent where Alvin had taken him when his wife was sick. He swung down from his horse and yelled in a loud voice, "Anyone home?"

The tent flap swung open and Alvin invited Brady to come in. There was a small fire burning in the center of the tent and the coffeepot was perking a fresh pot of coffee. Alvin was alone and Brady felt like this might be a good time to talk with him.

"I never got around to asking you what you were doing in Forge," Alvin said, as he poured two cups of coffee.

"You sound bitter," Brady said. "Did your wife's death came as a surprise?"

"She had been sick for some time," Alvin said as he sipped his coffee. "Our way of living doesn't leave much for our children to look forward to and my wife wouldn't turn loose of her ties to her Shoshone family. So we live like outcast in this Indian hating country."

"Alvin, I don't know if this is the time, but you did ask why I came here," Brady said. "I came here to offer you a proposition."

"Was this proposition going to be made before you saw our living conditions?" Alvin asked.

"I need your help Alvin, but I don't know quite how to ask for it," Brady said. "I might be getting myself in a fix that I can't get out of."

"Well ask," Alvin said. "It can't get much worse than the situation I'm in right now."

Brady explained about the ranch and how he planned to buy it and under what circumstances. He told Alvin it was the Reed Ranch that the Indian's had raided while they were on their scouting mission. He also told him there wasn't much left on the ranch. There were no cattle or horses left on the ranch but there was good water and close to ten thousand acres of pastureland. The captain and Brady felt the ranch could grow if the right people took on the job.

Alvin listened to every word that Brady said. He was staring into space as if he was trying to visualize everything as Brady described it.

“There’s a bunkhouse that was left standing and the corral seems to be untouched. The house shows signs of being damaged in places but there’s a roof and everything seems to be repairable,” Brady explained.

“What’s your proposition?” Alvin asked. “Seems like you have a fine thing going for you.”

“ I need you to get it started,” Brady said. “What if I give you a third of the ranch and asked you to run the ranch while I’m doing my business with the rangers? Right now I have no money to pay salaries for wranglers. I know I’m asking a lot from you. But I have a feeling that we can make something of this place if we could just get it started.”

“The town’s people ain’t going to do business with me,” Alvin said. “I’m a black man and Texas was on the loosing side of the war that freed men like me.”

“They’ll do business with me,” Brady said. “It won’t take them long to realize we’re partners and they’ll do business with you too.”

“If I take on this partnership,” Alvin said. “I’ll have to bring my wife’s family with me. They’re Shoshone Indians and they'll be the wranglers we'll need to get started. They're better cattlemen than any white man."

"Then you'll do it?" Brady asked.

"You have a partner even though he's black and comes with a lot of burden," Alvin said.

Brady wished he had seen Abbey before he had to leave, but time had suddenly become important to him and he had to get back to Abilene to close the deal on the ranch.

The rain had stopped and the people in the settlement were starting to stir around. It hadn't been enough rain to help the farmers and it wouldn't be long before the sun would make everything humid again.

Alvin watched Brady ride off and was wondering what the rest of the men would think when he told them they were going to work for a half-breed that was flat broke, yet owned enough land to run a couple thousand head of cattle and horses on it.

Brady rode straight to Captain Benson's office to make his report and to get his help in buying the ranch. When he walked inside the office Captain Benson was sitting at his desk.

"Brady, next time you knock before you enter my office," Captain Benson said, as he stood up and walked over to shut the door.

Brady tossed his hat on the floor next to his chair. He opened the cigar box on the captain's desk and took out what he called a stogy. He used one of the matches lying on the desk to light it.

"Make yourself at home," Captain Benson said. Then he watched Brady take a deep drag on the cigar. Immediately, Brady started coughing and gagging.

"Have you ever smoked before?" the captain asked, as he tried to hold back his laughter.

"No," Brady said between breaths. "I've seen it done and I wondered what it would be like." He started trying to put out the cigar.

"I should make you finish what you started," Captain Benson said, as he brought his hand down hard on Brady's back trying to help him regain his breath.

"I could never learn to suck on one of those things if my life depended on it," Brady said. "How people enjoy it is beyond me."

"I'll take care of the smoking and drinking if you'll stop fooling around with new experiments," the captain said.

Brady was still trying to clear his windpipe when Captain Benson's secretary brought in a glass of water and handed it to Brady. Brady grabbed the glass and swallowed its contents in one breath. Then he started to hiccup. Benson and the secretary laughed, as they both stood by and let Brady go through the steps of learning not to smoke.

When things settled down a bit more, Captain Benson and Brady talked about the financing of the Reed Ranch. They were to go to the bank and start the proceedings this same afternoon, just as soon as Brady was sworn in as a new Texas Ranger.

After the swearing in of Brady as a ranger, the captain brought up the subject of Otis and Frank Harper.

"Seems the town of Abilene had been putting up with a young gunslinger named Otis Harper. He has a brother named Frank Harper, who's the leader of a gang of outlaws up in no man's land that was called Oklahoma territory," the captain explained. "Frank Harper grew up to be an angry man that had turned killer and there was this feeling that if you messed with Otis Harper you were messing with his brother Frank."

"What made this Frank Harper turn bad?" Brady asked.

"Frank got in with a bunch of young hoodlums when he was fifteen years old." Captain Benson said. "They stopped a stagecoach and robbed the passengers of their traveling money. Probably got away with a few dollars. Then after that he tried cattle rustling, train robbery and then bank robbery."

"How did Otis get involved in all this?" Brady asked.

"Otis is a little slow in his head and he got hold of a gun one day and found out he could use it," Captain Benson said. "He became fast on the draw and he could put a bullet in the vicinity of where he was aiming. He got a lot of people scared of him and he enjoyed that power. He began pushing people around and if they pushed back Otis would remind them that his brother would be back in town one day. People then started avoiding Otis as much as they could."

"Seems like Otis had his bluff on the people in Abilene," Brady said. "Why would he go and kill someone?"

"There's a little redheaded dancehall girl named Dora that dances in the Wild Horse Saloon and Otis had feelings for her," Captain Benson said. "She never returned his feelings but Otis felt he had reservations on her. Last night Otis caught her upstairs with another man and Otis shot both of them."

"That's an eye-opener for a young man that thinks he's in love," Brady said. "What're you going to do about it?"

"I believe Otis will be hiding at his cousin's place near Deer Creek," Captain Benson said. "Otis can be dangerous and he shouldn't be on the loose. I believe you would have the best chance of bringing him back alive."

"Otis is the young skinny kid that hung out around the poker tables in the Wild Horse Saloon, isn't he?" Brady asked. "The one with the birth mark under his left ear?"

"That's him, and he's good with that gun he totes around," Captain Benson said. "Don't let him get to you with his boyish ways, because if you do, you'll be looking down his gun barrel in nothing flat."

After their business in the bank, Brady thanked Captain Benson and said, "I would like to ride out to my new investment before I leave for Deer Creek. I talked Alvin into coming in with me on the ranch. His wife passed away you know, so he'll be bringing some of her Seminole relatives with him to help get the ranch started."

"That's fine," Captain Benson said. "Alvin Simpson is a good man and you might remind him that if he ever needs any help, I'll be glad to lend him a hand."

"Alvin is going to be the ramrod of our outfit and I'm going to let him do things his way," Brady said, as he picked up his hat and headed for the door.

"Care for a cigar before you leave?" Captain Benson asked.

Brady shook his head and walked out the door, he was excited to be riding out to the ranch even if it wasn't up to par yet. He knew that if they were going to make a go of it, Alvin Simpson was the right ramrod for the job.

The first thing that Brady noticed when he rode up to the big gate was the entrance to the ranch had a new sign that read *B/A Ranch.*

The ranch house stood just down the road from the gate and he could already see a lot of improvements. The tumbleweeds had been removed from the front porch, the door had been put back on its hinges and all the broken windows had been replaced.

There were horses in the corral and some Indian wranglers stood around the corral watching one of their broncobusters trying to break a wild mustang. The mustang showed little hesitation in tossing the rider to the ground while the rest of the Indians laughed and clapped their hands.

Brady had to laugh along with the men as he rode up to the corral. When the Indians saw Brady they all held their heads down toward the ground. Brady knew they were trying to show their respect toward him so he swung down from his horse and shook hands with them, telling them he was Brady Wells, a partner with Alvin Simpson.

Alvin came out of the barn with a hammer in his hand. "Brady, we thought we would come a little early. We drove this bunch of mustangs in that we gathered along the way."

"I can't believe you've already started stocking this ranch," Brady said. "How many mustangs did you round up?"

"There's about thirty-five. We had ten stallions mixed in with them at one time," Alvin said. "Then a big black stallion came out from behind some boulders and separated the stallions from the mustangs and drove them off. Sure wish I could've got a rope on that big hunk of black horse flesh."

"There seems to be a good amount of horseflesh right here," Brady said. "I wasn't expecting you people to be here yet, let alone you bring all these horses."

"We left Forge shortly after you did," Alvin said. "We went to work as soon as we found tools and materials to work with. The Reeds kept things up pretty well and it wasn't hard to mend the fences and replace the broken windows around the house."

"I saw the sign at the gate but I couldn't make out the symbols," Brady said as he walked back to the barn with Alvin.

"That's Abbey's idea," Alvin said. "I was against it but she felt we needed some kind of brand so she designed that one."

"That's our new brand?" Brady asked. "The B/A Ranch? What do the initials stand for?"

"Brady and Alvin. Ain't that the dainty way for a woman to look at it?" Alvin said. "We can change it if you don't like it. Come on in the barn. I want to show you something."

"I like the B/A brand. It has a nice ring to it." Brady said, as he stepped into the barn behind Alvin.

"There's a complete blacksmith shop right here in the barn," Alvin said. "Now if we had a man who knew how to use this equipment it would save us a bunch of money in the future."

"You know I can use that equipment," Brady said. "One day I'll teach one of the men how to shoe horses. In the meantime, I'm going to ride around the ranch and get my bearings."

"Want me to ride with you?" Alvin asked. "There are many good spots on this ranch but there are some arroyos too."

"Don't want to take you away from your work," Brady said. "I can find my way around the ranch all by myself."

"I could help," Abbey said, as she entered the barn.

" I'm just passing time," Brady said. "I've no intentions of slowing progress on this ranch."

"The only progress we've made outside is the addition of the mustangs," Abbey said. "The women have been working inside the main house getting it ready for you to use when you come back to settle down."

"That'll be sometime coming," Brady said. "You and your father are to use the main house for your own convenience."

"You should see what the women have done with the house," Abbey said. "Have you been in the house before?"

"I looked it over before I bought it," Brady said. "I'm sorry it was in such bad shape."

Abbey took Brady by the arm and led him outside where the sun almost blinded him. She held on to Brady's arm as they walked to the ranch house. The stairs to the porch were in need of some repair but the porch itself seemed sturdy enough.

When they entered the house the sight took Brady's breath away. There were curtains over the windows, the hardwood floors had been scrubbed and there was furniture in all of the rooms.

Abbey gave Brady a first class tour of the main house and Brady was impressed. The kitchen was filled with odors of baked bread and apple pie.

"There are five women cleaning and cooking for the men," Abbey said. "There are seven men not counting my father, working on the outside of the house. Our families have three children that we're raising. We'll soon start planting a garden to grow our own food, but in the mean time I'll need you to fix us up with some sort of credit at the hardware store in town."

"Look Abbey, I'm on my way out of town in the morning," Brady said. "I have thirty-one dollars to my name. I'll give you twenty-five dollars and hope it'll last until I get back."

"Twenty-five dollars will be more than enough," Abbey said, as she took Brady's arm and led him into the kitchen. "I've been raised to handle money as if it were very scarce."bbey strolled through the kitchen and then led Brady up the stairs where all the sleeping quarters were. "There are five bedrooms up here and we didn't know how you wanted them separated. I told the families that the bunkhouse would have to serve as their living quarters until we could build them new ones."

"Abbey," Brady said. "If you're to handle the responsibilities of this house and your dad is the ramrod of the ranch, then you both will have to have a room in this house."

"My father said you were a fair man," Abbey said. "So I felt my father and I could sleep in the farthest two bedrooms at the end of the hall. You would use the bedroom directly across from us. We have two married couples that are my mother's sisters. I hoped you could see your way clear of letting them live in the main house until other arrangements are available."

"I'll be in and out of this house as I'm needed," Brady said. "I'll sleep in the bunkhouse with the rest of the men, when I stay overnight. You use my room for the other women and let's not argue about it."

There was a tear in Abbey's eyes as she turned her head toward the window to keep Brady from seeing her in a weak moment. "I must tell you now Mr. Wells," Abbey said. "I've dreamed of being the mistress of a large house like this one every since I was a little girl. I want to do you a good service. My father and I will always respect you for your kindness and we'll serve you well."

"My name is Brady, not Mr. Wells. I'm a partner with your father, not his boss." Brady said. "You don't work for me. You and your father are part owners and you can't keep thinking you owe me something because if anything, it's your family that I owe."

Brady heard someone downstairs and he left Abbey standing in the bedroom. He went down the stairs and out on the front porch where Alvin was siting in an old rocker smoking his corncob pipe.

"Want to tell me about the man your going after?" Alvin asked. "Seems like you could use someone to watch your back."

Brady spent a good hour explaining everything the captain had explained to him. Then the door to the house opened and an old Indian woman stuck her head out and let them know that supper was on the table.

Brady hadn't enjoyed a meal like this in several years. Chicken and mashed potatoes and apple pie. He enjoyed the best bake bread he had ever eaten and he smothered the bread with butter from the churn. Then it dawned on him. Where did the chicken and the cow's milk come from?

"The chickens and a couple old milk cows we brought with us," Alvin said. "We keep the chicken house full of hens and a couple of roosters so we can have eggs for breakfast. The two old cows are still producing milk but soon we'll need a bunch more to keep this large of group in fresh milk. One day we hope to slaughter our own hogs and beef, as well."

"I'm glad you're thinking ahead," Brady said, as he looked down at the apple pie and the cup of coffee Abbey had placed in front of him. "You must feel like a king Alvin with all these women waiting on you."

"They pull their load," Alvin said as he sipped his coffee. "We have enough workers for now but if things keep going the way I plan, we'll need even more. Maybe we can talk about that when you get back from your assignment."

Alvin and Brady finished eating and walked out to the bunkhouse and watched the small group of Indians playing a game that looked a lot like poker. They had small beads that they would wager on each hand and the one that ended up with the most beads got to sleep in the next morning. That seemed like a good deal to Brady but he wasn't going to get involved with their game at this time.

Alvin asked if everything was alright and the men laughed and said, "This is a good place and we'll work hard to stay here."

Alvin took Brady back to the house and showed him the room upstairs where he would sleep for the night.

The women had already brought in a large wooden tub and filled it with hot water. One of the ladies handed Brady a straight razor and asked him if he knew how to use it? Alvin got a laugh out of that as he ran the ladies from the room.

"Brady, I want to thank you for sharing this ranch with me and my family," Alvin said. "This is our first permanent place to call home."

"Don't get cow-eyed on me Alvin," Brady said. " When everything is said and done, I need you as much as you need me."

Alvin left the room and Brady couldn't wait to get his clothes off and climb into the hot tub. He had just submerged himself when the door opened and an old Indian woman walked in and took Brady's clothes. "I'll wash and dry them for you," she said as she left the room.

Brady lay soaking his body when the thought of Hannah Durham entered his mind. Where was she at this moment? Was she thinking about him too? Was she looking forward to coming home for a visit?

St. Patrick's day was coming up again and Brady started remembering the good time he and Hannah had celebrating that day. They danced into the night and Brady got a kiss on the cheek when he walked her home.

Now her mother and father looked at Brady as if he were trying to take their daughter away from them. They didn't have to send her away like that, he thought. Brady knew that Hannah was a special person and she needed to marry a special person. She might have already found herself a husband back east where she was attending school.

Brady broke his chain of thought when he started to rub the lye soap over his body. He got his face soapy and he pulled the straight razor across his face until every facial hair was gone. The water was starting to turn cool when Brady stepped out and started drying off. He used a brush that was on the wash basin table to brush his hair back over his shoulders.

He had long straight black hair that hung just below his shoulders and he tied it back from his face with a bandana. His hair surrounded a dark skinned face that was marked by a square jaw and a prominent nose that set him apart from his Indian heritage. He could look like a man of quality if he would just shorten his hair.

The door opened and in walked the two old Indian women with a pitcher in their hand. They went to the tub and started dipping out the water and carrying it down the stairs. Brady started to say something to them about his privacy, but then he stopped and sat on the bed letting the ladies finish their job.

The bed felt soft as Brady lay across it hoping that the old lady would return his clothes before to long. There was the sound of guitar music coming from the outside of the house. It was a very nice sound and Brady lay with his eyes shut as the music continued to filter into his room.

Then the sound of a voice singing like a nightingale started filtering into his room. Brady had never heard the song before and the words were not understandable but the soothing, mellow voice put Brady to sleep.

Brady didn't wake up when the old woman returned with his clothing and he didn't wake up when the music stopped. It wasn't until the sunlight filtered into his room and caused his eyes to blink, before Brady jumped from his bed and start to get dressed.

His thoughts of Hannah had made him over sleep. Why was it that life placed a burden on a person that they would have to carry the rest of their life?

The ranch was a step in the right direction to becoming respectable person, but he would always be a half-breed.

Chapter 4

Brady went down the stairs two steps at a time and entered the big living room where Alvin sat in an overstuffed chair smoking his corncob pipe.

Alvin had a grin on his face when he said, "You rangers keep strange working hours. Hope you don't mind me smoking in your house?"

"Alvin, when are you going to get it into your thick skull that this is our house? Not my house," Brady asked, as he followed Alvin into the kitchen.

"You late sleepers are always in a grouchy mood," Alvin said, before he sat down at the kitchen table motioning for Brady to sit next to him.

Abbey's Aunt Martha was always in a happy mood when she worked around the house, but this morning there was no smile on her face when she placed the men's breakfast on the table.

"I'm sorry for being late," Brady said, as he sat down at the table feeling guilty for over sleeping.

"Man sleeps as long as his body says," Martha explained. "I could have bounced you out of bed a long time ago, but I could tell that it's been a long time since you've had a real good nights sleep."

Martha had just finished frying the bacon when Alvin started passing the biscuits to Brady. "Your trip west will be a dangerous one unless you have someone watching your back," Alvin said.

"Everyone's needed here," Brady said. "The ranch is our first priority and you're the only ones around here that can make it pay off in the shortest period of time."

"When you made my family your responsibility," Alvin said, "It made you our responsibility also."

"The answer is still no, and the subject is closed," Brady said. "I'll be gone for some time and Abbey has what money I can afford right now. I hope she can make it last until I get back."

"Did I hear my name mentioned?" Abbey said as she entered the kitchen and poured herself a cup of coffee.

Brady was still amazed at how beautiful this young girl was. This morning she had her hair up in a bun and she wore a red flannel shirt that set off the dark smooth skin that spread across a perfectly formed face.

"I was just telling Alvin that I hoped the money you have will last you folks until I get back," Brady said.

"Don't worry about what's going on here at the ranch," Abbey said. "Alvin will take care of the ranch and Aunt Martha will keep the house going and I'll make the money last until you get back".

Brady stood up and held out his hand to Abbey as if he wanted to confirm the deal. Abbey laughed and reached up and pulled Brady's head down close to hers and rubbed her nose against Brady's and said, "That's how we sign a bargain in this family."

Brady looked at Abbey with goose bumps running up and down his spine. He hoped Alvin couldn't read his thoughts because he never wanted to embarrass anyone as much as he wanted to embrace Abbey at this moment.

"I'll have to remember that in the future." Brady said, turning his head away so the flush in his face wouldn't show. Then they all sat down to eat their breakfast but Brady couldn't clear his head of the thought of how beautiful this girl really was.

When Brady finished his breakfast he thanked the women and walked out on the porch to wait for Alvin to catch up. He wanted to talk with him on the way to the barn.

When the two men walked toward the barn, Brady told Alvin that if anything happened to him and he didn't come back, that he left papers with Ranger Benson that would leave everything to him and his family.

Brady's horse was already saddled and ready to travel when the barn door opened. It was Abbey with a burlap sack filled with food. "Got to keep the bread winner healthy," Abbey said, as she handed the sack to Brady. Then she winked and smiled at him over her shoulder, as she turned and walked out of the barn.

Brady felt embarrassed to let Alvin watch as his face turned beet red from Abbey's attention.

"When you leave here you have to start thinking Apache again," Alvin said. "Get your mind set for war and don't trust anything or anyone."

Brady tipped his hat to Alvin as he rode away, because they both knew in their hearts that they were more than just friends to each other were they were blood brothers.

There wasn't a cloud in the sky as Brady checked the placement of the sun. He had never started out on a trip so late in the day and he could feel the heat from the sun already.

His first day's ride ended next to a small stream that flowed very gently toward the south. There were enough rocks and wood lying around the edge of the stream for Brady to build himself a small campfire.

A cool breeze was blowing through the cottonwood trees and it cooled the evening air making it good for sleeping. The night passed with only the sounds of cicadas and night creatures that were heard and never seen. The lack of these sounds would've warned Brady that danger was near by.

The next morning Brady was up before sunrise. The wind had come up during the night and the small campfire was having a hard time staying lit. After building up the fire, Brady put on a pot of coffee and a small skillet of bacon. The biscuits had hardened over night and needed to be dipped in the grease to make them soft enough to eat, but all in all he had a filling meal.

After eating, Brady rubbed down his horse and gave him his fill of food and water. He took what was left of the coffee grounds and poured it on the fire. He rinsed the coffeepot and skillet in the stream before he filled his canteen with fresh water. Then he packed everything away before ridding on.

That afternoon Brady rode into a small town called Temporary. He chuckled under his breath because he felt it was well named. The town was almost a ghost town now and people were still moving out as he rode in. He stopped for a meal and some directions. The meal was satisfying and the directions were helpful as Brady replenished his supplies and rode back out of town.

The rest of his day was spent ridding through the dry, arid lands of west Texas. There seemed to be no useful reason for this land except to harbor lizards and to grow gourds. The sun was so hot it could bake a man's brains in hours if he didn't protect his head with some kind of cover.

Another week passed before Brady came upon the town of Deer Creek and he was looking forward to hearing some human voices again.

Deer Creek was bigger than Brady had imagined and it didn't look as if he was going to find Otis Harper as quickly as he wanted to.

Brady put his horse in the livery and asked the stable boy where he could find the nearest saloon. The stable boy told him the town counsel had passed an ordnance that prohibited drinking and gambling in town, so all these type places were located close together and east of Main Street.

Brady took a room at the Deer Creek Hotel and ordered bath water to be sent up to his room. The bath and a shave would take him to suppertime and after supper he would make his rounds of the saloons.

Brady felt good about the town ordnance because he didn't have to search the whole town for Otis. After stopping in three or four of the local saloons he finally found Otis sitting at a table playing poker with four other men. Their cards had been dealt and each man was checking his hand to see if he was going to bet or fold. Brady noticed the large amount of money in front of Otis and a thought came to him.

"Hi Otis," Brady said. "Did you find some more suckers to cheat out of their life savings? Them fellows you cheated in Abilene are still looking for you. The man that called you a cheater and you shot him for it, he died! His brothers are out trying to track you down right now." All this was said very nonchalantly as Brady moved around the table trying to look at each man's cards.

"You shut your mouth cowboy or I'll shut it for you," Otis said, as he laid his cards on the table and positioned himself so he had quick access to his gun.

"You ain't mad at me are you Otis?" Brady said. "I thought you were proud you killed so many men. Isn't that why you changed your name to the Abilene Kid?"

"I ain't never cheated no one out of one red cent or killed anyone that didn't need killing," Otis said, as he watched the other men stand up and start moving away from the table.

"I was wondering why you called yourself the Abilene Kid?" Brady said. "I know you're from Abilene and you're just a kid so I guess you did the right thing by changing your name."

"I ain't no more a kid than you are," Otis said, as he stood up from the table and pushed his chair clear of his legs. "I'm Frank Harper's little brother and you better not fool with me."

"Then why didn't you change your name to Frank Harper's little brother, instead of the Abilene Kid?" Brady asked. The crowd started laughing at that statement and Otis was showing more anger.

"You're trying to get me mixed up," Otis said, as he turned to the crowd and yelled, "Shut up or I'll shoot you all dead."

The saloon got quiet as the customers started backing out of the way. Otis turned back to Brady and said, "Why are you doing this to me? Don't you know my brother will kill you?"

"It's like this Otis," Brady said. "There's a warrant out for your arrest and Captain Benson sent me here to bring you back for trial. The warrant says dead or alive. I would prefer to bring you back alive, but that's your choice."

Otis couldn't believe that anyone would put himself in this kind of a position to arrest Frank Harper's brother. Otis knew that everyone was scared of his brother so why didn't this cowboy back off and let him be?

Brady walked over to Otis and suddenly slapped his face real hard. It came at such a surprise to Otis that he brought both his hands up to touch the spot that stung so much. It was then that Brady made his second move. Brady pulled Otis's gun from its holster, pointed it at him and said, "Turn around Otis, we're going back to Abilene so you can stand trial."

Otis kept his right hand over his burning cheek while he did what he was told. "Frank will get you for this, mark my word, Frank won't stand for you arresting me. You can't treat me like this." Otis kept repeating.

Brady shackled Otis's hands and led him from the saloon and across Main Street where he saw a sign that read *Sheriff's Office.*

There was no one in the office when the two men walked in. Brady found a set of cell keys hanging on a peg next to the cell entrance. Brady pushed Otis into one of the cells and removed the shackles from his wrists. Then Brady closed the cell door and locked it before he walked back into the main office.

The desk was cluttered with wanted posters and there was a list of things to do written on a piece of brown paper.

A dirty cup, that looked like it held coffee from last month's makings and it held down the brown paper. The rifle rack was empty and the potbelly stove hadn't been fired up in ages.

After checking the jail cell and seeing that Otis was settled in, Brady left the sheriff's office and walked toward the business area of town.

There was a small cafe located a block from the sheriff's office and Brady was hungry. He felt that his prisoner might want some food also.

The small cafe was empty of customers when Brady walked in, so he sat down on a stool at the counter. There was a chalkboard on the wall behind the counter that had a note written on it. *Today's special. All you can eat. Steak and potatoes served with apple pie. Two bits.*

The waitress was a small woman in her early fifties with a smile that could light up a room. She had already poured a cup of coffee and sat it in front of Brady.

"What can I do for you cowboy? Or should I say ranger?" the waitress asked, as she wiped down his section of counter.

"Got me a prisoner over at the jail and I was wondering if you could fix us both a meal? One to eat here and one to take with me?" Brady asked.

"Need cash for both meals," the waitress said. "The town doesn't pay too good for their prisoners food."

"I can handle that," Brady said. "By the way, where is the sheriff? The office looks like it's been vacant for some time."

"There's an old saying in this town," the waitress said. "When the going gets tough, the sheriff gets going, right out of town, that is." the waitress laughed, as she kept wiping the counter top.

"The town looks pretty quiet to me," Brady said, as he picked up his cup and took his first taste of coffee in a long time. "Good coffee,"

"I take pride in my coffee young man," the waitress said. "By the way my name is Dolly Pickings and I own this joint."

"Pardon me Miss Pickings, for my bad manners. My name is Ranger Wells and I came to Deer Creek to bring a man wanted for murder, back to Abilene to stand trial,"

"I admire you lawmen, but I wouldn't have your job for anything in the world," Dolly said, as she laid two large size steaks on her new wood burning stove.

Brady had finished his first cup of coffee when the cafe door opened and a large grizzly sized man walked in. His hat was filthy from the dirt that had settled on his hatband.

His shirt and pants were clean but well worn and the pants were being held up with a length of rope that rapped around his waste and hung almost to his knees. His boots were worn out and there were holes in the toes that showed he had no socks on.

"Luther Bogs," Dolly gasped. "What're you doing in my cafe? You were told to leave Deer Creek and not come back."

"Dolly, I'm hungry and I have no place to go," Luther said. "I've tried to find work and I've looked for some kind of shelter and no one will take a chance on me."

"You should of thought of that before you broke that cowboy's back," Dolly said. "The town is scared of you now."

"That was an accident," Luther explained. "He was beating me with that mule skinners whip and I had to protect myself."

"That's why the law turned you loose and told you to leave town," Dolly said. "If you don't leave Deer Creek someone will kill you and blame it on your temper."

"I don't have a temper," Luther said. "I just wanted to keep that cowboy from beating me to death. I know I have to leave town but I have no where to go."

"Can I break in on this conversation?" Brady asked. "I'll be glad to buy your breakfast if I can talk to you about taking on a job with me in Abilene."

"I'll do anything short of breaking the law," Luther said. "I'm a good worker and I can fight with the best of them. I can ride and shoot too, but no one will give me a chance."

"Dolly fix Mr. Bogs one of your specials and I'll pay for it," Brady said, as he shook the hand of one of the biggest men he had ever set eyes on.

"Hope you aren't sorry for what you're getting yourself into mister," Dolly said, as she placed Brady's food in front of him and started cooking Luther his steak.

Brady finished his meal and was on his fourth cup of coffee as he watched Luther gulp down his food. There was no telling how long it had been since the man had eaten. The prisoner's food had been placed on a tin plate and was ready for Brady to deliver it.

Brady paid for all the food and left a good tip besides. Dolly took the tip and slid it down the front of her dress and gave Brady a head nod as he opened the cafe door and let Luther lead the way back to the sheriff's office.

They crossed the street and walked over to the sheriff's office, Brady followed Luther through the door and headed back to the jail cells. Luther stood wide-eyed and was looking around like a small child interested in everything that was going on.

Brady gave Otis his food and returned to the office to catch Luther looking out the window with a strange look on his face.

"What's going on out there, Luther?" Brady asked, as he crossed the office to look out the window.

"There's a group of people gathering in the street out front. They seemed to be interested in what's going on in the sheriff's office." Luther said.

The crowd moved closer to the sheriff's office as Brady stepped out on the boardwalk. "Seems like we have a problem here in Deer Creek and I have a plan to clear up this problem," Brady said, as he looked at the crowd. They didn't seem to have a leader, yet they didn't seem to be in an angry mood.

"You have two men in that jail that don't belong in Deer Creek," one of the women said. "We're wondering if you're going to rid this town of 'um?"

"That's what I had in mind," Brady said. "If you people would let me spend the night here, I'll get them out of town first thing in the morning."

"You have until noon tomorrow," the woman said, "Then we're coming over here and run 'um out of town ourselves."

"You're very kind," Brady said, "I can have them fed and out of here before the sun rises and you people can be assured of that."

Brady stepped back inside the office and watched the crowd disperse, as the woman who did the talking, turned and walked into the small cafe where Luther and Brady had eaten their meal, earlier.

"That lady seemed to want me out of town pretty bad," Bogs said. "Wish I knew her reason, because I never seen her before."

"You're a big man," Brady said. "People have a problem with folks that are over sized and has the power to hurt them."

"I wouldn't hurt anyone unless they were hurting me," Luther said, as he watched the crowd start to disappear.

"I know that Luther. You look and sound like good man and that's why I would like to have you with me, instead of against me," Brady said, as he walked back toward the jail cells. "You use the bunk in that back cell and I'll take this cell next to Otis. We'll get a good nights sleep and leave town at first light," Brady said.

"Thanks for your help," Luther said, as he stretched his large frame out on the cell's bunk. The middle of the bunk almost sunk to the floor when he sat down on it, but it couldn't be very uncomfortable because Luther was sound a sleep almost as soon as his head touched the mattress.

Every day the early morning air was turning colder and on this morning there was very little difference. The coolness in the air woke Brady from a deep sleep. He wished he could just role over and go back to sleep, but he knew he had to get everyone fed and out of town before the town's leading citizens came calling again.

He woke Luther and Otis and placed the shackles on Otis. The three men walked across the street and into the small cafe. Dolly greeted them with a happy smile and started pouring all three a cup of coffee.

"Dolly if you could fill us up with enough food to last out the day," Brady said. "We'll be out of town before your high society comes to throw us out."

The three men ate their fill of steak and eggs and again Brady thanked Dolly, as she wished them God's speed on their journey back to Abilene.

The livery stable was lit up with one of the new kerosene lamps and all three men stood and stared at the light from the lamp for a good while. Then Brady asked the man that was pitching hay, "You got a horse big enough to carry this man on a cross country ride?"

"Got me a Missouri mule that can carry his weight all day and then some, but he's expensive," the stable owner explained.

"What do you call expensive?" Brady asked, as he followed the owner over to a door that led out into an open corral.

"There he is," the owner said, as he pointed out a mule that was so black he looked blue. "Only three years old and he's as fit as a fiddle."

Otis and Luther had followed Brady out into the corral and they stood and watched as the mule staggered and weaved as he tried to walk.

Brady placed his hand on the mule's neck and looked into his eyes. Then Brady bent down and rubbed the mule's chest and legs. Then he opened the mule's mouth and he busted out laughing. "This mule is dying of ragweed poisoning."

"What are you talking about?" the owner asked. "This mule came to me through a trade with a cross country wagon train."

"I'm sure he did," Brady said, as he laughed and turned around and headed for the door that led back into the stable.

"He'll last you about a week before he'll develop a need for sugar and molasses. Then before long he'll become weak and topple over."

The owner stopped in his tracks and said, "He's already developed those symptoms for sugar and molasses. The wagon master said he ate these sweet foods because he developed the taste back in Missouri."

Brady didn't say a word he just walked into the stable and started looking at some of the other animals that the stable owner had. "I won't tell the town's folk that you have a sick animal in your stable that might effect the rest of the animals in town."

"You wouldn't do that to me. Would you?" the stable owner said, as he took hold of Brady's shoulder and tried to turn him so he could look Brady in the eyes.

"I told you I wouldn't say a word about it," Brady said, "But I'd get rid of that mule as soon as I could find some sucker that would take him off your hands."

"You said the disease would probably last for a week or more didn't you?" the stable owner asked. "You said you were looking for a mule to carry the big man on a trip and then you didn't need him any longer, right?"

"What are you trying to say?" Brady asked. "Are you trying to push that sick mule off on me?"

"Look, you give me ten bucks for the mule and he's yours," the stable owner said.

"Wish I could, but that's like throwing ten bucks into a deep dark hole," Brady said, as he walked from stall to stall.

"What'll you give me for the mule?" the owner asked.

" I'll give you the ten dollars if you'll throw in that over sized saddle with the deal," Brady said.

"It's a deal," the owner said, as he picked up the saddle and threw it over the mule's back. "You boy's are leaving town soon aren't you?"

"Soon as you pack some feed into one of those grain sacks," Brady said. "The animals will need some feed on the trip."

The owner packed the toe-sack with grain, tied it with chicken wire and placed it behind the saddle on the mule's back. The mule stood weaving from side to side as if he was drunk.

"Mr. Wells," Luther said. "I can't stand here and watch you throw a way so much money on a sick mule. I can walk almost as fast as you can ride. I bet I can keep up with you on the trail without that mule."

"Well, look at it this way," Brady said. "We're helping out a neighbor and you'll get some rest while the mule last."

"Seems cruel to me," Luther said. "But it's your money and you're the boss, so I'll leave it at that." Then he placed his foot in the stirrup and swung himself into the saddle.

The three men pointed their animals to the southeast and rode out of town. The longer they rode the stronger the mule became and Luther couldn't understand it. By the time the first day ended the mule seemed strong and eager to keep moving. There was no stagger in his gait and the mule kept up with the other men without even breathing hard.

"Got you a good animal there," Brady said, as the three men pulled up beside a flowing stream to let the animals drink.

"Just a shame he isn't going to last very long," Luther said, as he rubbed down the mule while it drank from the stream.

"He'll last a long time if you take good care of him," Brady said, as he stretched his arms and kicked his legs to relive the stiffness.

"You said the mule was suffering from a disease," Luther said. "Now you 're saying he's going to be all right. Which is it?"

"Luther, the owner was going to try and make a lot of money off of a bunch of strangers," Brady said. "I just noticed that the feed the mule was eating was full of loco weed and that the mule had ate enough to make him a little dizzy. The rest was history and everyone came out with a good deal."

Luther threw his head back and started laughing. He slapped his leg as he thought about the way Brady talked the owner down to the right price for the mule.

"Are we ever going to eat again?" Otis asked. "I'm starving while you two are making jokes over how you cheated your fellow man out of his best animal."

"We have a couple more hours of sunlight left and I'm planning to make good use of it," Brady said, as he mounted up and continued to ride southeast.

The trip back to Abilene was an uneventful one. It lasted almost two weeks and it gave Brady and Luther a lot of time to learn more about each other.

When they arrived in Abilene, Otis was turned over to Captain Keith Benson of the rangers and the captain brought Brady up to date on what had taken place while he was gone.

Brady introduced Luther to the captain and explained how he was going to help with the work on the ranch. "You're going to be surprised at the new changes at the ranch," the captain said. "That young lady Abbey has already started making the ranch pay off."

"How's she doing that?" Brady asked. "We've nothing to offer anyone except for a few mustangs."

"I'm going to keep my mouth shut and let your own people explain things to you when you get back to the ranch." the captain said, as he reached for his hat and headed for the door. "Come with me to the bank and I'll catch you up to date on your pay."

When the men walked into the bank, Brady noticed the open door leading to Thomas Durham's office. There was a crowd in the office. Brady gave it little thought as he and Luther walked with the captain to the nearest teller's window.

Luther seemed amazed at the beauty and size of the Durham Bank. The people moving in and about caused Luther's head to turn in several directions. Then he stopped and focused on one person. She was a beautiful girl with long brown hair that flowed down her back past her shoulders. She moved with such grace that Luther just stood and stared.

"Hello Brady," the girl said, as she walked past the teller's window.

Brady stood with his mouth open. The sight of Hannah standing in front of him was more then he could take at the moment. He had to turn away from her so she couldn't see the tears that were building up in his eyes.

"Hannah, I'll be with you in a minute," Brady said, as he tried to hold his voice steady. "I have to get caught up on some business. Maybe we can sit down and catch up on some of the events that's been going on since you've been gone."

As Brady turned back toward Hannah he saw a crowd of people walking toward her. There was her father and mother, Doctor Robert Dewberry, Frank Spencer the lawyer, and others that Brady didn't even know. Brady knew he was out of his league with these people, but he made one more approach to Hannah. "Want to get together later this evening?" Brady asked.

"Brady, I'm short of time. I'll be catching the train back east the first thing in the morning. Couldn't we just write to each other sometimes?" Hannah said, as she turned and hooked her arms into the arm of Doctor Dewberry and Frank Spencer and they walked out of the bank.

Brady was crushed. He was having a hard time holding back his feelings, as he looked at Luther and motioned for him to follow him out of the bank.

"Let's get you some better clothes before we ride out to the ranch," Brady said. "There's a bath house across the street so you can clean up before you put on your new duds."

Luther looked like a wealthy cowpuncher when they got him cleaned up. They had a hard time finding a pair of boots that would fit. He was armed with a Henry rifle and a .44 revolver that he had to stuff in his pants because they couldn't find a belt or holster that would fit him.

The ride to his ranch was a quiet one and Luther seemed to understand as he rode his mule a few yards back to give Brady some privacy.

It was dusk when the two men rode into the gate of the B/A Ranch. The new gate was a beauty and the house and barn had been repaired. There was a new horse trough built underneath the well and Luther and Brady used the trough to let the horses drink.

A scream came from the house as they heard a door slam and a beautiful young girl came running up to Brady throwing her arms around Brady's neck kissing him on the mouth. "I'm so glad to see you," Abbey said, as she realized what she had just done. She knew she had no right to greet Brady in such a fashion.

"Hey Abbey," Brady said. "I like the way you welcome folks to the ranch. I want you to meet Luther Bogs, he's come to give us a hand with the heavy chores."

Abbey laughed, as she turned her head toward the sky to take in the size of the man standing next to Brady. "You are a big man," she said. "It's a pleasure to meet you."

"Same here missy," Luther said, as he took off his hat and turned it around and around in his hands.

Abbey took both men's hands and led them toward the house. "Papa you have visitors." She yelled as the front door opened and Alvin Simpson stepped out on the porch. He watched Abbey release the hands of the two men before she run into the house closing the door behind her.

Chapter 5

"Alvin, this is Luther Bogs," Brady said. "He's been down on his luck lately and I felt he might be a good man to have around. He says he's pretty handy around a ranch."

"Nice meeting you Luther," Alvin said. "We've more work than we can handle right now, so you'll be a welcome addition to the ranch."

"You have a nice place here Mr. Simpson," Luther said, as he leaned back against the porch railing observing the corral and other facilities on the ranch.

"You know this ranch really belongs to Brady, I just run it for him," Alvin said. "I also like to be called Alvin, not Mr. Simpson."

"I've never called my boss by his first name," Luther said.

"Brady is your boss," Alvin said, as he lit his corncob pipe. "I'll be making the work assignments every day, but Brady is still your boss."

The corral was filled with a number of mustangs that looked as if they could use some fattening up after living off the range.

"They need shoeing also," Alvin said, as he walked over and climbed the fence railing to sit on the top rail.

"Where did all these horses come from?" Brady asked. "Are there any more?"

"Indian Joe rounds them up off the open range," Alvin said "Yakima has enlarged our Longhorn stock by almost a hundred head. Both men have done a lot with what few wranglers they have helping them. Abbey has sold five head of cattle to the hotel restaurant and the local diner. She probably under cut their regular suppliers.

"Well that's a start," Brady said, "But we aren't going to make it by selling five head of cattle a year."

"She sold the army those eight wild stallions that Indian Joe brought in off the range," Alvin said. "We had them already broke for riding before we delivered them. Abbey even put some of the money in the bank."

Brady turned and looked at Alvin. "She put the ranch money in Thomas Durham's bank?" Brady asked.

"Is that a problem?" Alvin asked. "It wasn't much, not even enough to last us through the winter."

"Could be a problem," Brady said. "I just don't want Thomas Durham to know our financial status. He doesn't care much for us or this ranch. He doesn't want anything to do with us personally. He just wants to control our money."

"He's not getting much," Alvin said. "But I can sure tell Abbey to stop putting our money in his bank if that's what you want. By the way, I ran into his daughter Hannah in town and she asked about you."

"I saw her too and she spoke to me just long enough to tell me she was leaving on the morning train," Brady said, "She let me know that she would be spending her last few hours celebrating with her friends, Dr. Dewberry and Frank Spencer."

"Ouch," Alvin said, "That had to hurt. She has sure changed these past few years. Her stay in that Boston women's school has given her a different outlook on life."

"Her leaving and not wanting to talk to me did hurt a lot," Brady said. "I always thought she and I were a couple, but in the last few years I feel she has changed her mind. We've become strangers to each other."

"You know Brady, what money we have in the bank ain't going to get us through the winter," Alvin said, as he tried to change the subject. "We need more feed for the stock and wire for fencing and I could go on and on because we have more needs than we have money right now."

"I'm doing my best," Brady said. "I told you when we started this ranch it was going to be a struggle until we start to make it pay."

"Got time to shoe some of these horses?" Alvin asked, as he climbed down from the rail fence. "Your equipment's in the barn."

"Sure," Brady said. "Maybe it'll keep my mind off all my problems."

When the two men walked into the barn Brady fired up the forge while Alvin pumped the bellows to get the coals burning.

Just then Luther walked into the barn with a grin on his face. "Don't tell me you're a blacksmith too," Luther said. "I'm pretty good at shoeing horses myself."

"Good," Brady said. "You keep the forge going while Alvin stacks you some iron and I'll bring a couple horses in for us to shoe."

The rest of the day went well as Luther and Brady took turns shoeing most of the horses in the corral. It was getting dark when they shut down the forge and walked out to the horse-trough to wash up. Alvin hollered from the porch for them to hurry up and get ready for supper because he was starving.

"Luther you surprised me today with your horse-shoeing skills," Brady said. "You might have missed your calling by joining up as a cowhand."

"Mr. Wells," Luther said, "I believe I'll be help to you and Alvin because I'm also a good cowhand."

"Never doubted it a moment," Brady said, as he turned toward the house wiping his hands on his shirttail.

"You can always count on me," Luther said, as the two men entered the house and walked into the kitchen.

Alvin was already sitting down when Luther and Brady took their seat along side of him. Brady looked around for Abbey but he didn't see her. When supper was finished and the dessert had been served, Brady was still wondering where Abbey was. He leaned back in his chair and rubbed his stomach as he talked about eating to much. "Think I'll look up Abbey and talk with her about the ranch finances," Brady said.

"No need," Alvin said. "She has it well in hand. Beside she's in town at the doctor's office helping him with his patients today. She's working as his nurse three days a week."

"You didn't tell me that," Brady said. "When will she get back?"

"Before dark," Alvin said, as he stood up and pushed his chair back. "If she's too late, she'll stay overnight in town."

"I was worried because it's already dusk outside," Brady said, as he walked out on the front porch with Alvin following close behind.

Luther was still at the table eating his large slice of apple pie and washing it down with a large glass of milk. Coffee never did set well with Luther even though he could drink it on occasions. Luther wiped his mouth with his napkin and stood up thanking the women for an excellent meal. Then he walked outside and sat on the porch steps listening to Brady and Luther talking about the work Abbey was doing for the doctor.

"She's paid well," Alvin said. "She needs spending money and this is how she chose to earn it. The people respect her and the doctor treats her well."

"Do they know she has a black stepfather and an Indian mother?" Brady asked. "Do they know she too is a half-breed?"

"Why should they know?" Alvin asked. "Her skin is light colored like her white father and she speaks like the white man. She's more white than you are."

"I'm sorry," Brady said. "I know it's none of my business, but I just don't want her to get hurt when it comes to her choosing a husband."

"She won't be hurt," Alvin said. "She'll choose wisely and when she chooses a husband it'll be for the rest of her life, just like her mother did."

Brady stood up and walked toward the barn as he watched the sunset in the west. Brady could see a horse coming down the ranch road and he knew it must be Abbey. Brady felt like he made a fool of himself with Alvin.

Brady watched as Abbey climbed down from her horse and handed the reins to Luther. She ran upon the porch and hugged her stepfather then disappeared into the house. Brady knew he had to get over the feelings he had today and get both of these girls out of his mind.

Brady and Luther spent the night in the bunkhouse. The next morning when Luther woke up Brady was gone. The sun was peeking through the only window that brought what little sunlight there was into the bunkhouse. Luther dressed and walked to the large cookhouse where the rest of the hands were eating their breakfast.

When Luther picked up his tray and fell in line with the other men he couldn't keep from laughing at them for staring at his size. Some of the men dropped their tray, as they looked the big man up and down.

"I'll be working with you men for the time being," Luther said. "My name is Luther Bogs and I hope to get to know each and everyone of you in time. Did any of you happen to see where Mr. Wells went this morning?"

A small Indian boy walked up to Luther and was straining his neck trying to see up to Luther's face. Luther bent down and with one hand lifted the boy to his chest. "You got something you want to tell me?"

The boy grinned from ear to ear showing a mouth that was missing three teeth up front. "I hope we will be good friends," the boy said.

"I'm sure we will be," Luther said. "But we could be even better friends if you could tell me where Mr. Wells went this morning."

"He ate early and asked me to saddle his horse so he could ride into town. He had business with the ranger captain," The boy said.

"Did he say when he would be back?" Luther asked.

"No sir," the boy said. "He just told me to watch after the ranch while he was gone."

Luther laughed, as he sat the boy back down on the floor and said, "You had better do what the boss says."

The boy left running and the rest of the men seemed to except Luther as just another worker. After breakfast Luther went to the barn to see if there was anymore shoeing to be done. Alvin was in the barn talking with Indian Joe about which part of the hills he would ride that day to gather more horses.

Yakima was squatted on the ground marking out the area he would search for more Longhorns. There were other men standing around waiting for their instructions from Alvin.

Luther watched as Alvin sent each and every man on an important job for the ranch. There was branding, fence mending, seed planting, plowing, and soon more horses to shoe. Luther was surprised at the way Alvin selected the men for each job and the men respected Alvin enough to do just what he asked them to do.

When it came Luther's turn, Alvin said, "Abbey will be going into town today. Brady and I would like for you to ride with her and see that no harm comes to her."

"This, I would be glad to do," Luther said, as he turned and faced the noise that sounded behind him. It was the banging of the barn door against the wall. The wind had begun to blow and the door wasn't propped open or barred shut.

Abbey stood in the doorway with her hands on her hip, as the sun shown through the door putting a glow around her body. "Alvin," she said. "What is this talk about me having to have a bodyguard? I have no reason to believe that anyone would want to harm me or anyone else on this ranch."

"Brady's idea. He's only trying to look out for your safety in case there is a reason you might need some extra help," Alvin said. "It's better to be safe than sorry."

"I can do this job without anyone knowing that you're being watched over," Luther said. "As big as I am, I can still keep out of sight."

"You're sweet Luther," Abbey said. "But I feel like I'm loosing what privacy I might have."

"Could we try it for a while? If you see it's going to cause a problem I'll talk with Mr. Wells myself." Luther said.

"You've got a deal," Abbey said. "You might as well saddle two horses because I have to be in town by noon."

Luther did what he was told, except he saddled Abbey's horse and his Missouri mule.

The ride to town was a pleasant one because Luther liked listening to some of the stories Abbey told about her early childhood. When they arrived in town they left their horse and mule at the livery and agreed to be back at the stables in time to return to the ranch before dark.

Abbey walked over to the office of the local newspaper and picked up the latest addition. The headline read,

Otis Harper, brother of Frank Harper, was brought back to Abilene to stand trial for murder. A young ranger by the name of Brady Wells arrested him.

Abbey felt a cold chill run up her spine as she read the article. They were telling Frank Harper and his gang that the man responsible for his brother's capture was Brady Wells. They were putting Brady's life in danger.

She walked out of the newspaper office biting her lip until she almost brought blood. The smell of fresh air lowered her temper enough that she started looking around for Luther. She knew he would be some where within eyesight. She broke down and laughed when she saw Luther trying to hide that big body behind a post that was holding up the porch of the saddle shop across the street.

Abbey started walking over to the saddle shop and she continued to laugh, as Luther started to look for another place to hide. "Luther would you like to have lunch with me?"

"Me? Why I would be glad to Miss Abbey," Luther said, as he stepped down from the porch and walked with Abbey to the building that had *Cafe* written on the big plate glass window out front.

Abbey had to reach up to place her arm through Luther's folded arm while they walked to the cafe. When they entered, Luther chose a table next to the window then he pulled the chair out for Abbey to sit down.

"You're a gentleman," Abbey said, "We're lucky to have you working for us."

"Miss Abbey," Luther said. "I just want you to trust me because I need to be a friend to MR. Simpson, you and Mr. Wells."

"What has Brady got to do with you and I being friends?" Abbey asked, as she sat down in the chair Luther had picked for her.

Luther walked around to the chair on the other side of the table and started to sit down when he heard a loud voice from the back of the cafe.

"Don't sit down in that chair," the voice said. "Wait until I get you a chair from the back room."

Luther looked embarrassed as he stood waiting for someone to bring him a chair. When they did bring the chair, it was the biggest chair Luther had ever seen. "Who does this chair belong to?" Luther asked, as he sat down.

"That's Bernice's chair," the waitress said. "She uses it when she takes her lunch break. Her father owns this cafe and does most of the cooking."

"Tell Bernice that I thank her for the use of her chair," Luther said, as he twisted around in the chair admiring its width and strength.

Luther ordered a Mexican meal to be shared between him and Abbey. They were served tea and taco shells with butter and honey until the main course was served. The meal was more than enough to feed three people and Luther made the most of it.

Abbey was amazed at the amount of food Luther could put away. Then she noticed that Luther was staring at the batwing doors that led into the kitchen. When Abbey turned to look at what Luther was staring at, she noticed a beautiful dark headed girl staring back at Luther. The strange thing about the girl was she stood flat-footed and could see over the large batwing doors.

Luther hadn't blinked an eye when the girl suddenly disappeared from the doorway. Luther stood and started for the doors when a man almost the size of Luther stepped in front of him and asked, "Is everything alright?"

Luther stopped and looked at the large man standing in front of him. "Who was that girl I just saw?"

"That sir, is my daughter Bernice," the man said. "I would appreciate it if you'd return to your table and finish your meal."

Luther returned to the table but only to place a two-bit piece on the table. He assisted Abbey from her chair. "If you're ready Miss Abbey, we can leave now." The two walked out of the cafe still curious about the girl that had caught Luther's eye.

"We need to talk to Captain Benson of the rangers, before we return to the ranch," Abbey said. "I need to know where he's sending Brady for his next assignment."

"I believe that's Captain Benson leaving the barber shop," Luther said.

Abbey called out to the Captain, as she rushed up to his side. "I'm Abbey Simpson Mr. Benson, I sure would like a moment of your time."

"I know who you are," the captain said. "But I don't believe I know your friend."

"Oh, this is Luther Bogs," Abbey said, as she watched the captain look Luther up and down like he was a prize horse.

The two men shook hands and the captain said, "If you ever want to become a ranger look me up,"

"I have a job sir, I'm working for Mr. Wells," Luther answered.

"You're the new man Brady hired?" the captain asked.

"Captain, I need to know where Brady will be sent for his next assignment," Abbey said. "I also need to know how long he'll be gone."

"He's already left for Twin Forks this morning. He has been assigned to find Crazy Wolf," the captain said, "Crazy Wolf and a couple of his bucks jumped the reservation and have already killed one family in the Twin Forks area. The last we heard the three were hold up in the hills around Twin Forks."

"Did he take any help with him?" Abbey asked. "He can't fight off a bunch of wild Indians by himself."

"You know Brady as well as I do, Miss Abbey. You can answer that question yourself," the captain said.

Abbey turned her head to keep the two men from seeing the tears that were building up in her eyes. "All you men have to show is how tough you are while your friends wait to see if you're coming back home. Then you'll say it's all in a day's work. How stupid can men get?"

Abbey started walking for the post office with Luther following behind her. "You can go back to your hiding place," Abbey said. "Because I have some more stops to make."

Luther followed her but kept his distance. He didn't want her to turn her anger on him. When they reached the post office Luther found a spot in the shade across the street and sat down to wait for Abbey.

Abbey left the post office with the ranch mail in her hand then she went to the bank building where she entered the door that led upstairs.

Luther waited a while before he followed her up the stairs. He saw that she had entered Doctor Dewberry's office.

Luther knew when Abbey was angry and he knew she needed to blow off some steam. She needed to yell at someone and he knew he was the sounding board for her to yell at.

By the time Abbey left the doctors office, it was close to sundown and the ride to the ranch would last well into the late evening hours. So Abbey got two rooms at the hotel for Luther and herself.

The overnight rest did wonders for Abbey. She was already up and dressed when Luther came to her room to inform her that the hotel kitchen was open.

At breakfast Abbey had a worried look on her face but she carried on a happy conversation about how Brady and her stepfather became such good friends. She would dedicate her life to the B/A Ranch and do everything to make it grow into a working ranch.

Abbey knew that everyone was worried if there would be enough feed for the cattle over the winter. When winter did set in Abbey wasn't looking forward to the Christmas holidays unless Brady was able to be at home sharing in the happiness.

Abbey kept a happy face on the trip back home but Luther knew she was worried about Brady and his tracking of the Indians.

The weeks seemed to pass very slowly but soon winter started to set in. There was one snowfall after another and the men were struggling to keep the horses and cattle fed. Alvin had come down with a terrible cough that wouldn't go away no matter how they doctored it.

Brady had been gone for months now and the only time Abbey heard from him was when she went to the ranger's office to ask about him.

Ranger Benson would let her read his telegraphs and the telegraphs were always from Twin Forks. It seemed that Brady had been waiting for the winter to set in before he made an all out attempt to capture the Indians. In the summer the Indians had the advantage of surprise but in the winter the advantage changed toward Brady having the upper hand.

That Christmas and New Years found the Simpson family celebrating their second year on the ranch. Every member of the family and all the hired hands gathered around a large bond fire and gave thanks for their great success of the ranch. Little did Abbey know that the feed was running out for the livestock.

The New Year's celebration was a dance held in the center of town on New Years Eve night. Anyone who could play a musical instrument was asked to climb upon the stage and show off his musical talents.

It would have been a great hoe-down if Brady had been able to be there. Luther did get to meet his dream girl, Bernice. She was the daughter of the big man that owned the town cafe. She stood up to Luther's chin and she was every bit as pretty as Luther described her. Abbey found her sweet and charming and she hoped that Luther and Bernice could become more than just friends. Abbey spent her time dancing with Doctor Dewberry and some of the soldiers from the post, but she was glad when the party was over and she could return to the hotel.

Hannah Durham had returned to town and both Doctor Dewberry and Frank Spencer escorted her to the dance. She seemed to be enjoying herself. To Abbey, Hannah wasn't missing Brady at all.

Brady was on Abbey's mind most of the time and she missed him very much. Abbey kept herself busy around the ranch trying to make ends meet and taking care of Alvin who was getting weaker every day. She didn't know what the ranch would do if it hadn't been for Luther Bogs. He had taken over Alvin's duties since Alvin became to sick to work.

Luther spent days in the pastures looking for weak cattle that couldn't fend for themselves. He drove a feed wagon loaded with hay and water so he could tend the sick animals and nourish the weak cattle back to life, but the grain was getting low and the money was running short.

There was an envelope that Abbey had put on the kitchen cabinet that was addressed to Brady Wells. It had been there for a week or more and Abbey didn't know how important it was. The return address was to a lawyer's office in Denver Colorado.

"Aunt Martha," Abbey yelled. "Come to the kitchen, I have a job for you."

When Martha arrived in the kitchen she was steaming mad, "Girl, I've been meeting myself with all the work I've been doing in this house and you're screaming for me to come and do even more work."

"All I want you to do is witness me opening this letter to Brady," Abbey said. "It could be important and if it is I could have Captain Benson wire Brady in Twin Forks."

"I ain't going to witness you breaking the law for any reason," Martha said. "You're going to get yourself in a bunch of trouble."

"Just watch and see what I remove from this envelope," Abbey said, as she opened the letter and removed the contents.

There was a letter that explained a draft that was written on the Denver National Bank for the amount of five thousand dollars. Graven Burrow had signed it.

Dear Brady Wells;

We have hit a good vain of gold and it looks like we might have a few bucks coming to us over a period of time. This is your share so far and I wish you would give thought to selling your part to me so I can sell the mine to a corporation here in Denver. If you're willing to sell your part the money could turn out to be ten times the amount of this draft.

Your friend and partner; Graven

Abbey's eyes became very large as she looked at the draft in her hands. Five thousand dollars could save the ranch if she could get someone to cash the draft.

"Abbey that ain't your money," Martha said. "That money belongs to Brady Wells and he just might want to spend it himself."

Abbey ran upstairs and into Alvin's room. "Brady got a letter from Denver with a draft for five thousand dollars," Abbey said. "It's from a friend named Graven Burrow. It can save this ranch if I can get it cashed. Do you feel like riding into town? I might need you to sign for Brady."

"Do you think it's right for us to handle Brady's money without his permission?" Alvin asked. "I know it could save the ranch, but is it the right thing to do?"

"I believe Brady would want us to save the livestock above all else," Abbey said. "I'm going to town and get this draft cashed if it's the last thing I do. Do you want to come?"

Alvin pulled himself up from the bed and started getting dressed when Luther came walking in. Abbey handed Alvin his boots and walked over to Luther and led him out of the room.

"What are you doing Abbey?" Luther asked. "Alvin is sick and he shouldn't leave his bedroom let alone travel to town in weather like this." "Luther, it's our only chance to buy enough fed for the animals and food for the workers," Abbey said. "We have to take the chance. Please hook up the buckboard and put in a lot of blankets. We're going to try and save this ranch."

Luther did as he was told but he worried about Alvin the whole time he was hooking up the buckboard.

Martha cried as Luther and Abbey helped Alvin out the door and into the buckboard. She knew this might be the last time she saw her brother in-law.

The snow had slowed down and it was packed enough for the buckboard to roll through the light spots. There were times that Luther had to use his rope and the strength of his mule to help pull the buckboard out of some deep snowdrifts but the journey continued.

The trip took two hours longer then normal but they arrived at the Durham National Bank by early afternoon. The windows were still open when Abbey arrived and placed the draft on the teller's stand. "Would you please cash this draft with my stepfathers signature?"

The clerk looked at the draft and then told Abbey he would have to get Mr. Durham's okay. He left the window and went to Mr. Durham's office. When he returned, he refused to cash the draft without Brady Wells signature.

Abbey tried to explain the circumstances but the clerk wouldn't listen because of Mr. Durham's orders.

The three left the bank and went to the ranger station where they explained the situation to Captain Benson. They wanted the captain to wire Brady and get permission to cash the draft.

"Brady is on this mission and can't be reached right now," the captain said. "I've tried for over a week now and I'm getting no answer back."

"What are we going to do?" Abbey asked. "If we can't buy feed soon, the cattle will never make it through the winter. If we can't get supplies the workers may not make it through the winter either."

"Come with me," the captain said. "We can set up credit at the feed and hardware store. There's no reason to let the ranch fall apart."

The storeowners were more than happy to set up a line of credit after Abbey showed them the draft and Captain Benson vouched for it.

Luther rented two wagons and drivers to haul the feed and the supplies needed to finish out the winter. Luther left as soon as the wagons were loaded but Alvin wasn't in shape to make another trip back to the ranch in this type of weather.

Abbey took Alvin to see Doctor Dewberry for his cough and the doctor could only give him laudanum for his cough and fever.

"Doctor Dewberry, when will my stepfather start getting better?" Abbey asked.

"There are cases of consumption where people have made it through the stages of fever and coughing," the doctor said. "But I don't want to give you false hope. I would like to keep him here in my office over night. I'll put him on the exam table and fix it where he won't role off."

"I'll stay with him," Abbey said. "I don't want him to wake up without me being there."

"I have a couch you can sleep on," the doctor said. "I'll be here with him through the night. We must try to keep his fever down. We can use the snow to cool his body off."

Both the doctor and Abbey hauled snow up to the office all night long, but just before sunlight there was a rattle in Alvin's voice that told the doctor that Alvin was gasping for his last breath.

Abbey flung herself over her stepfather and cried when the doctor pronounced him dead. Abbey had lost the love of a great man that took her and her mother in when no one else even cared if they lived or died.

Chapter 6

The snow was still falling when Brady checked the weather outside of his makeshift lean-to. He had found signs that the Indians were using the trail below him for an access to their hidden cave. That's why Brady picked this spot to build his shelter. It was close to the trail and the only flat spot that was smooth and wide enough for the lean-to. He felt the Indians would return by this trail if the weather kept getting worse.

The wind was calm for the moment but it was only a matter of time before it would start blowing up another storm causing the snow to block his view of the trail below. He had to get closer to that trail to make sure the Indians were still using it. He tied two ropes together and secured one end to the tree just in front of his lean-to. Then he tied the other end around his waist, this way he could lower himself closer to the trail.

He made sure his clothing was dry and there was no skin exposed to the weather before he started his decent down the slope. The going was slow and cold, he could only move a few feet at a time or he might cause a snow slide that would give a warning to the Indians.

When he reached the rope's end he tried to focus his eyes on the area where the trail had last been seen. The snow was still falling and that forced him to use his gloved covered hand to block the snow from his eyes. It wasn't long before the cold blast of wind started infiltrating through his clothing.

The eerie feeling of no noise in this vast area of land was bad enough, but the feeling of the cold creeping through his clothing was making him very uneasy. How much exposure he got from this weather was going to make a big difference in his climb back up the slope. He had to make sure he started back before he became stiff and over exhausted. Any misjudgment now could mean his life.

He heard the whinny of a horse. He wiped the snow from his face until he saw the Indians returning to the cave. For months he had been able to keep one step ahead of them. Now he had to make his way back up the slope and wait out the snowstorm.

Pulling himself up by the rope was hard for him and he fought for every foot of precious ground. This became the hardest climb he ever had to make. The other end of the rope couldn't be seen and Brady was trying to judge his strength with how many feet he had to climb. The wind had started blowing much harder and it felt like it was pushing him back. This was no time for him to panic. He had to keep climbing. He tried to conjure up all the strength he had left in his body. He finally felt the tree that held the other end of the rope.

This gave Brady hope. He pulled harder until he raised himself to the top of the slope. Then he rolled himself over the edge and into the lean-to where his horse was still feeding on his feedbag. The horse made no sound when Brady crawled closer to the small fire he had left burning.

Brady pulled a canvas tarp over the opening of the lean-to, it blocked the wind from blowing in. The small space he shared with his horse began to warm up.

Brady lay close to the fire until he felt the tingling in his feet again, they had become numb from the cold. He began removing the layers of clothing he had on. When he was able to remove his boots, he rubbed his feet until the feeling began creeping back into them. Total exhaustion from the climb and his warm surroundings caused him to become very sleepy.

The night was going to be long, but not as cold as it had been. He packed his coffeepot with snow and sat it beside the fire so it would be ready for coffee the next morning. He removed the horse's feedbag and sat a pan of snow where the horse could drink when the snow melted.

Then Brady crawled into his bedroll and made himself comfortable hoping for a good night's rest.

After dozing off, a vision of Hannah Durham came into his mind. He kept reaching for Hannah but she kept moving away from him, laughing all the time. He kept pleading for her to stand still so he could hold her in his arms, but when he did reach her, she faded away into smoke that disappeared in the wind.

Brady was chasing Hannah in his dream when another face appeared. It was the beautiful face of Abbey Simpson. She was laughing and dancing around him holding out her arms and inviting him to come to her, but he could see Alvin in the background. Then he woke up in a heavy sweat, looking around the lean-to as if he was going to see Alvin Simpson standing there with a disappointed look on his face.

Brady picked up the coffeepot and took a long drink of melted water. He shook his head trying to clear his thoughts. These dreams kept appearing every night forcing him to watch the beautiful faces of Hannah and Abbey as they ran with him through the meadows of wild flowers and sat with him near the rolling brooks of the hillside. Every night ended in exhaustion before he would drift off to sleep.

Brady's eyes popped open the next morning when he heard his horse moving around in the shelter. He jumped up and placed his hand over the horse's nose as he listened for any noise from the outside. He heard nothing, but he started dressing himself so he could take a long look outside.

He was hungry and he needed some coffee, but he didn't want to take the chance of warning his enemies below. By the time he finished dressing the sun had appeared over the hill and he had already figured out that the weather was going to start warming up. He wanted to be in position to confront the Indians when they felt it was safe for them to leave their cave.

Brady climbed down to a rock that was a little above the Indian's cave and about fifty yards in front of it. There was no sign that the Indians had left the cave because the snow hadn't been disturbed around the entrance.

He checked his Winchester and placed a box of shells on a log next to him. Then he made himself comfortable. The boulder had kept the snow from piling up on this side and it was easy for him to wipe away any remaining snow. Brady felt he could stay warm and dry for the next few hours.

He leaned his Winchester against the boulder and cupped his hands around his mouth as he spoke in perfect Apache, "Crazy Wolf, Black Feather and Little Horse. This is Brady Wells, the ranger from Abilene. I've been sent to bring you back to stand trial for murder." The echo kept his words bouncing around the hillside.

There was no sound from the cave and there was no movement in the cave. Brady started having second thoughts about whether the three Indians were still in there.

"Crazy Wolf," Brady said again. "We can play women's games or we can talk like men but in five minutes I'm going to attack your cave." Again the echo kept repeating over and over what Brady said.

There was no return message and still no movement inside the cave. Could the Indians have left during the night and the drifting snow covered their tracks again? Could it be they were using another place to hide out in? Brady had searched these hills for months and this was the only logical place where all three Indians could hide.

Suddenly Brady saw movement in the cave. They were in there! It looked like they were going to make their stance inside the cave. He knew they were not giving up without a fight.

Brady kept a close eye on the cave entrance for the next few minutes then he aimed his rifle and fired at the spot where he last saw movement. There was no ricochet sound like he expected to hear which meant he had hit something. He followed with another shot but this time the ricochet sound was loud and clear. He kept moving his rifle and firing at different locations inside the cave opening. Two rapid fire, one slower, then three rapid fire, two slower. Brady didn't want them to learn the timing of his firing.

This went on for a good half-hour before Brady moved to another spot. He reloaded and started firing again. This time he started receiving fire from the cave, but they were firing wild and not anywhere close to him.

Brady tried to figure out how many guns were firing but he couldn't get an accurate count. He did figure out that the firing was slow and getting further apart. Which may mean they were running short on ammunition.

"I believe I've hit one of your braves Crazy Wolf," Brady shouted. "I believe I've got the advantage because I have the ammunition to keep up this firing for days."

Another shot rang out as Brady crawled to a different location, one that could cause the ricochet to move around the cave at a different angle. He started firing again as he moved the barrel of his rifle to fire at different positions in the cave.

Then a rifle appeared at the cave entrance, it had a rag tied to the barrel. "Don't shoot any more," the voice said. "We're dead."

"Who's speaking?" Brady asked. "Why do you say you're dead when you're talking to me? This is an old Apache trick to get me into the open so you can kill me."

"Your first shot killed my friend, Little Horse," the voice said. "Later, Crazy Wolf died from your bullets. Now I lay with a bullet in my stomach and it's my death wound."

"Pull yourself out into the open so I can check your words," Brady said. "I will not believe until I see."

A figure crawled out to the front of the cave and fell face down in the snow. Brady watched the Indian for several minutes trying to see any movement but none was made. "You're a good trickster," Brady yelled. "Which one is in the cave waiting for me to show myself?"

Still no movement and no sound came from the cave. Brady made his way back to his horse while he kept an eye on the opening of the cave. He wanted to entice the other two to come out, so he built a fire and made a pot of coffee. He drank it as he leaned against the boulder watching the cave opening. The sun was starting to set leaving long shadows across the trail and soon the shadow extended across the cave opening.

It was too dark for Brady to see the cave entrance from his distance. He found a dry spot between the two boulders he was using for cover and prepared for another long cold night. After feeding the horse he fixed himself a dry spot to spread his bedroll.

The night went much the same as all the other nights. Thoughts of Hannah would appear in Brady's dream and then drift off in a cloud of smoke. Then Abbey's sparkling eyes would appear then her beautiful smile and finally her whole face would appear in every beautiful pose imaginable. Then there was Alvin. Brady knew he had to stop thinking of Abbey or he would lose his best friend.

Sunrise brought another day of playing cat and mouse. If things went on like this the snow would be melted enough for a horse and rider to make his way out of these hills.

Brady climbed back to the lean-to and strapped the feedbag on his horse's head. Then he pulled chunks of beef jerky out of his saddlebags for himself. Brady went back to his lookout and surveyed the area in front of the cave as he chewed the beef jerky into mush and swallowed it.

The body of Black Feather was still face down in front of the cave. His body was iced over now from the cold.

There was no other sign of life in the area. Brady had to make a choice today. He had to check out the cave for any sign of life. The snow was melting and the trail could become an escape route for the Indians soon.

Then Brady got the surprise of his life. A huge black bear was waddling up to the cave entrance. Brady couldn't believe his eyes. Then a thought came to him. Maybe he could let the bear check out the cave. If he fired at the bear and ran it off he still wouldn't know if any of the other Indians were alive.

Brady stood quietly watching every movement the bear made. The huge bear kept a steady pace up to the cave entrance, then he stopped and sniffed at the Indian that was lying at the entrance. Soon the bear pawed at the frozen body and then it decided to move inside.

Brady couldn't see inside the cave but he soon heard a gunshot and a loud scream. Then after a few moments he saw the bear dragging a body out into the sunlight where he was going to settle down and have a good meal.

Brady opened fire on the bear hitting him several times in the chest. The bear stood on his hind legs stretching to his fullest height. Then he gave out a loud growl before he toppled over on the ground.

Brady watched to see if the second Indian was moving and like the first he lay very still without moving a muscle.

Brady felt this was his opportunity to give the cave a search. He moved down the hillside until he came to the crossing. He crossed over to the trail leading to the cave entrance. He kept his Winchester handy as he entered the cave very slowly. There was no sound or movement until he heard the horses moving around. He knew they were getting the scent of the dead bear and they were going to stay jittery until the odor was gone.

Brady found the third Indian leaning up against the wall of the cave with three bullet holes in his body. The hunt was over and the trip back to Twin Forks was going to be the best thing he had accomplished since he started the hunt for the three Indians he had a warrant for.

Brady brought his horse down to the cave entrance and got him to stand still long enough for Brady to tie a rope from the bear to the saddle horn. He could only hope that his horse could pull the bear close enough to the edge of the cliff for Brady to roll the bear over the side of the bluff.

The horse stood shaking his head and kicking his hind legs until Brady slapped him on the rump to urge him to move forwards. The ground was slippery and the bear was very heavy. Brady stopped urging the horse on and went into the cave and brought out one of the Indian ponies. He used the Indian's rope to tie the feet of the bear to the Indian pony. Then with a lot of encouragement the two horses moved the bear a few feet at a time.

Brady didn't want them to get to close to the edge, because if the bear went over, the horses would be pulled over too. There was a turn in the trail just ahead and Brady guided the horses around it stopping them just as the bear reached the edge of the turn.

After removing the ropes and securing the horses, Brady started cutting some giant size steaks from the side of the bear. His mouth was watering from just thinking about the good taste of bear meat.

Brady cut and wrapped the meat in his rain slicker and tied it to the back of his saddle. Then he picked up a large limb from the snow and used it as a wedge, prying the bear over the edge and down the side of the hill.

Brady tied each Indian on the back of an Indian pony and led the ponies back to his campsite. He removed the dead Indians and stacked them on the ground. He hobbled each of the horses and let them feed on the tall grass that stuck above the snow.

Then Brady built a stone wall high enough for a campfire. He found a flat rock that was big enough to lie across the stones. Then he built a fire under the flat rock and waited until it got hot enough to cook his bear steak. As the bear steak sizzled Brady seasoned it with the seasoning from his saddlebag. The smell was breath taking and he was looking forward to eating it.

It was the first decent food he had eaten since he had been in these hills. The sun was setting and the clouds were moving off to the northeast. The sky was filled with every color of orange you could think of. This brought more memories of Hannah and Abbey. He wondered what they would say after looking at this beautiful sight.

Brady shook his head to remind himself that he had to stop thinking of Abbey in any way except as a sister or close friend.

With a full stomach, his biggest dangers were behind him. Brady crawled into his bedroll in hopes of getting a full night's sleep. But it wasn't long before he started watching the faces of Hannah and Abbey beckoning him into their arms.

The night passed very fast and left the sun peaking over the hilltop lighting up the trail that would lead Brady back to town. Brady felt like he never closed his eyes.

The ride to town was a slow one because Brady had to pull the train of horses that were carrying the dead Indians.

The cold weather was helping by keeping the bodies from decaying so fast and holding the smell to a minimum. It took Brady less then a week to get back to Twin Forks. He enjoyed the bear meat every night except for his last night when he had only coffee and beef jerky left.

The last night on the trail Brady fell asleep without the thoughts of either woman on his mind. He woke rested and refreshed. After coffee and jerky for breakfast Brady continued his journey to Twin Forks where he turned the bodies over to the local sheriff.

Brady made his report to the sheriff and went to the telegraph office to send a telegram to Captain Benson.

The telegram that Captain Benson received was short and to the point.

Captain Benson.

Job completed. Captives dead and buried. Returning home by train.

Brady Wells.

Captain Benson saw Luther standing outside the hardware store and he knew that Abbey would be somewhere in the neighborhood. The captain checked the street for any signs of mischief and then headed over to the hardware store.

"Hey, Luther," the captain said. "Is Miss Abbey around? I need to pass on a message from Brady."

"I'll fetch her," Luther said. "She always wants news about Mr. Wells. If I didn't know better I would think there was something going on between those two except they seem to avoid each other when they're together."

Luther went into the hardware store and waited for Abbey to stop talking with the storekeeper before he told her Captain Benson was waiting outside to talk with her.

The bell on the door of the hardware store tingled as Luther looked up and saw the captain walking in with an angry look on his face. "You're going to make me stand out there all day aren't you?" the captain said.

"Captain Benson." Abbey said. "How have you been?"

"Just came to pass on some news," the captain said. "But Luther made me wait so long that I've forgot what the news was."

"Captain, I couldn't just bust in on Miss Abbey's conversation," Luther said. "Besides, I was listening to the girls talking about Miss Hannah coming home to get married."

"Hush now Luther," Abbey said. "Don't you go around spreading rumors. It's bad enough with us women doing it." Everyone got a laugh out of that.

"Brady sent me a telegram," the captain said. " Something about taking the next train back to Abilene."

"Did you hear that Luther?" Abbey said. "Brady is finally coming home."

Luther liked to see Abbey happy because her smile spread sunshine all around the store. Her laughter caused goose bumps to run up and down his spine. It was the first time she had laughed since Alvin died.

"When captain? When will Brady be home?" Abbey asked, as she ran to the mirror that was hanging on the center post of the store. She started patting down her hair as she waited for the captain's answer.

"It'll depends on the train schedule," the captain said. "He could be here now."

"Luther why aren't you at the train station waiting for him?" Abbey asked, as she grabbed Luther's hand and started pulling him toward the door.

"Miss Abbey, I just heard about his arrival just now myself," Luther said, as he followed Abbey out the door and toward the train station.

"The train could have come and gone while we were piddling around in that stupid hardware store," Abbey said.

“Miss Abbey, the train rings its bell and sounds its whistle when it arrives at the station and I haven’t heard a bell ring or a whistle all day,” Luther said.

“All that proves is you’re hard of hearing,” Abbey said, as she started to run toward the train station. “Hurry Luther he might have arrived by now.”

The station clerk looked up when he saw Abbey and Luther enter the station.

“Where’s the train?” Abbey asked.

“What train?” the station clerk answered.

“The one bringing Brady Wells back home,” Abbey said. “The one from Twin Forks.”

“There isn’t a train due here until tomorrow,” the clerk answered. “They’ve had some trouble down the track and they wired ahead that they wouldn’t be here until noon tomorrow.”

For some reason Abbey burst out crying. She ran outside the station to keep anyone from watching her cry. Luther walked to the window and looked out watching Abbey sobbing deeply as she wiped the tears from her face. Luther gave her some more time before he walked out on the porch.

"Got a bug or something in my eye," Abbey said. "They need some way of keeping those bugs out of the train station."

"They shore do," Luther said. "You know, if we start home now we could make it back to the ranch before dark. We could eat and get a good nights rest and be back in town before noon tomorrow."

"That sounds like a good idea," Abbey said, as she wiped the tears from her face and walked toward the livery.

"Luther, I just got a little excited when I heard Brady was going to be away for another day and it just got to me," Abbey said.

"I miss him too, just not in the way you do," Luther said. "He's the only man that has ever put full trust in me and I ain't ever going to let him down."

They walked to the livery and Abbey saddled up her horse while Luther saddled his mule. It was a sad ride back to the ranch but Luther did get Abbey to thinking about the arrival of the train tomorrow and she started perking up some.

Abbey sat out on the porch nearly all night thinking about all the things that could happen when Brady got off that train. She was going to drown him with kisses and tell him just how she felt about him. Then they would get married and live happily ever after. Only if that could be true she thought. It was a wonderful dream.

With her eye lids getting heavy Abbey climbed the stairs to her room. She loved her stepfather and her mom, but now they were both gone. She knew she wouldn't stand a chance with Brady because of his childhood sweetheart Hannah Durham.

Sleep came to her the minute she hit the bed. It seemed she had just laid down when her Aunt Martha started shaking her to get up. Abbey looked into the mirror and saw the lines under her eyes from the lack of sleep and she was angry with herself for staying up so late.

What would a man like Brady ever see in a woman like her? Abbey thought. With Alvin gone Brady could ask her to take her family and leave this place. The place she had grown to love so much.

Abbey entered the kitchen with a look of despair on her face, yet she hummed a tune as she poured herself a cup of coffee.

"Martha did the mail arrive this week?" Abbey asked.

"I sat it on the bedside table in your room," Martha said. "Only thing of any importance was an invitation for Brady to attend the wedding of Hannah Durham to Frank Spencer."

The shock of that news caused Abbey to drop her coffee cup and it splattered all over the kitchen floor. Abbey over looked the mess and ran out of the kitchen and up to her bedroom. The mail was on her bedside and the invitation was lying on top of the stack.

Abbey quickly opened it and read the contents. The wedding was less then a week away and Brady was invited. Abbey knew that this was going to be another set back for Brady and she couldn't imagine how it was going to affect him.

She placed the invitation inside her shirt and stuffed her shirt tale inside of her pants. Just like a country hick to be wearing a plaid shirt and britches to meet the most important person in her life.

Luther was waiting for Abbey at the bottom of the stairs. "We're saddled and ready to go when ever you are," Luther said.

"We must leave now," Abbey said. "I must deliver the bad news to Brady before anyone else does. Maybe I can soften the blow."

Luther grabbed some biscuits and bacon and wrapped them in his bandana before he followed Abbey out of the house. They went straight to the barn where their horses were saddled and waiting.

The ride to town seemed much longer than in the past. Abbey was thinking of Brady and the last thing she wanted was to deliver him sad news.

When they arrived at the train station there was no one standing around and Abbey thought that to be very strange.

The station clerk came outside to put up the arrival time of the next train and Abbey asked him where the train from Twin Forks was?

"It came in late last night," the clerk said. "They got their problem fixed so they just pulled out later than usual."

"Did Brady Wells get off that train?" Abbey asked.

"Yes ma'am." the clerk said. "Captain Benson met him."

Abbey turned and started running toward the ranger station as Luther thanked the station clerk for his information.

Just as Abbey arrived at the ranger station Captain Benson and Brady walked out the front door. Both men removed their hats as Brady said, "Hi Abbey, you look like you're in a hurry."

"Brady Wells, why can't you do things normal like other men?" Abbey said. "We have been waiting for your train to arrive for two days and you question my reasons for being in a hurry."

"Your temper's showing," Brady said. "Guess that means you missed me just a little bit?"

"Brady, I have no reason to miss you," Abbey said. "You stay gone all the time and the folks at the ranch only get to see you twice a year."

"Well I'm here now," Brady said. "I got the information about Alvin and I'm sorry I had to miss his funeral. Captain Benson said you handled yourself well and I'm proud of you."

Abbey stood looking at the one man she respected as much as Alvin and she was tongue-tied. Why did this man have such an effect on her?

"Has the captain talked to you about a situation that I think you'll be a perfect solution for?" Abbey asked, as she tried to change the subject.

"Can't say that he has," Brady answered. "Why don't we go to the cafe and discuss the ranch situation over a steak dinner?"

"I know just the place," Luther said, as he guided the party to Merit's Cafe.

The atmosphere was much better in the cafe and everyone but Brady knew why this cafe was picked.

Brady stood up from his chair as the tallest woman he ever saw approached the table. "Welcome to our café Mr.

Wells," she said, as she curtsied to the group. "I'm Bernice Merit and I'll be your waitress."

All the men were standing with their hats in their hands as they stared at the pretty lady that was going to serve them. They all stood looking Bernice Merit straight in the eyes, except for Luther who had to tilt his head down just a little bit to see her eyes.

"Bernice, you've got to change your looks if you're going to get a different reaction from these lugs," Abbey said. "They never greet me in such a fashion." The girls started laughing as the men replaced their hats and sat down.

"Your daily special sounds good to me," Brady said. "Plus a pot of coffee."

Captain Benson and Luther agreed on the same thing. Abbey ordered a much lighter meal to eat while they discussed the ranching business.

"Brady I want you to run for the office of the town marshal," Abbey said. "I want to run your campaign and I want you to start making speeches very soon."

"Whoa little girl," Brady said. "I know you're ambitious and I admire you for that, but you're forgetting that half-breeds aren't very popular in west Texas and we have a ranch to run."

"This half-breed is very popular in this town," Abbey said. "Tell him captain. Tell him how he's building a reputation among the town folk. The way you handled yourself with Otis Harper and the way you killed the most dangerous Indians in Texas is only a start in your run for marshal."

"Let's not jump too far ahead," Brady said. "I need to thank Thomas Durham for all his help when you were in an emergency situation. Then I hear we have a wedding to attend."

Chapter 7

Abbey watched Brady's face as he listened to the preacher pronounce Hannah Durham and Frank Spencer husband and wife. She could see the hurt in Brady's eyes when he watched the two in a loving embrace. Abbey thought if there were someway she could relieve him of his pain, she would.

All through the wedding party Brady never showed his emotions. The cake was cut and everyone seemed to be having a great time. The band played dance music while the newly married couple started the first dance. Then the crowd joined in. Abbey stood beside Brady praying he would ask her to dance.

Luther and Bernice walked up to Abbey and asked, "Why aren't you two dancing? They're playing such beautiful music."

"Brady hasn't asked me yet," Abbey said. "I believe he thinks I'll step on his feet or want to lead him on the dance floor."

"Nonsense girl, you two start your dancing," Bernice said, as she pushed the two toward the dance floor.

Brady took Abbey in his arms for the first time and guided her gracefully across the dance floor. She couldn't hold back the tears as she lay her head on Brady's chest.

Abbey wanted the music to last forever. She kept holding Brady in her arms even after the music stopped. She felt safe and warm in his arms and she wanted to remain there forever.

"We need to clear the floor until the music starts again," Brady said. "The band has to get a breath between songs."

"You're going to dance with me again?" Abbey asked. "I didn't believe I could keep your attention that long."

"Seems you're the only one that'll dance with a half-breed," Brady said, as he led her off the dance floor.

"You've got to lose that attitude," Abbey said. "There's no better man in this room than you, and you know it."

Abbey had hopes that the party would never end, but it started breaking up by midnight. The folks from the B/A Ranch had reserved the second floor of the hotel for their members and they started to drift in that direction.

Brady had wondered off and Abbey was looking for him. She found him talking with Hannah's father, Thomas Durham.

"You could've cashed that draft and helped Abbey to keep the ranch running but you chose to be a banker instead of a friend. I'll never forget your treatment of me and my friends."

"Your friends," Mr. Durham said. "You're running an Indian reservation out there, not a ranch. The town's tired of Indians and half-breeds trying to take over our town."

"We'll keep your words in mind too, the next time you need our business." Brady said.

"No one wants the business of a bunch of Indians," Mr. Durham said. "I'd rather starve before I cater to your bunch."

Brady turned to Abbey and took her hand as the two walked away from Thomas Durham and his family.

The walk to the hotel was a silent one until Abbey brought up the subject of the election coming up. She just felt that Brady could be elected the new town marshal.

Abbey had wanted Brady to run for town marshal ever since the office became vacant, but she had a hard time convincing Brady to throw his hat in the ring.

When Brady did decide to run, Abbey ran his campaign feverishly. She had Brady making campaign speeches and joining in on town meetings every day.

The election was quickly approaching and the word was out that Brady could win the election by a landslide. Abbey had worked hard and Brady worked hard trying to keep up with her tough schedule.

September first, eighteen hundred and seventy, Brady took over the job as Marshal of Abilene.

Being the marshal kept him busy, but never like the ranger work, where he traveled most of the time and still faced harden criminals. As a ranger he had made seventy-five arrests and a third of them had been wanted killers.

As the Marshal of Abilene, most of his troubles were handling drunks, bar fights and family problems.

Abbey came into town on a regular basis and kept Brady posted on how Luther was managing the ranch. Her reports were always positive and she praised Luther on his abilities. He was handling the workers as good as Alvin did and the workers respected him.

Abbey had just left Brady's office when she ran into Hannah Spencer. At first Hannah was trying to hide her face from Abbey because she had a big bruise just under her left eye. "Hannah are you having a problem with your marriage?" Abbey asked.

Hannah broke down crying and Abbey put her arms around her knowing they had to get off the street. Abbey took Hannah over to the cafe and guided her to a back table where there wasn't much traffic. When Hannah sat down

Abbey went to the counter and asked Bernice for a glass of water.

When Abbey returned to the table with the water she asked Hannah if there was anything she could do for her?

"No," Hannah said. "I wish you would keep this meeting our little secret. I don't know why I had this awful breakdown. It's not very lady like of me." "Hannah is Frank hurting you?" Abbey asked.

"Only when he's drunk," Hannah answered. "But lately he seems to be drunk most of the time. Please Abbey you can't say a word. I need a friend to talk to and you have been the closest thing to a friend that I have in this town."

"Would you like to go somewhere else where it's more private?" Abbey asked. "You could get some of your problems off your shoulders by just talking."

"Maybe later," Hannah said. "I just need some more time to think on it. I never dreamed marriage could be this bad."

"Anytime," Abbey said, as she helped Hannah up from her chair. "I'll always be available to listen to anything you have to say. But remember, always protect yourself from being hurt."

Hannah smiled and walked to the front of the cafe. Then she stopped and said, "Keep working with Brady. He'll be a great man one day."

"He already is," Abbey said, as she watched Hannah leave.

There was sadness in Hannah's eyes. There were rumors that Frank Spencer was gambling away all their savings and even some of Thomas Durham's money.

When Abbey left the cafe she finished her shopping and picked up some sewing materials for her aunt. They were keeping up the mending of the clothes for the workers and it was really becoming a chore for them. She knew they all could use some help but now wasn't a good time to bring it to Brady's attention. The ride back to the ranch gave her time to think about what was going to happen to her and her family now that Alvin was gone.

When Hannah left Abbey she went home and found herself crying as she ran upon the porch. Her mother met her at the door and took her in her arms. "What's wrong, Hannah?"

"Mother, I can't go on with this loveless marriage," Hannah said. "Franks is nothing but a gambler looking for a way to get rich fast. I hate him."

Thomas Durham looked very angry as he sat on the sofa reading the Abilene newspaper and listening to the two women talk. Finally, he walked out of the house and made his way to the Golden Rod Saloon where he found Frank Spencer sitting at a table with four other men. They were playing poker and it looked like Frank was on the short end of winning again.

This pot was large and the betting was still going on. Frank looked up at his father-in-law and made a remark, "Hang around old man I've made my hand and I may need your financial backing."

"Frank get up and go to your wife," Thomas Durham said. "She's at home every night by herself while you're losing every penny you have."

"My luck has changed," Frank said, as he counted his money and raised the pot five hundred dollars.

"You can't make that kind of bet," one of the gamblers said. "We're here to pass some time away not to get rich fast."

"Put up or shut up," Frank said, as he covered his cards with his hands and looked around the table.

There was a stranger sitting in the game and he had the coldest eyes Thomas Durham had ever seen. His hat was pulled down over his eyes as he kept looking around the table. He studied his cards for a long time before he laid them face down on the table and counted out five hundred dollars and placed it in the pot. Then he counted out five thousand dollars and raised the pot.

"You know there ain't that kind of money at this table," Frank said. "This is just a game among the local towns people."

The stranger placed those cold eyes on Frank, "How many of your towns people had the five hundred dollars to call your bet?"

"Five hundred dollars is a lot less then five thousand dollars," Frank said, as he squirmed in his chair.

The stranger was still staring at Frank when he said, "Shut up and put up or the pots nine."

"Thomas give me five thousand dollars," Frank said. "You'll have it back right after I call this hand."

"That's crazy Frank," Thomas Durham said. "That's ten years wages for a cowhand and I'm not going to do it."

"If you love that daughter of yours you'll cover this bet," Frank said, as his eyes looked straight into Thomas Durham's eyes. "Can't never tell when she might have a bad accident."

Thomas Durham took out a blank piece of paper, and then he looked at Frank. "You take this money because I'm buying your law business. You win, you have your business, you lose and I want you to divorce my daughter and get out of town." Then Thomas Durham wrote a note for five thousand dollars and tossed it in front of Frank Spencer.

Frank grabbed the note and tossed it on the table. "It's a bet mister because I can't lose either way." He laughed out loud as he told the stranger to read 'em and weep. He turned over a full house of aces and nines.

The stranger stared at the hand in front of Frank and then he grabbed Frank's arms before he started dragging the money from the table.

"That's a real good losing hand," the stranger said, as he turned over a royal flush using the last ace in the deck.

"You can't have a royal flush," Frank yelled. "You're cheating. That ace was on the bottom of the deck when I dealt."

The stranger stood up and reached for his gun. "No man calls me a cheater."

Frank reached for his gun but he was to slow. He never cleared leather before he was falling backwards from the pressure of a bullet hitting him in the chest.

The saloon got very quiet as the stranger picked up the money placing it in his saddlebag. Turning to the crowd he said, "You all heard him call me a cheat and you all saw him get a fair draw. He died from a fair gun fight and I hope you all tell the marshal the same thing." The stranger kept his gun pointed at the crowd as he made his way to the batwing doors.

Brady had heard the shots that came from the Golden Rod Saloon and he pulled his Starr Double-Action Army .44 revolver to check its load. Then he walked across the street and watched as a stranger made his way out of the saloon.

When the stranger reached the street he looked up and saw the marshal coming his way. His first thought was to mount his horse and make a run for it, but he knew if the marshal was any kind of a gunfighter at all, he could shoot him out of the saddle before he got his horse turned and moving. He felt his best bet was to face the marshal head on.

"I need you to drop your gun belt," Brady said, as he walked very slowly toward the stranger.

"It was a fair fight marshal," the stranger said. "He called me a cheat and we both drew and I was a might faster."

"If that's true you won't mind dropping your gun belt while I check things out," Brady said. "At least long enough for me to talk to a few witness."

"If they don't see things my way," the stranger asked. "What then?"

"You'll be going on trial for murder," Brady answered. "If you're not guilty of the crime, then you're on your way out of town."

"Haven't got time for that trial marshal," the stranger said. "Make your peace with your maker and then draw."

"Your choice," Brady said. "I've already made my peace so when you're ready, make your move."

The stranger saw the batwing doors open and felt this was a good enough distraction for him to make his move. His gun just cleared leather when he felt a blow to his chest. He felt as if a sledgehammer had hit him in the chest causing him to step backwards until he fell to the ground.

He felt a stinging sensation in his chest and he started to cough up blood before he even realized he had been shot. That's impossible he thought. There's no man faster on the draw than himself. There was a dim light that lit up the right corner of his eyes, then moving to the left. It became brighter every inch it moved, until he sat with his head-hanging limp to his chest.

The batwing doors of the saloon swung open again and the crowd rushed outside to look at the stranger sitting on the ground. He was so balanced that he couldn't fall over. He looked like he was taking a nap.

"Move aside," Brady said, as he pushed his way closer to the stranger. Brady stopped and picked up the man's gun before he checked him for any sign of life.

"Get the undertaker," Brady said, as he stood up and turned to the crowd. "Does anyone know this man?"

"That's Snake Peterson from New Mexico territory. He was riding with the kid last time I seen him," one of the men said.

"You're right," another man said. "He was faster with a gun than the kid himself. He was faster than any man I ever saw up till now."

"Seems like we have our own fast draw right here in Abilene," a man said, as he started explaining to the crowd how fast Brady had cleared leather.

Brady questioned all of the men involved in the poker game and he kept the stranger's winnings as evidence. If there were to be a hearing he would turn the money over to the judge. If not, the money would go to the church as a donation.

By the time both bodies were taken away, all the witness had been questioned. Brady went to his office and wrote up his report. It explained how two more men died of violence, one in the streets of Abilene.

Brady had watched as Thomas Durham walked out of the saloon staring at him after the shooting. Then he headed down the street toward his home.

Brady hadn't been in his office long before Abbey came running in. "Brady are you alright? I just heard about your gun fight."

"I'm fine," Brady said. "I was just doing my job."

"Typical man," Abbey said. "You nearly got yourself killed and you say, all in a days work. Maybe there'll be more gunfights tomorrow and maybe you'll win them too. Then there comes the gunfight that you don't win."

"Abbey, you ran my campaign to become the Marshal of Abilene," Brady said. "What's gotten into you?"

"I didn't realize that all this killing went with the job," Abbey said. "I want you to hand in your badge right now and come back to the ranch with me."

"You don't mean that," Brady said "I've got a job to do and you aren't making it any easier crying over an incident that's already over."

"Come on Luther," Abbey said. "We're not wanted around here."

The two walked to the livery and made ready for the ride back to the ranch. Abbey was crying and babbling that every man she became involved with ended up dead. It became a long ride back to the ranch.

The streets were dark when Brady finished his nightly round of the business section. Nothing had changed after the shooting. The Golden Rod Saloon was playing music and passing out drinks just like nothing had happened. The town folks were home getting ready for another day. The bank had a light on in Mr. Durham's office. Seemed like Mr. Durham was spending a lot of time at work now days.

Then Brady saw movement in the alleyway beside the bank. He pulled his Army .44 and pointed it in the direction of the movement. A woman step from the shadow of the building. It was Hannah.

"What are you doing out at this time of night?" Brady asked. "You should be home with your parents." Hannah wasn't very sturdy on her feet. She had been drinking and she started slurring her words, "Franks dead," she said. "Can you and I start having picnics at the old frog pond again and talk about us getting married?"

"No, Hannah," Brady said. "To much water has passed under the bridge." Brady slipped his revolver back into its holster and placed his arm around Hannah to keep her from falling.

"Brady, I can't go on like this," Hannah said. "I need you to help me to get myself back on track. I need to be the person I was before I married Frank Spencer."

"Stop drinking and go back to work for your father," Brady said. "He can keep you busy enough to get your mind off things for a while. There'll be other men in your life."

"It's that Abbey woman isn't it?" Hannah said. "She's the reason why I've lost you. She came into your life and changed your feelings about me."

"No Hannah," Brady said. "You changed both of our lives yourself."

Brady heard the bank door slam shut while he stood holding Hannah by the shoulders. It was Mr. Durham, who came walking out of the bank. "I can't turn my back a minute before you're making up to my daughter. Can't you wait until her husband is cold in his grave."

"Your daughter was waiting for you to get through with your work," Brady said. "So she can walk home with you."

"My daughter has turned out to be a drunk," Mr. Durham said. "She gives no thought to what you and your kind would do to our reputation, so she drinks."

"Daddy stop it," Hannah yelled. "It's you who can't stand the thought of someone being happy because you're feeling so miserable yourself."

Mr. Durham walked over and pulled Hannah from Brady's arms and started walking her in the direction of his house. "Stay away from my daughter you half-breed," Thomas Durham said, as the two walked away.

Brady felt sorry for Hannah as he listened to her father scolding her for being seen with a half-breed on the streets.

The streets were unusually quite at this time of night and Brady needed some coffee. He walked over to the Merit's Cafe.

When Brady walked in Bernice greeted him with a big smile and said. "Sit yourself down hero. One coffee coming up."

"You can cut the hero bit," Brady said. "Have you talked with Abbey this afternoon?"

"Luther and I were talking about your little shootout when she came walking into the cafe," Bernice said. "She was in a terrible way. She was crying and mumbling about this was all her fault."

"Her fault!" Brady said. "How in the world did she figure this was her fault?"

"She helped to get you elected marshal, so she feels she helped to place you in danger," Bernice said, as she placed a cup of coffee in front of Brady.

"You said you've been talking with Luther today," Brady said. "When does that man find time to work?"

"Just because you're having a bad day marshal, don't you go firing off on Luther. He's always working for you," Bernice said

"Sorry," Brady said. "I know he has my best interest in mind. It's just this job is so demanding and I would like to be out on the ranch doing something useful for a change."

Brady pulled a coin from his pocket and tossed it on the counter. "Thanks for being there Bernice. I just needed to talk to someone."

Brady left the cafe and walked to the boarding house where he was staying. Inez Brown, the owner of the boarding house, was in the kitchen getting things ready for tomorrows meals. She served two meals a day and Brady sure did like eating at her table when he could.

"Brady, have you had anything to eat today?" Inez asked. "There's a couple of pieces of chicken left from supper and I can heat up the mashed potatoes and corn."

"Sounds great Inez but I'm too tired to eat," Brady said. "Got to get an early start tomorrow. I'm falling behind in my paper work."

Brady took the stairs two at a time as he made his way to his room. Inez had lit the oil lamp before Brady came in.

The room had been cleaned and the bed had clean sheets on it. Brady was so tired he barely undressed before he fell into bed.

Thomas Durham walked the floor of his bedroom going over the events of the day. Frank Spencer was dead and that was good news. Hannah wouldn't have to put up with his gambling any more. The money he spent paying off Frank's gambling debts was causing him a problem. He had used a lot of the investor's money to pay off all those gambling debts. Now he had to figure some way to put the money back.

Then there was the half-breed that the town elected marshal. He was the cause of all his other troubles. He had to figure some way to keep his daughter from seeing this half-breed because he wasn't fit to marry her. Then there was the matter of Hannah's drinking. Seems like everything was going wrong at the same time.

Then a thought came to his mind. What if the tables were turned? What if the half-breed started having his own troubles? Maybe a little trouble would keep the marshal's mind off of his daughter and things could get back to normal again.

Thomas Durham pulls a sheet of paper from his desk drawer and sat down to write a letter to an old friend.

To Wade Weston

Care of the post office

San Antonio, Texas

Got me some trouble in Abilene and need your kind of help. There's a marshal that needs to be put in his place. Could be worth a thousand dollars to see him and his kind run out of town. If you're interested meet me at Antelope Springs on Monday of next week and we can work out some plans.

T.D.

The letter was sent and Mr. Durham started setting his mind on different ways of getting rid of that nests of wild Indians that was running the B/A Ranch. Thomas Durham had wished many times that he had never sold that ranch to Brady Wells.

On the day of the meeting with Wade Weston, Thomas Durham had come up with a plan that could ruin Brady and get rid of his Indian friends at the same time. Raids on the ranch until Brady goes broke trying to keep the ranch above water.

This was discussed with Wade Weston when he arrived. Wade told Thomas Durham that it would take more money to hire the men he needed to complete the task.

You get one thousand dollars now and one thousand dollars when you're finished with the job. Here's five hundred for your expenses. That's twenty five hundred dollars ant that should be enough to hire anyone in Texas.

Wade Weston took the money and left. He rode to Devil's Bend, where his gang was waiting for him. He explained the situation to his men and they made plans to ride to Brady's ranch the next morning. They would look over the layout, then go from there.

The six men left for the B/A Ranch before sunrise and made camp just west of the ranch by sundown. They made camp in a dry gulch where they couldn't be seen from anyone without them riding up accidentally.

They started looking over the range the next day. It looked simple enough. They counted about five hundred head of cattle on the range and maybe seventy-five horses. Two old Indian scouts were all they had looking after the heard. They planned to make their first raid on the ranch early the next morning.

Yakima was waiting for Indian Joe as he rode up to bring him some fresh supplies. Yakima raised his right hand in a greeting as Indian Joe climbed down from the wagon.

"Luther has asked if you need anything more from the ranch?" Indian Joe said.

"Yes," Yakima said. "We have visitors and I believe they have come to make a raid on the cattle. They are hiding in the dry gulch just over the hill."

"You are sure of this?" Indian Joe asked.

"As sure as the birds fly," Yakima said. "We can drive the cattle to lookout point in the valley and when the rustlers come we could catch them in a crossfire."

"You have the thoughts of a great leader," Indian Joe said. "I will relay the message to Luther while you move the cattle. We'll be waiting at lookout point when you arrive there."

The two Indians locked their hands on each other's arms and made their pack. They all would depend on each other to keep up their assignment.

The ride back to the ranch was much faster than the ride to the pastures. Indian Joe was giving out the Indian yell when he arrived at the ranch. Everyone had heard his yells and they all came running to the corral where Indian Joe stood up in the back of the wagon waiting for all to come.

Luther waited until the rest of the crew had arrived before he asked Indian Joe what was going on and why the yelling.

"There are six men hidden in the dry gulches in the east pasture. They'll raid our cattle in the morning," Indian Joe said. "Yakima is moving the herd to look out point tonight. We must be on top of look out point by morning to ambush these cattle rustlers."

"You have done well and your plan is a good one," Luther said. "Now we'll split our forces and cover both sides of look out point. Indian Joe, you take three men and cover the north side of look out point. Iran, you'll take the others and cover the south side. I'll cover their retreat."

"Everyone meet me at the barn and we'll issue you ammunition," Indian Joe said, as he climbed down from the wagon and made his way to the barn.

Abbey grabbed Luther's arm and asked if she and the women could help.

"Yes," Luther said. "Start boiling water and making bandages in case we have casualties.

Abbey ran to the house and explained what the women had to do. She knew they had only a short time to get things done.

The women of the house were busy with their assignments while the men cleaned and checked their weapons. There could be no miss fires in the morning.

Luther met with all the men in the barn to explain what was going on and how this ambush was to take place. Luther sent Indian Joe and his crew out first. They would travel quickly and quietly to their positions. Fifteen minutes later, Iran and his crew would leave. Fifteen minutes later Luther would travel to his position. By sun up the trap should be set.

The women watched as each group left. They stood where they could touch each mans hand as he rode to his death or his glory. Luther tried to give the ladies encouragement as the men rode out.

The plans were good but there was always room for unexpected things to happen and Luther hoped he covered all things that could happen but he knew he hadn't.

Chapter 8

Wade Weston started waking up his gang long before sunrise. He had the coffee brewing because he wanted the men wide awake and alert before they took on the job of rustling the B/A cattle. Wade had already made arrangements for the railroad to buy the stolen cattle sight unseen. The deal was, he and his men had to deliver the cattle to the Junction City station just down the line from the Abilene station.

The men started moving around the camp trying to get the early morning stiffness out of their joints. Wade noticed the sun was beginning to beat down on them even before they finished their coffee. He knew it was going to be another scorcher and the cattle would be restless.

Jake Patterson was placed in charge of this raid. Wade Weston sure didn't want anyone outside of his men to know he was involved. There was no telling how long he may have to stay in Abilene before he finish his job of destroying Brady Wells and his band of Indian wranglers.

Jake had given the orders for the men to mount up and follow him out of the gorge. The path was so narrow they had to ride in single file. When they reached the top of the narrow passage the first thing they noticed was the cattle had been driven to another location.

The men spread out and rode around the area trying to locate which direction the cattle were headed. All the signs pointed west. Jake rode back to explain what had happened to Wade and what he felt went on during the night. He felt the Indians had moved the cattle to a different grazing pasture over night. He also felt his men could catch up with them before the sun was directly over head and if they did, it could be a break for them, because the Indians guarding the herd would never expect a raid at this time of day.

Wade listened to the change in plans. He gave his approval, then left the rest of the job for Jake to handle on his own. Wade left instructions where he could be located before he rode back to Abilene to meet with Thomas Durham. He had to make sure that he was seen around town during the time that the rustling took place.

As the rustlers moved west toward the cattle, Jake kept his eyes open for any sign of danger. After an hour of tracking he saw the pass that divided the twin hills. It seemed to separate one pasture from the other. The gorge surrounded the west end of the pasture before it curved around the north side separating the pasture better than a fence its self. The hills on the east and south side completed a perfect grazing spot while guarding the pasture from other intruders.

As the rustlers rode closer to the hills they could see the cattle mingling at the far end of the pass. Jake gave the men the order to keep their weapons handy while they rode through the pass and to spread out and make sure there were no witnesses left alive.

The rustlers were within fifty yards of the herd when a voice rang out from the hillside above them, "You're surrounded and have no chance of getting out of this pass alive. Don't make the wrong decision. Throw down your guns and maybe we can talk this out."

Jake yelled out to his men, "Every man for himself," as he took the first shot toward the men hidden on the hillside. The rest of the rustlers started firing, as they turned to make their way back out of the pass. Then both sides of the hills erupted in gunfire, as the rustlers were shot from their saddles or their horses shot from under them.

Luther used the large rocks at the opening of the pass to hide behind. His Henry rifle was firing at a rapid pace as the rustlers came riding in his direction.

The sound of the gunfire was deafening and the smell of gunpowder was nauseating as several minutes passed. What seemed like a turkey shoot to Luther soon came to a halt. The pass became very quiet, almost to quiet. Everyone waited for the smoke to clear before they made their move down the hill. Then an awful sight appeared before them. Men and animals were laying in the pass. The only movement was from four of the horses that had withstood the gunfire.

Luther turned those horses back toward the cattle and tried to calm them down while the men in the hills rode down to give him a hand.

Indian Joe took a head count of the B/A riders and everyone was counted for. There were no injuries and the shock of the excitement was starting to wear off.

Luther told Yakima to ride back to the ranch and bring back a flat bed wagon so the crew could load up the dead rustlers and take them to town. While Yakima was gone Luther checked all six of the rustlers and found four of the rustlers' dead. One was shot up pretty bad but was still breathing and another suffered from a head wound. A bullet had taken off his left ear.

Indian Joe pulled a medicine pouch from around his neck. In it was a small jar filled with a smelly solution that looked like goose grease. He began putting the grease into the wounds of the wounded rustlers. He covered the wounds with bandanas he gathered from the men. In the meantime Yakima had returned with the wagon.

The men started placing the dead rustlers on the flatbed wagon, covering them so the flies wouldn't swarm in mass numbers. They took special care of the one wounded rustler, they wanted to keep him alive as a witness to what happened, along with the earless rustler.

The rustler that lost his ear was given a horse and told to follow the wagon back to the ranch. Luther kept a good eye on this rustler because he knew he could get valuable information out of him when he had time to question him.

Yakima drove the wagon to town after Abbey joined them for the trip. Her curiosity was getting the best of her. This was the first cattle rustling in the area for over two years. The herd wasn't big enough to make them a bundle of money, so what gives? All sorts of reasoning were running through her mind but none of them made any sense.

Luther and the B/A riders stopped at the jail to drop off the one prisoner with the missing ear. The marshal wasn't in so they locked the prisoner in a cell and hung the key back on the nail by the outside door. Then they drove to the bank and carried the wounded rustler up the stairs to Doctor Dewberry's office. He was still breathing but that was about all.

Doctor Dewberry met them at the door and escorted them back to the examination table. He was cleaning up for the examination when Abbey went in the back room and changed into her nurse's uniform. When she returned to the examination room she told Luther and Indian Joe to go find Brady.

Thomas Durham and Wade Weston stood in Durham's office looking out the window watching everything that was going on outside of the bank. They couldn't imagine what had gone wrong.

Indian Joe followed Luther back over to the sheriff's office and when they entered the office Brady stood up with a startled look on his face. "Is there something wrong?" Brady asked.

"Not any more," Luther answered. "We had a group of rustlers camping out in the dry gulch last night. Yakima and Boca noticed them when they arrived. They kept an eye on them until Indian Joe arrived with supplies."

"We decided to moved the cattle to the west pass," Indian Joe said. "We felt this was a good place for an ambush."

"Quick thinking," Brady said. "Looks like a successful mission. Did any of our men get hurt?"

"The ambush went off just like we planned," Luther said. "None of our riders were killed or wounded. We killed all but two of the rustlers. One of them is in Doctor

Dewberry's office right now getting patched up. The other one is in your jail cell."

"There's no one in any of my jail cells," Brady said. "When I came into the office the front door was open but I thought someone just forgot to close it."

Luther walked back to the jail cells and looked around. They were all empty. Then Luther walked out of the room and checked the nail where he hung the keys. They were there as if they had never been touched. "That's strange Brady," Luther said. "We did put that rustler behind your bars."

"Never doubted it at all," Brady said. "Let's go over and pay a visit to our rustler friend in Doctor Dewberry's office. Maybe he can shed some light on things."

"Abbey and Doctor Dewberry doesn't want us over there until they get through with whatever they had to do to the rustler," Luther said.

"Then let's go to Merit's Cafe and I'll treat you boys to what ever Bernice has on the special menu."

Luther was all for that. He and Indian Joe hadn't had time to eat since late last night, plus he wanted to see Bernice again. It had been a while since he had been in town.

They got a friendly greeting when they entered the cafe. Bernice was glad to see all of them, but she was especially glad to see Luther.

The men ordered the cafe's special dinner of steak and red beans with a large slice of apple pie thrown in.

Bernice was putting the meat on the stove when the door opened and Thomas Durham walked in with a man that no one had seen before.

"Sheriff, this is Wade Weston from San Antonio," Thomas Durham said. "He wanted to report that six of his men were missing. They were riding out to inspect the Richards place when they disappeared. Wade wanted them to look the place over because he was thinking about buying it and starting a horse ranch."

"Could these be the same men that tried to rustle our cattle this morning?" Luther asked. "If so you'll find all but two at the undertaker's office. One rustler is being patched up at Doc. Dewberry's office and you probably were the one who turned the other one loose from his jail cell."

"That can't be true," Wade Weston said. "These men have worked for me for years and not one of them has ever turned a crooked hand."

"You calling me a liar?" Luther asked, as he stood up from his chair and walked toward the two men.

"Stop it Luther," Brady said. "Seems like Mr. Wade here has a legitimate complaint. I'll need to check out his credentials of being a land speculator. I'll wire San Antonio and find out about Mr. Weston's horse ranching business."

"Why are you wiring San Antonio?" Thomas Durham asked. "You have your murders right here in this cafe. I wouldn't put it past you to be their leader in this crime."

"You're pushing your luck Mr. Durham," Brady said. "If I find out you or your friend here had anything to do with the rustling this morning I'll put you both away for a long time."

"You're threatening us when your Indian friends are running around Texas murdering white people."

"You have no call to make those kind of accusations," Brady said. "When our captive wakes up I'll make him talk and when I do you best have no knowledge of this rustling."

"I knew you would protect your murdering Indian friends over the honest citizens of this town," Thomas said, as he led his friend out the door of the cafe.

"What's got into that man?" Luther asked. "He sounds like he's on a mission to smear your name around here."

"We do have our differences," Brady said, as they all sat back down. "Let's eat, I'm starved and the food's getting cold."

Eating and talking wasn't Luther's way of enjoying a meal, so Brady waited until he had finished his meal before he started asking Luther to fill in the blanks.

Not long into their conversation Abbey walked into the cafe with Doctor Dewberry. They walked over to the table where the three men were setting.

"Who's watching the rustler?" Brady asked.

"No one," the doctor answered. "He has been sedated and he won't wake up until morning. Beside he needs the rest."

"Is your office open?" Brady asked.

"No," the doctor answered. "We locked it because of the medicine we have stored in some of our cabinets."

"Give me the keys," Brady said. "I need to get a guard on him until we have a chance to question him."

The doctor pulled out his keys as everyone followed Brady over to the doctor's office. The door to his clinic was standing open, it had been kicked open and the rustler inside had been smothered with his own pillow.

"What's going on?" Luther asked. "First our prisoner is turned loose and now the only remaining witness to the rustling has been murdered. What're they trying to do?"

"We'll know soon," Brady said, as he searched the dead body for any kind of identification. "Can't seem to find anyone that knew either of the two rustlers. Only Wade Weston and Thomas Durham."

"There's a crowd gathering in front of the mayor's office," Abbey said. "Thomas Durham is telling the crowd that the marshal and his Indian wranglers are responsible for the death of four land speculators."

The crowd was chanting, "*Only good Indian is a dead Indian.*" Then they shouted for the mayor to withdraw the marshal's badge and let an honest marshal arrest the murdering Indians that killed the white land speculators.

"Luther take the men back to the ranch," Brady said. "Get ready for a fight if things turn bad here in town."

"What are you going to do?" Abbey asked. "You'll be all alone if the mayor swings to their side."

"I'm going to Captain Benson and explain what has happened," Brady said. "If he can't help, I'll take steps to stop this bunch of cattle rustlers myself."

When everyone was gone and Brady was back in his office he heard the office door open and there stood John

Spencer, Mayor of Abilene. "Got time for a town meeting without the town getting involved?"

"What's on your mind mayor?" Brady asked. "Are you getting some heat from the town counsel? Seems like Thomas Durham is ready to call in some of his chips."

"I can handle the town counsel," John said. "But everyone in town owes Thomas Durham and he is calling in notes if the people don't ask for your badge."

"Not necessary," Brady said. "Ask and you shall receive. I would like to bring Captain Benson up to date before you take my badge."

"You do what you have to do," John said, as he turned to the door. "There's nothing personal about this Brady. When we get this mess cleaned up you'll get your badge back."

"That's okay, John," Brady said. "I've needed this break to get me back at what I do best, ranching."

After the mayor left, Brady went to Captain Benson's office. He was standing by the window looking into the dark. "Come in Brady," Captain Benson said. "Want a cigar?"

Brady smiled and sat down in an overstuffed chair. "Got me a problem with Thomas Durham and his sidekick Wade Weston. Seems they want the ranch back and the Indians ran out of town."

`"Tough situation with Thomas Durham," Captain Benson said. "But his sidekick is wanted in about every state but Texas. Seems Texas was his birth place and he wants to keep out of trouble here."

"He's already in trouble here as far as I'm concerned," Brady said. "He planned to rustle my cattle and I'm going to prove it."

"You might start at the railhead over in Junction City," Captain Benson said. "There has been no crime committed except for the death of the land speculators. But I have heard rumors that someone was going to deliver a herd of cattle to the Junction City railhead this week. The railhead was going to pay cash for the cattle. Then they were going to deliver the cattle to St. Louis, Missouri. That's only rumor."

"I'm turning in my badge tonight," Brady said. "But I'll be following up on every lead I get until I get this mess cleaned up."

Brady left the ranger's office and went to Mayor Spencer's home. When he knocked on the door the mayor's wife answered and asked Brady in for a cup of coffee. The mayor was in his den talking with a young lady that turned out to be Hannah Spencer, the mayor's daughter in law.

When Hannah saw Brady, she jumped to her feet and asked "Brady, what are you and my father doing? It's as if you're trying to destroy each other."

"You had better ask your father," Brady said. "He has a feeling about Indians that goes far past just a grudge. Here's my badge mayor and I'll be out of your town before sun up."

"Brady don't be ridiculous," Hannah said. "Tell him mayor, he has to remain in town for my sake. Why can't we let bygones be bygones and return to the same people we were?"

"Talk to your father about that," Brady said. "Right now I'm out to see what he has done that he doesn't want the people of this town to know about."

"Brady don't take that route," Hannah said. "I love you both but Thomas Durham is my father and I will stick by him no matter what."

"Now you see how the past effects the future." Brady said. "I'm the outcast in this picture and your father will never let me live it down."

Brady left the room with the mayor holding the marshal badge and Hannah crying for him not to go. What was left for him? Only his ranch, and Thomas Durham was trying to take that away from him too.

A trip to Junction City could help shed some light on things Brady thought. He needed to persuade some of the old rail hands to help him put this puzzle together, but he needed to inform Luther of his plans before he left. He rode to the B/A Ranch with all kinds of thoughts running through his head and all of them kept coming back to Thomas Durham.

There was still some sunlight left when Brady rode up to the B/A corral. He saw Luther talking with some of the wranglers. Seems that there were some talk going around town that the marshal's job was being turned over to Wade Weston. If that were true, the ranch hands had to get ready for an unfriendly visit from the marshal and his hired gun hands.

"Luther," Brady said. "I just left town and nothing has been done about replacing me as the town marshal."

"Just something that Indian Joe came back with when he talked with Lou Roles over at the telegraph office," Luther said. "There has been a bunch of gunmen gathering in town lately and I believe they're here to run everyone off this ranch and let Durham reclaim it for his bank."

"I want you to keep a lid on this until I get back from Junction City," Brady said. "If I can get the proof that

Durham or Weston are behind all this rustling I can call in Captain Benson and his rangers."

"We'll fight for this ranch," Luther said. "This is a home for many people. Speaking of that, you should go to the big house and let Abbey know what you're up to."

Brady walked to the ranch house and as he walked up the steps of the porch, Abbey opened the front door and stepped out on the porch. "I didn't know if you were going to come to the house or not." Abbey said. "Since Alvin passed away I haven't been able to tell if you wanted me and my family to leave or stay and help you with the ranch."

"Abbey, one third of this place belonged to Alvin," Brady said. "Now that one third belongs to you and your family. You'll always have a home here."

"I'm sorry about Hannah and her father," Abby said. "I know you have feelings for her and that her father is keeping you two apart and I do know she has feelings for you and she'll come to you in the end."

"Abbey, I've got to ride to Junction City," Brady said. "I promised Alvin that I would take care of you and your family but I need to get information from the railroad at Junction City to help me gather prove that stealing our cattle was planned long before the death of Wade Weston's speculators."

"I know. I'll be worried every minute you're gone," Abbey said. "Stay out of harms way and come back safely."

Brady tipped his hat and walked down the steps to his horse. He swung himself up into the saddle and rode away from the ranch.

Abbey stood with tears in her eyes, thinking there was no way she could explain her feelings to Brady when she knew he loved Hannah so much and why not, she was his school girl sweetheart.

Brady wasted no time in going to Junction City. He knew it was only a matter of time before Wade Weston would use his authority as town marshal to try and drive the Seminole Indians off the B/A Ranch. Then he would use the law about Indians not being able to own land, to turn the ranch back over to Thomas Durham.

There were signs going up in Abilene warning the people that the Indians that were in town could be dangerous. They belonged on a reservation, not on the streets of Abilene. The law didn't specify which Indians or what tribes and Wade was going to use this law to force Abbey's family off the ranch and on to a reservation.

Brady rode into Junction City at dusk and he went to the sheriff's office the first thing. When he entered the sheriff's office there was a conversation going on between the sheriff and another man wearing a U. S. Marshal's badge. The sheriff paused for a moment and asked how he could help Brady.

"I'm Brady Wells from Abilene and I'm here for some information on a man named Wade Weston."

"What about Wade Weston?" the U.S Marshal asked.

"This is U.S. Marshal Tad Hunter from Washington D.C.," the sheriff said. "I'm Sheriff Gresham from right here in Junction City."

"Nice to meet you both," Brady said. "But I have a problem that has cost me my job and is in the makings of costing me my ranch and its all because of a man named Wade Weston."

"Wade Weston is a wanted man in almost every state but Texas," Marshal Hunter said. "Washington has sent me to gather enough evidence to arrest him."

"What can we do to help you cowboy?" the sheriff asked.

"I need one of you to come with me to the railroad station to talk with the section head," Brady said. "I have a gut feeling that this Wade Weston planned on selling my cattle to the railroad even before he tried to rustle them."

"I'll walk with you over to the station house," Marshal Hunter said. "I would like to get some more information on this man myself."

Brady filled the marshal in on what was happening back in Abilene and the threat Wade Weston was making against his friends that were helping him to get started in the cattle business. He explained that many of his friends were Seminole Indians that came here from Florida more then ten years ago.

The marshal didn't say a word, but he did listen, as if he felt some kind of awareness for the people Brady was talking about.

There was no trains scheduled to leave or arrive in Junction City until tomorrow morning. The station keeper was filing papers as a younger man was mopping the wooden floors.

"How can I help you?" a man asked from within his ticket station.

"My name is Brady Wells," Brady said, as he stood next to the window and watched the man's eyes as he talked to him. "I have reason to believe that you made a deal to buy cattle from Wade Weston of Abilene last week."

"Never heard of the man," the manager said. "Can't make deals for the railroad myself, that's left up to Mr. Roberts."

"Where can I find this Mr. Roberts?" Brady asked.

"His office is in the back room of this building," the manager said. "But he isn't in right now. He's having lunch with a friend over at the hotel restaurant."

"How will we know him?" Brady asked.

"He wears a bowler hat and he'll be the largest man in the restaurant," the man said, with a grin on his face.

Brady thanked the man before he and the marshal left the station for the hotel restaurant. There were a lot of buildings in town but the hotel was the tallest of them all. That made it easy to spot.

The restaurant was almost empty when Brady and the marshal walked in. They spotted Mr. Roberts right away. It sure was true, he was the largest man in the restaurant. When Brady and the marshal made their way to his table the big man stood up and looked down at both men. He had a grin on his face and he held out a big hand for the men to shake. "What can I do for the law today?" Mr. Roberts asked.

"We need to ask you some questions," Brady said. "But if this isn't a good time we can wait."

"This gentleman at my table is Mayor Burnside," Mr. Roberts said. "He has granted me an audience for a short period of time. But if you would like to join us, it'll be okay, we have no secrets from each other."

"That's good," Brady said. "Because I need to know who the man was that signed a contract to sell you a herd of cattle two weeks ago."

"I signed no contract to buy any cattle this past month," Mr. Roberts said. "In fact we haven't shipped any cattle from here in several weeks."

"You didn't ship any cattle because my men caught on to the rustling and put a stop to it before it ever started," Brady said.

"I, sir, do not participate with those who rustle cattle," Mr. Roberts said. "If you continue to accuse me of this awful crime then I will have to challenge you to a bout of fisticuffs."

"What do you think he said?" Brady asked his marshal friend.

"I think he said he was going to kick your butt," the marshal said, "Unless you stop calling him a crooked station manager."

"Mr. Roberts," Brady said. "I have to except your challenge to a fist fight because I know you made arrangements to buy stolen cattle with Wade Weston."

"Mr. Burnside, will you be my second in this little transaction?" Mr. Roberts asked.

"Be glad to," Mr. Burnside said. "But I feel that we must let this gentleman know that you were the heavy weight champion of the world at one time."

"Look," Brady said. "If I whip you, I get the information I need. If you whip me, I don't question you any more. Deal?"

"Deal," Mr. Roberts said, as the four men made their way out of the restaurant and into the street in front of the hotel.

One of the men in the restaurant ran up and down the street yelling for everyone to come and see Mr. Roberts mangle the young kid from Abilene.

The crowd kept gathering while Mr. Roberts removed his jacket and shirt. The muscle in his body made him look like he was deformed. His back looked liked it was hunched over because of the muscle that the shirt and coat had hidden.

Mr. Roberts walked around the crowd flexing his muscle and showing how the muscles in his arms could be moved up and down just by the way he clutched and turned his fist.

"Mr. Wells," Roberts said. "What are the rules for this fight? There must be some standard set for the people to know that I stuck within the rules when I tear you apart."

"The best thing about a good old cowboy butt kicking is there are no rules," Brady said. "How ever if you're afraid I'll take advantage of you, then you can set your own rules."

The crowd laughed, as the young cowboy stood in front of Mr. Roberts looking like a man that thought he might have a chance.

"Brady, are you sure you want to go along with this charade?" his marshal friend asked. "This man's a professional with training on how to whip your butt in one easy lesson."

"Your rules of having no rules, suits me fine," Mr. Roberts said, as he placed his arms in a bent position in front of his chest and face.

The crowd held their breath as they prepared themselves for a bloody brawl that could leave the young cowboy injured for life.

Brady watched Roberts move around like a cat sneaking up on a small mouse. His arms cocked and a smirk on his lips. There were signs of saliva trickling from the corner of Mr. Robert's lips.

Then the unexpected happened. Brady brought his right leg up and planted his boot between Roberts's legs. There was a loud groan that came from Mr. Roberts's mouth, as he bent to protect his groin. That gave Brady another opening to Robert's face. He brought up the same boot the second time and it landed on Mr. Robert's chin bringing him back up to a standing position.

The crowd began to yell get him as Brady jumped into the air and landed a kick with both feet on Mr. Robert's chest sending him reeling back on to the crowd. The crowd helped Mr. Roberts back into the center of the ring that had been formed by the on lookers.

Brady again leaped into the air and locked his legs around Mr. Robert's neck and brought him to the ground with a loud thump. Brady kept tightening the muscles in his legs until he heard Mr. Roberts start to choke. Then he asked Mr. Roberts to say uncle.

Mr. Roberts started prying Brady's legs apart and Brady knew that this man wasn't going to stay down for long. Loosing his grip Brady let Mr. Roberts climb to his knees before Brady unleashed an upper cut that should have brought down a bull.

Mr. Roberts leaned back on his hands and looked Brady in the eyes. Brady knew he had to finish this quickly or he stood the chance of being killed with a barrage of fists coming from Mr. Roberts.

Brady had learned a trick taught to him by a Chinese army cook. He had never used it before but he needed to try something before Mr. Roberts regained his strength.

Brady opened his right hand and turned it where the edge of his hand would land in the spot where he directed it. He swung and hit the side of Mr. Roberts's neck staying away from the windpipe. Mr. Robert's head tilted forward. Then Brady opened his left hand and brought it down on the back of Mr. Robert's neck sending him face down in the dirt.

The fight was over. Brady and the marshal carried Mr. Roberts to the hotel and sent for a doctor. By the time the doctor arrived Mr. Roberts was starting to come around.

Chapter 9

The doctor had made his examination and determined that Mr. Roberts had nothing broke and was going to recuperate from the whipping he had just received.

"I believe we have a confession coming from you," Brady said. "You were going to tell me of your contact with Wade Weston."

"Marshal," Mr. Roberts said. "Can I go to jail for what I'm about to say?"

"That depends on how deep you're in with this gang," the marshal answered. "I represent the government and if your involvement in this cattle rustling ring has been harmful to the government, then I'll have to arrest you."

"You'll be getting in deeper if you don't tell us what involvement you had with Wade Weston," Brady said. "He's already been involved in one killing and there could be more. Do you want to hang along side of him?"

"I've never been involved with that gang except to buy cattle," Mr. Roberts said. "Wade Weston came to me almost a year ago to show me how the two of us could make a lot of money and he would be the only one taking the chances."

"How many transaction have you made over the past year?" the marshal asked. "Do you have any paper work to show these transactions?"

"Maybe five transactions, " Mr. Roberts said. "And I have the paperwork to prove it, because I had to protect myself from being suspected of fraud by the railroad."

"I'm interested in the B/A cattle transaction," Brady said. "Did you keep proof of that transaction?"

"Come to my office and I'll show you all the information I have on Wade Weston," Mr. Roberts said. "By the way, who taught you how to fight?"

"The Fifth Cavalry and the Apache," Brady said. "I picked up a few tricks on my own."

Mr. Roberts had a well-organized office and his records were in such an order that he pulled Wade Weston's records with only one try. Everything seemed to be in order. The records showed transactions starting from a year back and ran to last weeks raid on the B/A cattle.

Marshal Hunter took the records and informed Mr. Roberts. "Don't leave town, Marshal Hunter said, "If there's a trial, we'll need you to testify against Wade Weston and his gang of rustlers.

"What are your intentions now?" the marshal asked Brady, as they left Mr. Robert's office. "You know you can't take the law into your own hands."

"Somehow Wade Weston is tied in with Thomas Durham," Brady said, "I just need to find out how."

"You're going to need back up if you plan to ride back into Abilene," the marshal said. "If I deputize you then we both would have a reason to go into Abilene to search for more evidence."

"They would kill you for helping an accused killer," Brady said. "I think we should split up and go into town separately and we would get our information from more then one source."

"Whatever you say," the marshal said, "But I would feel better if you went in to Abilene under the protection of a badge."

"I'll get my badge back," Brady said, "But I'll do it my way."

The two men left Junction City with the same idea of arresting Wade Weston but they wanted to make sure they got all that was involved at the same time. Brady rode toward the B/A Ranch to meet with Luther, while Marshal Tad Hunter made his way into Abilene.

The ranch hands were hard at work when Brady arrived. The wranglers building barricades around the ranch house gave Brady the idea that the ranch was in danger of being raided. Luther met Brady at the barn and started explaining their actions.

"The mayor has given Wade Weston the town marshal's badge," Luther said. "Wade has already formed a posse to come to the ranch and arrest the men who took part in the killing of those rustlers."

"How much time do we have before we can expect their visit?" Brady asked, as he walked his horse into the barn to rub him down and see he got food and water.

"Don't know an exact time," Luther said. "But we're trying to get the women and children out of here before they come."

"Great idea," Brady said. "Take them to the ranger station and Captain Benson will see they are taken care of."

"We have a lookout at eagles point near the road from town," Luther said. "They have a mirror that they'll use to warn us during the day and they'll build a large campfire to warn us of their arrival during the night."

"Looks like you have about everything covered," Brady said. "I'm going back into town and see what else I can dig up about Wade Weston and his hired guns. I want to see how much Thomas Durham has to do with this mess."

"They'll kill you on sight," Luther said. "They'll give no mercy to any of us. They've placed extra taxes on the stores and they've made all business pay protection money. They've gotten way out of hand."

"There's a federal marshal in town by the name of Tad Hunter," Brady said. "He'll try and keep a lid on things until we gather enough evidence to make an arrest."

There was a movement inside the barn that made both men lookup. It was Yakima. He had entered the barn unnoticed and had heard the conversation between Luther and Brady.

"This Tad Hunter," Yakima said. "He's a tall man with a scar down his left cheek? Walks in deerskin boots and carries an old Henry in a deerskin saddle pouch?"

"Very good description of him," Brady said. "His scar has almost faded away but everything else matches. Do you know him?"

Yakima stood silent for a moment. Then turned and walked out of the barn. He had a strange look on his face and he seemed like he was in a trance.

"Strange fellow," Luther said, "But the best man to have around in time of trouble."

"I would like to spend the night and go into Abilene in the morning when I'm fresh," Brady said. "No reason to let anyone else know my plans."

The two men left the barn and walked around the ranch checking on the barricades to make sure the safety of the ranch was being taken care of. Yakima was talking with Indian Joe and they looked as if they had a difference in their feelings.

When Luther and Brady walked up the conversation between the two men stopped. "Yakima, is there something I should know about this federal marshal?"

"There was a time when the soldiers in Florida controlled the lands of the Seminole," Yakima said, as he looked into the eyes of Indian Joe.

"Go on," Brady said. "Don't keep anything away from me that might prove useful in the future. I'll be working with him when I reach town."

"The Seminole wouldn't give up their land or their fighting when the soldiers came to destroy them. The chief of the tribe was called Gray Wolf, the Hunter. The army called him the Hunter when they referred to him, and they referred to him often,"

"He was like smoke." Indian Joe said. "He slipped through their fingers on many occasions."

"The army chased the Seminole deep into the swamps where the army couldn't take their big cannons," Yakima said. "Then Gray Wolf the Hunter would strike at the army from ambush."

"The President of the United States wanted Gray Wolf the Hunter and his warriors destroyed," Indian Joe said. "Gray Wolf the Hunter had a wife that was sick and couldn't travel. Her only son, one that Gray Wolf the Hunter called Tadpole, stayed with her in a camp site near the swamp."

"The army got desperate," Yakima said. "They raided the Indian camp and took Tadpole and his mother captive. The two were used to bribe Gray Wolf the Hunter and his men from their hiding place."

"Yakima and myself were in that group that surrendered that day," Indian Joe said. "We were told to leave Florida or we would all go to prison."

"Gray Wolf the Hunter died on the trail," Yakima said. "His wife and son were pulled from the group and placed on an Indian reservation in Florida."

"We lost track of them for over a year," Indian Joe said. "Then one day Alvin showed up with Gray Wolf the Hunter's wife and a child that they had named Abigail. There were no questions asked and the three were welcomed into the group with open arms."

"We were told of the man called Tad Hunter," Yakima said. "He had become a lawman and was known as The Hunter that always got his man. He's also the son of Gray Wolf the Hunter."

"Seventeen years later you showed up and offered us a way to survive on our own labor," Indian Joe said. "You know the rest of the story."

"All of this said. You still haven't told me what Tad Hunter has to do with all this." Brady said.

"Alvin escaped from the reservation with his wife and his adopted daughter," Yakima said. "Because the two year old son of Gray Wolf the Hunter was offered to the commanders wife in exchange for their safe escape."

"Alvin never lived that down," Indian Joe said.

"The scar was placed on the boy's cheek by an eagle claw. The eagle came down from the sky and made a grab at the boy before flying off into the wild," Yakima said, as he lowered his eyes and mumbled, "I know the marshal is the son of Gray Wolf the Hunter and he goes by the name of Tad Hunter. Short for Tadpole."

"If what you say is true," Brady said, "And Tad Hunter is who you think he is, it would make him Abbey's older brother."

"Now you see why we talk of this man," Yakima said. "We must wait and let time tell us the true story."

"For right now," Luther said. "We must keep preparing for the new town marshal and his hired guns. Don't stop until we have enough barricades to stop an all out attack."

Meanwhile Tad Hunter made his appearance at the livery in Abilene. The livery boy took his horse and directed him to a good place to eat. When he arrived at the cafe he was waited on by one of the tallest waitress he had ever set eyes on. Tad stood flatfooted and looked her right in the eye. She was also beautiful, "I have found my dream girl," Tad said.

"Marshal, you're very flattering," Bernice said. "But I have a boyfriend that stands a head taller than I do and he's all I can handle at the time."

"Seems like I'm always late for the pretty ones," Tad Hunter said, as he ordered the day's special along with a pot of coffee.

When the meal was served Tad Hunter introduced himself and asked her if she knew a Brady Wells.

"Marshal, I hope to marry a man that works for Mr. Wells," Bernice said. "As far as I'm concerned he's the best thing that has happened to Abilene in ages. The mayor had no right to remove him from his job and the town's paying for it now."

"What do you mean by paying for it now?" Tad Hunter asked.

"This new marshal has added extra taxes to the business people," Bernice said. "Then they're charging protection money for protecting us from them. Now they want to drive out all Indians and mixed bloods so they can purify the town."

"Your friend Mr. Wells seems to have some mixed blood in him," Tad said. "Can that be why you're so angry?"

"Brady Wells grew up right here in Abilene," Bernice said. "He was raised at the fort by the army and he's as straight as they come."

"How about your bank president?" Tad asked, "Is he as straight as they come too?"

"Thomas Durham is a man of wealth," Bernice said. "He feels that there aren't to many men that are good enough for his daughter and that includes Brady Wells."

Tad Hunter finished his meal and drank the pot of coffee before he paid Bernice and thanked her for the conversation. He walked out of the cafe with his stomach full and his curiosity running wild. Why was Wade Weston given the marshal's badge without an election? Why had Thomas

Durham and Wade Weston become such close friends? Why had the law gone against the Indians? Why was the town business forced to pay heavy taxes that were levied on them by the new marshal?

Tad Hunter kept all these questions in his head as he headed over to the mayor's office. When he entered the office he came face to face with an older man that was just leaving. He seemed to be in his mid fifties and in very good shape. The man tipped his hat and left the office.

"Can I help you?" a voice said from a doorway that led to a large office.

"I'm looking for the mayor," Tad Hunter said, "I was told his office was up here among all the other offices."

"I'm Mayor John Spencer. How can I be of assistance to you?"

"I'm the federal marshal assigned here, by the government, to investigate what the government feels is blackmail, extortion and cattle rustling." Tad Hunter said.

"I have no recollection of any of that going on in my town," the mayor said, as he led the marshal into his office.

"You fired you're newly elected marshal and assigned a gentleman from out of town to fill his job," the marshal said.

"It is said, that our newly elected marshal was leading a bunch of wild Indians against the town people," the mayor said. "I was told that he and a band of Indians killed five men and wounded another. The new elected marshal claimed that the men were rustling his cattle and they had to protect their cattle from being rustled."

"You have solid proof that this incident of cattle rustling didn't happen?" the marshal asked. "You must have since you already got rid of your marshal."

"Thomas Durham, who incidentally, is the owner of the town bank, introduced me to Mr. Wade Weston, who was a cattle buyer for a company in Denver, Colorado."

"You verified this information with Denver?" Tad Hunter asked. "You must have done that since you found Wade Weston capable to handle the job of town marshal."

"Well, I really took the word of Mr. Durham," the mayor said. "He's an up right citizen of Abilene and has been for years."

"When the town marshal started placing extra tax burdens on the local business you didn't question why?" Tad Hunter said.

"The marshal had to call in special deputies to help him enforce the law and that cost money," the mayor replied.

"Did it not dawn on you that these special deputies were hired gun hands?" Tad Hunter asked. "Or did you give Wade Weston a free hand to do as he pleased?"

"Why are you asking me all these questions?" the mayor asked. "I have to do what the towns people want me to do."

"It's the towns people that are requiring you to do this?" Tad Hunter asked. "Or is it Thomas Durham and Wade Weston that are requiring this to be done? Why are you letting them charge the businesses protection money?"

"I'm doing my best without getting myself killed," the mayor said. "I can't handle these men by myself and neither can you."

"I will get to the bottom of this," Tad Hunter said. "You better hope that you have kept your nose clean because I'm going to bring this group down."

"Please, if I give you some extra information, would you drop any charges against me?" the mayor asked.

"That information better be a breaking point in this case," Tad Hunter said, "Or you'll be standing with these men in front of a federal judge."

"Thomas Durham has been robbing the bank of its investors money so he could pay off his son-in- law's gambling debts," the mayor said. "Then to get his money back he tried betting on the horses."

"You have proof of this?" Tad Hunter asked. "I can't go on hear say. I need solid proof."

"Thomas Durham has a safe in his home where he keeps his personal information," the mayor said. "It's behind the wine shelf in the basement. His bank records are kept there while a second set of record are kept in the bank vault."

"This information will go good for you if you haven't left anything out," Tad Hunter said, as he left the mayor's office.

Tad went to the telegraph office and wired his office in Washington to send a bank auditor to come to Abilene. After leaving the telegraph office, he went to the bank and filled out a card to open himself an account. The young lady that waited on him was beautiful. She had big blue eyes and a smile that would light up a dark room.

"Mr. Tad Hunter," the girl said. "How much would you like to deposit with us?"

"I have a thousand dollars to deposit now but I'm expecting more in the near future," Tad Hunter said.

"Good, we're always glad to have a new resident to use our facilities for their financial safety," the girl said.

"I'm new in town," Tad Hunter said. "It would be nice if I could get someone to show me around Abilene."

"My name is Hannah Durham," the girl said. "My father owns this bank and I'm sure he wouldn't mind if I became your welcoming committee."

Marshal Tad Hunter couldn't believe his good luck of meeting such a pretty young lady as he left the bank and went to the marshal's office.

When he entered the marshal's office he looked death in the eyes. The man behind the desk reached for his gun. His second mistake was to try and duck a guided bullet that was directed to the deputy marshal's badge that hung on his vest. The bullet struck the deputy in the chest knocking him from the office chair where he landed face down on the floor.

The office door opened again and Tad Hunter had already moved to the back of the door to wait and see if it was friend or foe.

The man who entered went straight to the body lying on the floor and knelt down to see if his deputy was alive. It was then that Tad Hunter stepped out from behind the door.

"Hello Mr. Wade Weston," Tad said. "Bet you didn't know that a wanted man with a wanted poster on him just walked in here and stole a deputy's badge and pinned it on."

"You got that right," Wade said. "What's brought you to the town of Abilene, marshal?"

"The federal government was asked to send a marshal to investigate robbery, fraud, cattle rustling and even murder, here in Abilene" Tad Hunter said. "They chose me for the job."

"Well, you're barking up the wrong tree if you think me or my deputies had anything to do with any of that," Wade said. "In fact your help isn't wanted or needed in Abilene."

"Not your choice," Tad Hunter said. "Better get your wanted prisoner buried before he creates another problem."

"You stay out of my business," Wade Weston said. "You could become a wanted man right along with the last marshal of Abilene."

Tad turned and walked out of the marshal's office with a lot of his questions answered. There was a crooked marshal in Abilene that had some very crooked deputies. They carried out the orders of a crooked leader, name unknown.

Hannah was busy rushing around town trying to get her hair done. She also needed a new dress and new shoes. It had been so long since anyone had paid her any attention. Her husband had been dead a long time. Brady wouldn't forgive her for marrying Frank Spencer and her father wouldn't let her date just any man. Now this man was a representative of the federal government. Her father couldn't have a thing against this man.

Captain Benson made his daily appearance in the bank and watched as Hannah closed her window in the middle of the day and rushed out the front door of the bank, as if the bank was on fire.

"Captain Benson," a voice said to him. "Can I have a moment of your time?"

Captain Benson looked around and saw Thomas Durham standing in front of his office door. "Sure, I'll be right there."

Thomas Durham met Captain Benson with a handshake and a Havana cigar. The captain loved a good smoke and these Havana cigars made a good smoke.

"What can I do for you Mr. Durham?" the captain asked. "Been a while since I last saw you in your office."

"I know all that and I'm trying to make up for all the work I've let slide," Thomas Durham said. "That's why I called you over. I needed to ask you about the reason you feel that Brady Wells went bad."

"Brady Wells doesn't have a bad bone in his body," the captain said. "Who ever started the talk about Brady and his Indian friends being killers, didn't like Brady or the Seminole wranglers in the first place."

"I heard it came from reputable sources," Thomas Durham said. "I know one of the sources was the new marshal of Abilene."

"You said reputable sources," the captain said. "There's nothing reputable in a cattle thief and murder that has been handed a badge."

"If you feel this way about the new marshal, why don't you arrest him," Thomas Durham asked. "He came here highly recommended."

"He would be highly recommended if someone wanted some cattle stolen," the captain said. "He would be highly recommended if there were to be a town take over too."

"Are you pointing fingers at anyone Captain Benson?" Thomas Durham asked. " If you are, you had better have plenty of proof or that person could have your job too."

"I can't arrest Wade Weston until I find him breaking the law in Texas," Captain Benson said. "But when I can prove he broke the law, I'll arrest him and all of his henchmen with him. Including anyone who might be connected to him through other sources."

"There was a federal marshal in my bank earlier," Thomas Durham said. "He wanted to open an account."

"Hope you haven't stepped on the governments toes," Captain Benson said. "There are no state barriers for those federal marshals to follow."

"He asked my daughter out on a date," Thomas Durham said. "Does that sound like he has a warrant for my arrest?"

"Walk lightly and keep Wade Weston in front of you," Captain Benson said. "He's like a rattler, he makes his biggest noise just before he strikes."

Captain Benson had a feeling that Thomas Durham was behind all the trouble that had come up in the last few days, but he had no proof.

Thomas Durham had gone back into his office and shut the door when Captain Benson saw Wade Weston heading for Thomas Durham's office as fast as his legs would take him.

Captain Benson left the bank after he watched Wade Weston enter Thomas Durham's office. The first thing he saw after going outside was a tall, broad shouldered cowboy walking down the boardwalk with Hannah Durham hanging on to his arm.

Captain Benson crossed the street and stepped up on the boardwalk just in front of the couple. They stopped and Hannah spoke up as he arrived.

"Hi, Captain Benson," Hannah said. "I would like you to meet Federal Marshal Tad Hunter from Washington, D.C."

"My privilege," Tad Hunter said, as he shook Captain Benson's hand. "I've followed your adventures by reading about your reputation as a Texas Ranger."

"I heard the government sent a federal marshal to Abilene," the captain said. "Do they want you to check up on me or the things that's going on in our town?"

"No reflection on you or the rangers," Tad Hunter said. "We know your boundaries and the regulations you have to follow to bring in a local bandit."

"You feel we have a bandit in our presents?" the captain asked.

"Yes sir," Tad Hunter said. "A bandit, a rustler, a fraudulent person and maybe even a killer."

"Can you two carry on your conversation on your own time?" Hannah asked, "This is my time, so let me finish showing the marshal around Abilene?"

"Nice meeting you captain," Tad Hunter said, as Hannah pulled him on down the boardwalk toward the local cafe.

Captain Benson stood and watched the two young people walking away from him. He knew the government had sent this marshal to take control of the problems in this town.

He knew that this man had a reputation with firearms of all kinds. But is he man enough to tame a town like Abilene?

Brady had finished his meal and had joined the men on the front porch. They all had a pipe or a cigar and the smoke was clouding up the air. The night air was turning colder and everyone knew that winter was just about to move in. But it was Indian Joe who brought up the subject of winter-feed and if there was money to carry them through the season.

“Sure there is,” Abbey said, as she and her aunt walked out on the porch. “Hi Brady, they didn’t tell me you were going to pay us a visit.”

“Didn’t know it myself,” Brady said. “Not until I found myself half way here when I left Junction City,”

“Brady are we in trouble with the law?” Abbey asked. “What in the world made the mayor take your badge?”

“Misunderstanding,” Brady said. “And until I can get some more information on Wade Weston, I might as well be chasing my tail.

“Clearing the reputation of the B/A Ranch is as much as saying you’re fighting for our reputations,” Abbey said. “Where did we go wrong? Our cattle was being rustled and we stopped the rustlers who were doing it.”

“I wished it was all that easy,” Brady said. “We’ve been accused of killing cattle buyers, not cattle rustlers. The men that could tell the town the truth were let loose from jail or murdered by the rustler's own hands. Yakima, you've got to ride into town with me in the morning. It'll be dangerous, but we can ride in from the south and enter the ranger station from the back way, maybe Captain Benson can help us find the rustler that got away."

"Good idea," Yakima said. "I'll never forget his face and one of the rustlers called him Jake."

"Has anyone ever heard the name Jake being used in town before?" Brady asked.

"Old Jake Dickinson from the Dickinson spread," Luther said. "He's all most sixty years old and he walks with a limp. But he still has both ears."

Everyone stood and stretched before they headed for the bunkhouse or the ranch house. "Brady can we talk?" Abbey asked.

"I've got plenty of time for talk," Brady said. "I've been wanting to ask you about how things were going here without Alvin around pushing the wranglers."

"You don't have to worry about the jobs getting done," Abbey said. "Luther has slid right in as boss man and is doing a great job with the working hands."

"Glad to hear that," Brady said. "I felt he had ramrod material in him when I first met him."

"We have enough money left from your friends loyalty," Abbey said. "We'll be all right until the spring round up and our next drive to the railroad should be profitable for us."

"You know Abbey," Brady said. "We've come a long way since Alvin past away. At first I didn't think we could make it without him. Then your family stepped up the pace and followed Luther as if it was Alvin and now we're on the verge of making a profit for the first time."

"Brady, will my family and I always be welcomed here on the B/A Ranch?" Abbey asked. "I don't feel like all of us are holding our own when it comes to working everyday. There are children to feed, women that are to old to work and men that don't have cattlemen skills. There are only a few men that are earning their wages for the rest of us, like Yakima and Indian Joe."

"Abbey, I promised Alvin that I would watch after you and your family," Brady said. "And as long as I live you all will have a home at the B/A Ranch."

"That's very good of you Brady," Abbey said. "But I wished it was for other reasons than a promise you made to my stepfather."

"Abbey, I don't know if this will help," Brady said. "But I've loved you since the time I first saw you standing in men's britches, a red plaid shirt, Indian boots and holding a smoking Henry rifle and the way you stared down a bunch of crooked outlaws."

Tears came to Abbey's eyes, as her heart seemed to come to a complete stand still. These were the words she had dreamed of hearing every since she had set eyes on Brady. What he was saying, took her breath away.

"Brady you'll never know how long I've waited for you to say just those words," Abby said, as she walked up to Brady and stood on her tiptoes, pulling his head down so she could feel the first kiss she ever placed on a man's lips.

Brady returned the kiss and remembered the dreams he had while he was hunting down the Indians. It was just as he imagined it.

Chapter 10

Early the next morning Yakima had the horses saddled and was waiting for Brady so they could ride back to town. The weather had turned colder over night and the sun still had over an hour left before it would make its appearance.

The ride to Abilene would give both men time to run things through their heads while deciding on their next move.

Why did the rustlers pick the B/A Ranch to rustle cattle when there were larger ranches with more cattle throughout the state? Why did Thomas Durham back the word of a stranger over the word of a hometown marshal? Why did Wade Weston and his gang come to Abilene? Then there was this question of where did they come from?

Brady was hoping to get all these questions answered before he lost control of his ranch over the crazy idea that he and his men were responsible for the death of five so called, cattle buyers. Thomas Durham had to be the controlling figure in this transaction, but why was he tied in with this bunch of gunslingers?

Brady and Yakima rode into town from the south to avoid being seen. There was no one hanging out behind the ranger station to watch them ride up. The back door of the ranger station was unlocked and Yakima followed Brady through it. There was a lot of excitement going on in the station when they walked in. A band of renegade apaches had left their reservation again and another cattle ranch had been attacked. Two of their wranglers had been killed while the Indians made off with several horses and a few head of cattle.

Captain Benson was getting ready to make a trip out to the ranch that had been raided, to see if he could pick up the Apache's trail. Then he saw Brady and Yakima come through the back door.

"You boys arrived just in time to help us track down a raiding party of apaches," Captain Benson said, as he led the two men into his office.

"Like to be of some service," Brady said. "But Yakima and I have a mission of our own to deal with."

"Do you two happen to know about a federal marshal that arrived in Abilene a day or so ago?" the captain asked.

"I met a Marshal Tad Hunter in Junction City just before I left there," Brady said, "He mentioned that he was headed this way, but I didn't know if he had arrived yet."

"He's here and he's noising around in Wade Weston's business," the captain said. "If I didn't know better I would say he has already placed a cocklebur under Weston's saddle."

"Good for him," Brady said. "Any idea where we might find the marshal now?"

"Try the bank," the captain said. "Seems he has set his sights on Hannah Durham as well. But remember, you're considered a wanted man here in Abilene and the new town marshal might just shoot you on sight."

"I'll take my chances that Wade Weston will not try a thing unless he has a huge advantage and no witness" Brady said. "Yakima and I'll keep ourselves in sight of witness so Wade and his hired guns won't shoot us in the back."

"I'll be out of town for a week or two," the captain said. "Ranger Burt Gibson will be in charge while I'm gone."

"Keep to the high country captain, you'll stand less of a chance of being ambushed," Brady said. "The apaches like the high ground too. It gives them control of anything or anyone below them that tries to ride through their land."

"I'll keep that in mind," the captain said, as he watched the two men leave his office headed for the Durham Bank.

When the two men entered the bank several people stopped to see if there was going to be any kind of a ruckus.

Marshal Tad Hunter was talking with Hannah when the two men walked up and removed their hats, as they made their greetings.

"We meet again marshal," Brady said. "Tad Hunter I would like you to meet Yakima. He's the brother of Indian Joe who married Suma of the Seminole tribe."

"You seem familiar to me for some reason," Marshal Hunter said. "Have you ever been east of the Mississippi River?"

"I lived in Florida during the swamp wars," Yakima said. "I had the privilege of fighting along side of my second brother, Gray Wolf the Hunter, chief of the Seminole tribes."

Tad had a pail look that came over his face, then he turned to Brady and said, "I've got a lead on Wade Weston. He was in Junction City selling cattle to the railroad a week before the cattle rustlers attacked your herd.

"Not much to go on," Brady said. "But it's a start. Yakima got a good look at the rustler that got away. We feel that he's still in town and if he is, we'll find him."

"There's a feeling that Wade Weston has found himself a partner here in town and the two are squeezing every penny out of the people of Abilene," Marshal Hunter said.

"Any idea who that might be?" Brady asked. "You do know it has to be a local boy."

Marshal Hunter glanced over at Hannah and shook his head in a negative manor. "Who ever it is has a lot of pull in this town," Marshal Hunter said. "Because they don't ask questions when he wants something done."

Brady took the hint that Tad Hunter didn't want to talk in front of Hannah, so he tipped his hat to Hannah and let her know he enjoyed seeing her again.

Hannah took Tad Hunter's hand and smiled real big as she looked into his eyes and said, "Tad has graciously asked me to attend the Thanksgiving Day celebration with him. I do hope you'll be there Brady."

"Thanks for reminding me," Brady said. "I wouldn't miss it for the world. Turkey and stuffing, plus all those pies, couldn't miss all that."

"I bet you can eat your weight in Pumpkin pie," Hannah said, as she started leading Tad Hunter down the wooden walkway.

"Tad Hunter is the son of Gray Wolf the Hunter," Yakima said. "He has the mark on his left hand. The brown mark of the wolf's paw."

"That's called a birthmark," Brady said. "Because it looks like a wolf's paw is coincidental."

"This sign appears on all the men of the Hunter tribe," Yakima said, as he turned his hand over for Brady to get a look at his birthmark.

"Yakima Hunter, brother of Gray Wolf the Hunter," Brady said. "Uncle of Abbey Hunter Simpson, born of the She Wolf Hunter, Gray Wolf the Hunter's sister."

"Now you know the whole story behind the Hunter tribe of the Seminole Indians," Yakima said. "You can believe we have traveled far for our freedom and we'll continue to fight for that freedom."

The two men walked over to the town barbershop where Brady sat down in a wooden chair to wait on a customer that was sitting in the barber's chair. He was propped back and had a hot towel around his face. "Be with you fellows in a minute or so," the barber said. "This shave won't take long."

"We're here for some information," Brady said. "My friend here has come a long way to find a friend of his named Jake."

"Jake who?" the barber asked. "There are several Jake's in town right now. In fact I'm shaving a Jake right now."

Brady reached over and yanked the towel from the man's face that was waiting for his shave. "Hey what are you doing?" the man asked.

Yakima took a good look at the man before Brady handed the towel back to the barber. Brady apologized to both men. Then he asked one more time, "Is there any more men named Jake that are new to Abilene, say in the past two weeks?"

"There's a strange Jake over at the Red Horse Saloon," the unshaven man said. "He's been staying in a shack behind the saloon with one of them bar girls named Lilly. Seems the marshal wants to keep him out of sight for a while. Heard Lilly is making a fortune keeping old Jake Patterson occupied.

"Know which shack the two are staying in?" Brady asked.

"Sure," the unshaven man said, "They're in the shack with the smoke coming out of the chimney."

Brady flipped a two bit piece to the barber and said, "The shave is on me and my partner." Then they left the barbershop and headed for the shacks behind the Red Horse Saloon.

"Yakima, you go around back and see to it that no one leaves by a back door or window," Brady said. "I'm going in the front way."

There was a window in the back of the building but it was so dirty that Yakima couldn't see inside. He went to the window and placed his ear to the thin glass and waited until he could hear Brady.

Yakima heard the door being kicked open as the people inside started yelling. "Who're you to be kicking our door down?" the woman asked.

"My name is Brady Wells and the two of you have just enough time to get dressed before I haul you to jail." Brady said.

"You ain't the marshal of this town and you can't make me get dressed," Jake said, as he sat down on the unmade bed.

"Your choice," Brady said, as he brought the barrel of his .44 down on the side of Jake's head. "Now, do you want to go to jail necked?" Brady asked the girl. Lilly was hurrying around to get dressed.

Yakima walked into the shack and took a piece of leather strap from his belt to tie the hands of Jake Patterson. Before he was finished the girl was dressed. Brady placed Jake over his shoulder and carried him out the door with Lilly and Yakima following behind him.

Brady stuck to the alleyways to maneuver his prisoner to the ranger station. Burt Gibson watched as the four entered the back door. Jake was taken to one of the empty jail cells and Yakima took Lilly to the conference room.

Burt Gibson entered the room with Brady. Everyone sat down at the conference room table across from where Lilly was setting. Then Brady started questioning the bargirl about her acquaintance with Jake Patterson.

"They gave me ten dollar a day to keep that good for nothing nincompoop occupied. They wanted him out of sight of any nosey lawmen," Lilly said. "But especially you and your Indian varmints."

"These Indian varmints are going to send you to prison for murder," Brady said. "When you help a wanted killer, it makes you an accessory to murder. That means you get to serve the same time as the murder himself."

"You can't do that," Lilly said. "Tell him Ranger Gibson, he can't do that because I ain't done nothing wrong?"

"You do know that Brady Wells was the marshal of Abilene before your friend Wade Weston got to town?" Burt Gibson asked. "He was also a ranger under Captain Benson and he knows what he's talking about. So I would suggest you listen to him."

"Look Brady, marshal Weston said, that there were some people interested in Jake. He offered me a lot of money to hide Jake," Lilly said, "I took the money and we stayed hidden as much as we could. That's the whole story."

"What other people did you come in contact with?" Brady asked. "Wade Weston must have brought some of his men around with him when he made contact with you."

"None I could name," Lilly said. "They all stayed out of sight except for his banker friend that kept giving him orders about getting rid of Jake before he became a liability, whatever that is."

"You actually saw and heard Wade Weston and Thomas Durham making arrangements to get rid of Jake Patterson?"

"If that's what you want to call it," Lilly said. "They were in the saloon when I heard them talking and Wade told me to keep my mouth shut or he would see that I would get planted on cemetery hill."

"You go back to your shack. I'll send Yakima with you," Brady said. "He'll tie you up before he leaves and that should let your friends know you had nothing to do with the disappearance of Jake."

Yakima left with Lilly while Brady and Burt Gibson went into the cell to question Jake Patterson. He was setting on the bunk with a blanket rapped around him concealing his nakedness. "Where're my clothes?" Jake asked.

"You didn't seem to want clothes at the time of your arrest," Brady said. "So I brought you in the way you were dressed."

"You didn't arrest me," Jake said. "You kidnapped me with a deadly weapon, forcing me to leave without my consent. You'll go to jail for that, because I know my rights."

"That might be true," Brady said. "But I have a gut feeling that you'll be hung as a cattle rustler long before I get put in jail. But you might have a way out of this if you give us evidence on Wade Weston and his band of outlaws."

"You're shooting in the dark if you think I'm going to talk to you fellows," Jake said, as he turned to walk into another empty cell that the ranger left open. "I'll take my chances with my friends as you call them. They got me out of jail once and they'll do it again."

"Brady, we can't hold this man on suspicion," Burt Gibson said. "We need hard evidence that he was involved with the cattle rustling."

"I know," Brady said. "We're going to take him out of here and hide him until his trial comes up,"

They both heard the back door open again and when they looked up Yakima stood in the doorway with his face painted like a wild Indian on the warpath.

Yakima grinned at the prisoner and made the sign of death as he pulled his finger across his neck. "I'll take good care of the prisoner when we get him away from town where no one can hear his screams." Yakima said.

"You can't do that," Jake said, as he backed up against the back wall of the jail cell. "Torture isn't legal in America."

Yakima just stood there smiling as he kept staring at the prisoner. "We Indians have been practicing the slow death every since you white men arrived on our land," Yakima said. "We now can cut you many times and still keep you alive for questioning."

"Ranger Gibson," Jake yelled. "Don't let them take me from this jail cell. They'll kill me just to make me talk."

"The only way I can keep you in jail, is if you confess to a crime," Ranger Gibson said. "Anything you want to say? Or do I turn my head while this Indian drags you to his torture tent?"

"Look I haven't been with the gang long enough for me to tell you anything about them," Jake said, as he sat down on the bunk.

"You were in on the raid of my cattle," Brady said. "Are you going to admit to that?"

"We were told these cattle were bought on credit," Jake Patterson said. "We were to round them up and bring them back to the bank until the bank got their money from their loan."

"Why did the railroad in Junction City pay your boss for the herd you rustled?" Brady asked.

"Look I was just told to help bring the cattle to town and put them in a holding pen until someone picked them up," Jake explained.

Yakima pulled his knife from its scabbard and swung his arm around with the speed of a cat. The tip of the knife struck Jake on the cheek and split his skin enough that the blood ran down his cheek.

Jake's eyes opened wide, as he placed his hand over the cut. He felt the blood that was still oozing from his cheek. "They can't do this to me?" Jake yelled.

"Sorry Jake, I didn't see a thing that happened," the ranger said. "These boys asked you a question and you made a joke of it. I believe it made the Indian mad. I don't think he liked your joke."

"You're going to let them cut me up like a thanksgiving turkey?" Jake said, as he moved away from Yakima.

Yakima grinned and brought the knife up to the cut on Jake's cheek. He scraped some blood from the cut and smiled. Then he took Jake's hair and pulled his head back placing the tip of the knife to his Adam's apple.

"Look Brady, if you guys are going to skin this guy, I want you to do it away from this office, the ranger said. "I don't want him bleeding all over the floor." "You can't do this, it's against the law" Jake said. "Wade will take you guys to the gallows if you harm me."

"Why would a town marshal care about a town drunk?" Brady asked. "We've already set your girlfriend free. So there'll be no one to even miss you."

"Move dead man," Yakima said, as he pulled the knife across Jake's throat enough to bring fresh blood but not deep enough to slit the throat. Then Yakima started pulling Jake toward the door by the hair on his head.

"No, don't let them do this," Jake screamed, as Yakima put more pressure to the hair and pulled Jake off his feet. "Stop, I'll talk," Jake said, as he held Yakima's hand to keep him from pulling his hair completely out.

"No more funny stories or I'll not stop Yakima next time," Brady said. Then Yakima pushed Jake back onto his bunk. "Please don't talk," Yakima said. "I like skinning white men."

"We have a hide out in Oklahoma Territory where any outlaw can come to get the law off their trail," Jake said. "We call it the devil's campsite. There's one way in and one way out and you don't want to be caught in-between."

"Jake we don't have time for you to brag on your different hide outs," Brady said. "We want to know who put you up to stealing our cattle."

"I don't know and that's the honest truth," Jake said, as he held his arms in front of his head to keep Yakima from grabbing his hair again.

"You better give us more information then I'm hearing right now," Brady said. "I'm loosing my patients."

"We were at the campsite when Wade rode in with the information that we were to go to Texas and help a friend out with some local problems," Jake said. "No names were mentioned. There were six of us who volunteer. We thought six was enough to handle some local cowpunchers that couldn't stand up to our guns."

"You came with Wade Weston without knowing who hired you?" Brady asked. "You're dumber than I thought."

"We have to trust Wade to get the money and pay us off," Jake said. "He has never failed us before, so why should he fail us now?"

"So as far as you were concerned," Brady said. "Wade Weston brought you here to rustle some cattle and your job was done."

"That's right," Jake said. "Then these savages turned up and killed every one but Hank and I. That's why Wade finished the job by smothering Hank and turning me loose from jail. I was suppose to hide out for a while and then go back to the devil's campsite."

"Did you get that down on paper?" Brady asked the ranger.

"Got it all," Ranger Gibson said. "Now Jake we have enough information from your confession to put you in jail and save your life from all of those savages. I want you to sign this paper now."

Brady and Yakima left the ranger's station looking for Wade Weston when Hannah and Marshal Hunter walked up. "Finding any information on the cattle rustlers?" the marshal asked.

"The man that was locked up in the town jail and later turned loose, has been found," Yakima sad. "He is now under arrest and is being held by the rangers."

"Get any useful information?" Tad asked. "So far everything is circumstantial."

"He has tied Wade Weston to the cattle rustlers but he hasn't given up the person who put this all together," Brady said.

"Why do you think there is another person involved?" Hannah asked. "Seems to me you have your cattle rustlers and you should stop at that."

"Wade Weston was in Colorado when he was contacted by someone in this town to come and shut down my ranch," Brady said. "They're not going to stop with the cattle rustlers being arrested. They'll hire others and continue rustling until the B/A Ranch is closed down forever."

"You think it's my father, because he was against us going together while we were children?" Hannah said. "You're wrong. My father isn't a vengeful man and you know it."

"You may be right Hannah," Brady said. "But what if he was behind all this? He could bring down the B/A Ranch and this whole town of Abilene with it."

"Marshal," Hannah said. "You have the authority to stop these crazy accusation that Brady is applying about my father. I want Brady arrested for conspiracy."

"Hannah," the marshal said, "All the evidence we have is pointing to your father being involved. The only thing we're looking for now is motive. Why is your father so set against the B/A Ranch and Brady's ability to run the marshal's office here in Abilene."

Hannah took a swing at Tad with an open palm, but he blocked her arm before she landed the blow to his face. "I thought you were different from all the other men in this town," Hannah said. "I thought you had some feeling for me and my family."

"I do Hannah," Tad said. "When this is all over and the cattle rustlers are caught. I want to be able to come to you with an apology or the facts."

Hannah walked off leaving the men standing in the street watching her as she disappeared from the street in front of her father's bank.

At the same time the far end of the street started filling up with riders. At the head of the riders was Wade Weston. They started to spread out over the street as they rode closer to the three men.

"You're wanted for murder in this town," Wade Weston said, as he held up his right arm for his men to stop their advance. "You can come peacefully or we can drag you in by your heals. Your choice."

"I'm a U.S. Marshal sent here from Washington to try and solve the problem that Abilene is having with cattle rustlers." Tad Hunter said.

"Cattle rustling isn't a government problem," Wade said. "That means you have no jurisdiction in this town. The problem is local and your Indian friends are guilty of murder. It is my duty to bring them in for trial."

"We have your friend Jake locked up at the ranger station and he has confessed to helping you to rustle the B/A cattle," Brady said. "You have some innocent towns people acting as deputies and they'll go to jail for firing upon a U.S. Marshal."

"They have been deputized and they'll kill your marshal if he tries to resist arrest," Wade said.

"Hold on there," one of the riders said. "We want no part of killing any U.S. Marshal. We came to help arrest Brady and his bunch of Indian friends."

`"If you don't have the stomach to stand up for the law, then get out of here and let the law get its work done," Wade said.

About half of the riders turned their horses and rode away. Leaving Wade with about seven men counting himself.

Yakima smiled and said, "You have enough time to go get help, because we have the advantage, now."

"Let me explain what he's saying," Brady said. "If there is the slightest move for your guns we will add to the number of graves that are on cemetery hill."

Just then the door to the ranger's office opened and Burt Gibson walked out with a double-barreled shotgun in his hand. "Gentlemen the streets of Abilene will not be turned into a battle ground," the ranger said. "I suggest that you all take your leave from the streets and gather somewhere else."

"This isn't over," Wade Weston said. "You'll be dangling from the end of a rope or lying face down in the street before I'm done."

"Brady, you'll have to take your problem off the streets of Abilene too," Ranger Gibson said. "The mayor isn't happy with the way things are turning out and he'll force the rangers to take sides before a war breaks out in his town."

A loud banging noise came from the alleyway next to the ranger's building, it caught Yakima's

attention, as he turned and pulled his gun from it's holster.

"They're building your gallows," Wade Weston said, as he slipped his gun back into its holster and rode away.

"Their building the stage for another celebration next week," Brady said, as the group of men moved out of the streets.

"What's you're next step?" Marshal Hunter asked.

"A visit to my ranch," Brady said. "I would like for you to see the ranch and meet the people who run it."

"These people will be the last remaining relatives of your father Gray Wolf the Hunter," Yakima said. "You have a sister that lives on this ranch. Her name is Abigail Simpson."

"My adopted parents told me so little about my real father," Tad Hunter said. "I knew of Yakima and his brother by the stories that were told while I was growing up."

"You were given to your adopted parents so they would turn their head while your father's sister escaped with her new born baby," Yakima said.

Ranger Gibson wished them all good luck as he went back to the ranger station. Brady knew that if something didn't happen soon to prove that cattle rustlers had attacked the B/A Ranch, Wade Weston would take control of the town and drive the Seminole Indians off their land.

A young boy was cleaning the livery when the men went for their horses. Otherwise the stable seemed empty. Marshal Hunter noticed straw moving from one of the stalls when he yelled, "Take cover."

The three men fell to the floor of the stable. Brady rolled to his right pulling his revolver as he kept his eyes open for any sign of danger. Marshal Hunter had pulled his gun and fired two bullets into the straw that was stacked inside the middle stall. Yakima had leaped inside an empty stall and had pulled his knife and let it fly at a shadow that moved into the light just as the marshal fired. Shots came from the rafters as Brady placed two bullets into the flash of light that was formed from the barrel of the guns.

There was silence as they listened for any other movement. Then came the sound of crying as the stable boy showed his emotions from the danger that had just took place.

Marshal Hunter walked over to the stall that he just fired into and used his foot to uncover two men that smelled like a brewery. They had guns in their hands but they never got to use them. Yakima's knife had gone into one man's chest that had made the shadow on the wall. The knife went deep enough to leave the man struggling for breath. In his hand was a poster crumbled up into a ball.

Brady climbed the ladder to the rafters and pushed two dead men down to the stable floor. They smelled like they too had bottomed out a barrel of rot gut whiskey.

When Brady climbed down from the rafter Yakima handed him the wadded up poster he found in the hand of the man that was still alive. It read,

$100.00 Reward for any man who brings in Brady Wells dead or alive. $50.00 Reward for any of his Indian friends dead or alive. All Rewards paid in gold by the town marshal.

Marshal Wade Weston.

"Takes a real low individual to hand out these type of posters," Marshal Hunter said. "Bounty offers can last awhile even after a man is cleared of wrong doing."

The barn door opened and Wade Weston stood in the opening with his deputies. They had their guns drawn and a grin on their faces. "We have you now," Wade Weston said. "Drop you're guns. Then you can make yourself comfortable in our jail."

A crowd started gathering outside the livery where they stood and watched as the new town marshal escorted the three men toward the marshal's office.

"You got this all wrong," Marshal Hunter explained. "These men were waiting for us to enter the livery so they could collect on your illegal bounty offer."

"Shut your mouth marshal," Wade said. "You might get shot for trying to aid these wanted killers to escape. That's what you're doing aren't you?"

"You shoot a federal marshal and you'll never rest easy ever again," Marshal Hunter said. "You'll be hunted down like any other animal."

"The men in that livery were ambushed by you and the half-breed, along with his Indian accomplice."

"That's a lie and I can prove it," Marshal Hunter said. "Come here kid. Tell this representative of the law what happened in that livery."

"Like the marshal said," the boy answered. "When these men entered the livery, the other men come out from under their cover and tried to gun them down. But the marshal and his friends were to quick. They had their weapons out and firing before the other men could get off a shot."

"When you try to get someone killed you shouldn't have witness," Marshal Hunter said. "This young man was a part of the danger that you've set up with your reward posters. You best pull them before some innocent person dies and I have to place you and you're men under arrest for manslaughter."

"You might have nine lives," Wade said, "But you've used most of them and I intend to have your badge before this is over."

"That or the other way around," Marshal Hunter said, as he stared down Wade Weston.

Chapter 11

During the ride to the ranch, Yakima and Brady brought Marshal Hunter up to date on what had happened to his mother and her family after they left their land in Florida.

Marshal Hunter couldn't have been more than five years old when all this took place, yet he had memories of his mother, Indian Joe and Yakima. He also remembered his mother's sister Martha Sigils. But there were no memories of him having a sister.

The sun was setting by the time the men reached the ranch and there wasn't much activity going on. Indian Joe walked from the porch of the ranch house over to the barn to greet the three men. There were several empty stalls available in the barn for their horses. Each man unsaddled his horse and rubbed it down with loose straw while they carried on a conversation with Indian Joe. Then Luther Bogs came into the barn.

When Marshal Hunter saw Luther his first words were, "Wow, do you gentlemen always keep a giant around to guard your barn?" While his eyes scanned Luther from head to toe.

Brady laughed, "This is Luther Bogs our foreman," Brady said. "Luther, I want you to meet Tad Hunter, Abbey's brother."

Luther stood in amazement for a moment then extended his big hand to the man that had just sized him up. "You're welcome to the B/A Ranch, if you're looking for an invite," Luther said.

"Thanks for the offer," Marshal Hunter said. "Brady and Yakima have brought me up to date on everything except they didn't tell me about the young giant."

"Don't let Luther's size fool you," Yakima said. "He's much meaner then he looks." Everyone got a laugh out of that.

When the horses were fed and watered, Yakima and Indian Joe began asking questions about the marshal's adventures for the past fifteen years. How he became a federal marshal? Where did he make his home now? What happened to his adopted parents?

"You're true Seminole Indians," Marshal Hunter said. "You talk to much and ask to many questions to be from any other tribe."

"We also fight like true Seminole warriors," Yakima said. "We'll stick with our friend Brady Wells and we'll defend his ranch and our home to the death."

"No one will ever question your ability to fight," Tad Hunter said. "Nor will your loyalty be challenged by me."

A woman's voice came from the porch of the ranch house, "Where is everyone? Supper is getting cold and we still have work to do before it gets to dark to see."

"That's the real boss around here," Luther said. "She can have the men jumping to her tune before I can get a word in edgewise." All the men got a kick out of that statement coming from the big man with a lot of fear for a woman.

"If she's the authority around here then we had better get a move on," Brady said, as he led the rest of the men to the house.

Abbey's eyes lit up when she saw Brady leading the crowd of men. She jumped down from the porch and started running toward the men. "When did you get here Brady?" she squealed, as she ran into his arms.

"Excuse me gentlemen but I have some time to make up," Brady said, as he lifted Abbey up in his arms and placed a kiss on her waiting lips.

"Got a pockets worth of information and I thought I would come here and share it with the rest of you folks before I decide what to do," Brady said. Then he lowered Abbey back to the ground and placed his arm around her shoulder, as he walked with her back to the house.

"Any of this information going to help our cause?" Abbey asked, as she walked beside Brady with her arms wrapped around his waist.

"We'll all have a long talk after supper," Brady said. Then he led Abbey and the men into the large dinning room. "This is Tad Hunter everyone, Yakima says he's a long lost relative."

Marshal Hunter stood looking at Abbey while she returned that same stare with fixed eyes. There was silence in the house as the two just stood trying to recall each other from earlier days. Then Abbey walked over and extended her hand to the marshal. He took her hand in both of his and said, "The little one with the big eyes."

"Do you remember me from so far back?" Abbey asked. "What does big eyes mean?"

"I remember watching my mother being dragged from the room with a little baby girl in her arms," Tad said. "The little baby was so tiny but she had big, wide open eyes."

"Mother died from consumption a few years back," Abbey said. "Alvin didn't live much longer after her death. Yakima and Indian Joe have been with me all my life, but neither of them have never mentioned that I had an older brother."

"You're disappointed," the marshal asked. "You never expected a brother and now that you're face to face with one, you're disappointed."

"I'm no such thing," Abbey said. "You're welcome to this house any time and I'm sure you'll be welcomed into my heart very soon."

"The food is already cold," Martha Sigils said, as a tear ran down her cheek. "Luther you start the food moving around the table. Brady, you sit over by Mr. Hunter. Yakima you can grab another chair if you want to eat at the table with the rest of us."

The evening meal went well even though there were so many eating around the same table. The talk was light and there were only questions asked until after the meal. The men were still seated drinking the last of the coffee when the questions started.

"I noticed the barricades around the ranch house," the marshal said, "Expecting company or is this standard for this part of Texas?"

"Wade Weston has made some threats about the only good Indian being a dead one. We felt he should be taken at his word," Yakima said. "We'll be prepared if and when he and his men decide to carry out their threats."

"What about this celebration you're going to tomorrow?" the marshal asked. "Is it a big thing in these parts?"

"It use to be a big thing when I was growing up," Brady said. "The town got together every year to pick out the best wrangler in town and they rewarded him with prizes."

"Did you ever win any of these rewards?" the marshal asked. "After watching you defend yourself with guns and fist these last few weeks, you must have given the men around here a run for their money."

"I've competed in some events and in most cases won my share," Brady said. "But enough of that, I don't compete any more."

"Are you going to the celebration with Hannah Durham?" Brady asked. "She used to be the bell of the St. Patrick's day celebration."

"You and Hannah were high school sweethearts, weren't you?" the marshal asked.

"We ran around together a lot until her father became a well know banker, then he wanted his daughter to marry a man with a traceable back ground," Brady said. "I was a half-breed with an Indian father and a mother that had committed suicide."

"I believe your telling me that if I wish to remain a friend of Hannah Durham and her father, I had better keep my background to myself," the marshal said

"She's a good woman and she'll make someone a good wife one day," Brady said. "But she'll never be a wife of mine for many reasons. Can we move our conversation out on the front porch?"

The whole gang went out and sat on the front porch. They were enjoying the night breeze that was blowing in from the south. You could almost smell the ocean water from the wind that was blowing in from the Gulf of Mexico. The conversations were about Florida and the land the Seminole Indians occupied before they were driven from their lands. Most of the Indians wound up in Oklahoma Territory, but Alvin led his group to Texas and here they would stay.

The darkness had blanked the ranch house when Indian Joe stood and said good night. The rest of the hands followed him to the bunkhouse, along with Brady and Tad Hunter. The ladies went into the house. They all felt that tomorrow would be a long and busy day.

The next morning when breakfast was over and the buggies were hooked up. Brady watched as Luther rode up from inspecting the barriers around the ranch. "We're going to be short handed with everyone going to the celebration," Luther said.

"Relax Luther," Brady said. "Even Wade Weston and his bunch of cut-throats wouldn't miss this celebration." There were seven grown ups and five children from the B/A Ranch headed into town for the celebration and this was going to leave the ranch very short handed. Everyone was involved, as lookouts for danger when they were on the ranch, now there would be twelve fewer lookouts. Luther was nervous but he went along with Brady's reasoning about Wade Weston and his bunch of deputies being involved with the celebration also.

The town was already starting to come alive with games and competitions when the B/A group arrived in town. The children were so excited that they started jumping from the wagons before they came to a complete stop.

Tad Hunter looked over the crowd in the streets and the gathering at the courthouse hoping to see Hannah among them. The bank seemed to be empty at the time, Tad thought the bank might have closed for the festivities, When the B/A group did come to a halt, it was in front of a large portable shelter with canvas stretched over a supporting framework by poles, ropes, and pegs. There was sawdust scattered on the floor of the tent to keep the dust from blowing all over the place. The folks unloaded and started setting up tables for the picnic baskets that were brought to feed the party for a couple of days.

Yakima and Indian Joe rode with Brady to the ranger station. They wanted to see how their prisoner was getting along.

Burt Gibson, the ranger in charge, met them in his office and talked with them about how he was keeping the prisoner safe until a trial could take place. There had been talk of a jailbreak but nothing worth checking out. There was also talk that Thomas Durham had wired the ranger's main office in Dallas for a wire to release the prisoner to the local law enforcement.

"Hang on to him as long as you can," Brady said. "We'll keep trying to find something on Wade Weston and his gun hands."

"Did you know that the local stage line was carrying a bank auditor from Denver?" Burt Gibson asked. "He's due here today."

"Marshal Hunter must have requested him?" Brady said. "I like how that man works. Let's get back to observing our local law at work, Weston and his bunch, hopefully, will take the day off."

Luther found Bernice Merit strolling through the haberdashery shop looking at the latest merchandise. She was with Hannah Durham and the two seemed to be enjoying themselves when they noticed the big man blocking the entrance to the shop.

"Luther Bogs!" Bernice said. "What brings you off your little ranch on the prairie?"

"There's a celebration going on in town and I thought you might want to go to the dance with me tonight," Luther said.

"This celebration has been going on every year since I don't know when," Bernice said. "Why is it that this is the first time you've asked me to go to the dance?"

"Please Bernice, don't give me a hard time," Luther said. "I've had a job to do and it's getting worse since the local law seems to be against the ranch."

"Sorry Luther," Bernice said. "I just miss you so much every day because you stay out on that ranch for weeks at a time."

"Luther, did Marshal Hunter come into town with your group? Hannah asked.

"Just left him about five minutes ago," Luther said. "He's expecting someone important to arrive on the stage today."

"I'll catch up with you two later. I'm going to the stage depot to see Marshal Hunter," Hannah said, as she lifted her dress and petticoats and ran out the door.

When the stage arrived, Marshal Hunter stood waiting for the passengers to depart the stage. Hannah came running up to the marshal and gave him a big smile as she too watched the people step-down from the stage.

A short stocky gentleman dressed in a tailored broadcloth suit, a black bowler hat and black boots, stepped down from the stage and walked straight to Marshal Hunter. "We meet again," the man said. "You are keeping me in business."

Marshal Hunter turned to Hannah and introduced her to the gentleman, "Hannah Durham, I would like for you to meet Frank Faust. He's a bank auditor and a federal marshal himself."

"You sent for an auditor?" Hannah asked. "You're having my father's bank audited aren't you?" There was a look of astonishment on Hanna's face.

"Hannah, I need to clear your father from this mess right away," Marshal Hunter said. "The only way I can do that is to call in an auditor and show the people your father is running a sound bank."

"You can go on with your investigation," Hannah said, "But you'll do it without my consent. I never dreamed you would ever consider my father to be criminal." There was no doubt that Hannah meant every word she said, as she turned and headed home to inform her father of the new information she had received.

The sun was changing the color of the western sky as it set. The March winds were blowing in from the north but that wasn't why Marshal Hunter felt a cold chill run up and down his spine.

"Bad timing?" Faust asked. "Seems like there is no good time for an audit."

"Do you have your authorization to do this audit?" Marshal Hunter asked.

"I always come prepared," Faust said. "I'll be in the bank first thing in the morning and I will have some kind of an opinion by the end of the week."

Men were putting on their jackets as the women placed shawls over their shoulders. The night air was going to be cold for the dance but no one seemed to mind the weather."

When the music started Brady noticed that Marshal Hunter was standing with a man that he had never seen before. There was no Hannah Durham with him. In fact there was none of Thomas Durham's family around at all

Brady walked over to the marshal to ask about Hannah and the marshal went into detail about calling in the auditor to check the finances of the Durham Bank. That's why Hannah wasn't with him. She's fighting mad about this audit.

"I haven't seen Abbey around all day, either," Marshal Hunter said. "Can there be a problem with your love life?"

"She went over to help Bernice Merit get ready for the dance," Brady said. "They should've been back by now."

"I've informed Frank Faust that the audit will start the first thing in the morning," Marshal Hunter said. "I hope you're wrong about Thomas Durham stealing from the bank to pay off debts."

"You may not believe this," Brady said. "But I hope I'm wrong too. Hannah needs a break to give her fresh hope. I feel you have helped her some in gaining that hope."

"There was no hope in her eyes when she left me a while a go," Marshal Hunter said. "She was as mad as an old wet hen."

The men walked over to the shelter of the tent and Marshal Hunter introduced Mr. Faust to everyone except Luther Bogs and he wasn't around.

The band started making a loud noise that drowned out the spoken word. The couples were gathering on the stage and the party seemed to be getting under way.

Luther heard the music start up when he walked up to the cafe door. He was hoping that the girls were dressed and ready to be escorted to the dance. From the corner of his eye he saw a shadow of a man moving out of the alleyway toward him. Then a gun barrel was shoved into his rib cage.

"Guts and glory gets you six foot of property on cemetery hill," the voice said. "Put your hands in the air and step away from that door."

"Got no quarrel with you gents right now," Luther said. "But if you keep this up I'll have to squash you like an ant."

Luther saw the shadow of an object coming down on his head. He raised his left arm to block the blow but the object was heavy like an ax handle and Luther heard the bone in his arm snap. The pain was felt clear through his body. Luther managed to keep his feet as he took his right arm and swung at whoever was behind him.

The arm caught flesh and Luther felt the person fall backwards enough that Luther made his turn and brought his big fist down on another man's head. He heard bone snap as the man doubled up on the ground. There were enough men grabbing at him that he didn't notice the man from the alleyway. He pointed his gun and fired a shot that brought

Luther to his knees. The burning sensation was felt threw out his body just before he lost consciousness.

When Luther regained his consciousness he reached for his head. It felt like it was as big as a wagon wheel. There was blood from a gash that almost split his head wide open. He felt like he was going to pass out again. Everything kept spinning around. It was then that he heard Brady ask, "What has happened here Luther? Where are the girls?"

"I don't know," Luther said. "I came to escort them to the dance and I was jumped by a group of men that must have had ax handles in their hands. Next thing I know I'm laying here with you yelling in my ear."

"There are two men laying here beside you," Brady said. "One has a busted head the other one has a broken neck."

"Sorry Brady," Luther said. "There were to many of them and when I got shot I lost count of everything."

"You did well Luther," Brady said. "The men left behind are wearing deputy badges. That in it's self gives us a place to start. Yakima get a doctor over here now. The bullet put a gash in Luther's head."

The cafe door had been busted open and it remained open as Brady pulled his gun and very slowly went inside. There were no sign of a struggle until he reached Bernice's room and it looked like a stampede passed through it. The girls had put up a fight but it looked like the intruders won the war.

"There's money in the cash box," Marshal Hunter said, as Brady came back into the cafe area. "Their motive wasn't robbery."

"When did you get here?" Brady asked. "The room's a mess. The girls gave them a fight but they had no chance with all those men."

"They're going to be hard to find tonight," Marshal Hunter said. "If we try to track them down we could pass them up. Our tracking could force them to do something we would all regret later."

"Marshal, you wait until tomorrow when you can gather a posse," Brady said. "But I'm going to try and stay close to those kidnappers to make sure they keep their mind on running and not on the girls."

"Good idea," Marshal Hunter said. "Keeping their mind occupied could save the girls a lot of grief."

Brady bent over and checked Luther's head one more time before he went to the livery and saddled his horse. He had plenty of ammunition but he was short on food and water. He would have to make good with what he had. He didn't want to fall to far behind the kidnappers or they might settle down with a night of pleasure on their mind.

There was enough light left in the sky to show sign that the kidnappers had left town from the west. They weren't even in a hurry to get away. Their horses were moving at a walking gate and there seemed to be a large number of them. Maybe fifteen to twenty men were in on the kidnapping. Brady knew that the men were trying to draw him out of town so they could kill him once and for all. Now they had succeeded, Brady would follow them until he had the satisfaction of killing Wade Weston or die trying.

About three miles out of town the darkness crept over the land and Brady knew it was going to be nip and tuck from here on. He kept his eyes open for a campfire or a light from a lantern, anything that would show him what direction the kidnappers were taking the girls.

The sun was gone and the darkness was blinding. There wasn't enough light to see the head of the horse he was riding. His only chance was to let the horse have his head and hope that they didn't run over an arroyo or fall into a gorge.

After about a half-hour of riding blind from the darkness, Brady pulled his gun and fired two shots into the air. He was hoping he was within earshot of the kidnappers and they would keep their minds on the gunshots and off the girls.

After another half-hour of wondering around in the dark Brady fired two more rounds. Then he pulled up on the horse's reigns. Brady could hear water moving through a stream. The noise was soft but it was moving water. Brady climbed down from the horse and started leading him toward the moving water.

The smell of water became strong and Brady dropped the reigns and let the horse lead the way. When the horse pulled up and started drinking from the stream, Brady knelt and felt for a place so he too could get a drink of water. This was Elk Creek that ran through old Dan Miller's place. There wasn't enough water to maintain cattle but there was enough water to keep a person alive.

Dan Miller lost his family to cholera and left this place over two years ago. The house was left empty of people but it still held the furniture and makings of a home. This could be where the kidnappers were going to hold the girls until they received other orders.

Brady knelt beside the stream trying to figure out just where the Miller house sat in accordance to the stream. The stream ran north to south and it split the Miller land almost in half. The house set more to the west, close to Pine Tree

Ridge, a ridge that dropped a hundred yards straight down and it gave you no warning of its drop off spot.

When Brady left town the wind was blowing in from the south. It was hitting him in the back right now and that meant the house was some where to his left. Now all he had to do was follow the stream until he ran into the pine trees, then it was a guessing game.

Brady fired another round of two shots and mounted his horse. He turned him to his left and gave him his reins. The flow of the stream kept coming from his right side and the horse seemed to be on a straight line to somewhere but he was the only one to know just where he was going.

"There goes those shots again boss." Gabby Taylor said. "Those shots are coming closer to the hideout too."

"Someone out there is playing a mind game on you," Wade Weston said. "The idea is for us to stay awake all night waiting for the next shots and no one gets any sleep. If that happens, we won't be as alert tomorrow as we should be."

"That's an old Indian trick," Bob Pool said. "I bet those people out there are Indians and they're hunting for scalps."

"You can bet all of those people out there are Indians," Abbey said. "Their leader is a half-breed Apache, called Brady Wells and he won't stop until you're all scalped. He'll have you all in his sights before the sun sets tomorrow, he might have you targeted right now."

"Shut up woman, before I take a liking to you and show you what a white man can do to make a woman howl for more," Bob Pool said.

"There's no reason for standing watch out side," Wade said. "You can't see a foot in front of you and neither can that half-breed."

"An Indian is like a wolf at night," Bob Pool said. "When I was a scout in the army and we were chasing Geronimo and his band of cut throats, we camped one night in the foothills to rest the horses and just before sun up the next morning we were awakened by a high screeching yell. Looking around we found several of our men dead from having their throats cut during the night."

"Pool, we don't need one of your night time stories to put us to sleep," Wade Weston said, as he heard two more shots that sounded like they were even closer than before.

"Cover that window with a blanket," Gabby Taylor said. "If he is some one out there he could see the light for miles."

"The men in the barn have a fire going to keep them warm," Bob Pool said. "If they make it hot enough they'll be sending a warning light to the half-breed too."

"Shut up," Wade said. "We'll hold the girls long enough to send a message to Marshal Hunter to drop the bank audit and get out of town. Then we'll take over and make our fortune off the town folks."

"The rangers won't let you continue your thieving ways." Abbey said. "Captain Benson isn't the type man to take orders from you or any other crooked snake. Besides, you aren't going to leave this place alive any way."

Wade Weston doubled up his fist and struck Abbey on the chin knocking her to the floor where she lay unconscious.

"Let me take her to the bedroom and make a woman out of her," Bob Pool said. "She's nothing but a mouth anyway."

"You leave her alone," Bernice said. "She'll have Brady Wells string you up to a tree and skin you like a wild animal."

"Get some sleep Bob," Wade said. "These women are not to be harmed in any way. They'll be our way out of here if things get rough. They'll be the reason for the U.S. Marshal to leave town and they'll be the reason for the Indians to keep their distance."

The men started settling down by finding them a place to rest their heads. They knew they had to face the enemy tomorrow. Two more shots were fired as the kidnappers lay with their eyes open waiting for the next round of shots.

The men in the barn were starting to get uneasy with the shots being fired every half-hour. They felt the shots were coming closer and closer even though they couldn't see a foot outside the barn.

Brady's horse seemed to be following the stream even though he was given no directions in which to go. Now and then he would stop, raise his head and shake it as if he was trying to stay awake or could he smell danger ahead? Then the horse stopped and stood very still. There seemed to be a new smell in the air. It was smoke.

Brady swung down from the horse and took hold of the stirrup with his left hand as he slapped the horse on the rump with his right hand. Walking beside the horse they both moved closer to the smell of smoke. It was time to fire off another round when Brady saw the twinkle of light just ahead. The sound of the shots didn't seem to carry as far in the dark now that the fog was moving in, but it didn't need to because Brady could see the light of their fire from where he was standing.

Brady tried to turn the horse in the direction of the light as he kept his grip on the stirrup. The horse wasn't ready to make a turn and Brady was afraid he would whiney if he was forced to go in a different direction.

Soon the horse reached a clump of pine trees that stood between them and the light. Brady hobbled the horse with a strip of rope long enough to keep him close to the trees but yet give him room to munch on the grass growing around the outside of the tree line.

Brady lay down on his belly and moved very slowly toward the light. What made the light twinkle was some of the men were still awake and were moving back and forth in front of a fire. There seemed to be nothing in the darkness except the light. It could be from a barn with an open front or a light shinning from the window of a house. What ever it was Brady was going to explore it.

Chapter 12

"We have an hour of darkness left," Marshal Hunter said, as he used the light from the kerosene lamp to check his pocket watch.

Yakima and Indian Joe stood beside their horses watching the Marshal as he paced back and forth in the livery. Their bows were hanging over their shoulders along with their quivers that they were filled with arrows. Their rifles were in their scabbards hanging from their saddles, their pistols were in their holsters and tied down to their leg. Each one had a canteen of water that hung from his saddle horn.

"Indian Joe and I'll start now," Yakima said. "Boca will know how to get in touch with us on the trail."

The marshal knew that time was going to be a factor and if Indian Joe and Yakima could pick up the trail before the rest of them he was all for it.

Luther was tightening the girth on his mule when the two Seminole Indians rode off. Luther's head was heavily bandaged and his left arm was in a sling. His head still felt like it was the size of a watermelon and it had a constant throb like a toothache. His stomach was swirling around as if he was going to be sick. He knew he had let the girls down and he wanted to be there if and when they were rescued.

The Seminole Indian named Boca rode up with a pack mule that was loaded down with supplies. "There's enough light to get us started," he said, as he turned in his saddle and watched Ranger Burt Gibson ride up.

"I can't afford to take any of my rangers and leave the town unprotected," the ranger said, "But I'll go along to give you one more gun."

"Brady has been on the kidnapper's trail all night," Marshal Hunter said. "Yakima and Indian Joe left just before you rode up. Luther, Boca, you and I will make up the total number of the men that we have to face up to a band of killers that out number us about five to one."

"I wouldn't doubt that Brady will have the odds cut down some before we catch up with him," Luther said.

The clouds were moving in causing the fog to form in the low areas. The trail was going to be hard enough to follow without the clouds and the fog. The men knew that Indian Joe and Yakima would find the outlaw's trail no matter how hard they tried to cover it up.

The four men rode west in the direction the kidnappers took during their escape. Everyone would keep their eyes open for any signs left behind by the large group of riders.

After three hours of hard riding the men started worrying that they might have missed some signs that would've led them in another direction. If they had to back track they would loose valuable time. Then like a beacon in a storm, Boca pointed to a piece of cloth that hung from a tree with two knots tied in it.

"They're still moving west," Boca said. "We can travel faster now that we know that Brady is showing us the way."

"Marshal Hunter," Ranger Gibson said. "How did Boca know that the kidnappers were still moving west?"

"The Seminole Indian use knots to tell direction," Marshal Hunter said. "One knot equals east, two knots west, three knots north and so on."

"Boy do I have a lot to learn," the ranger said, as he moved his eyes over the flat terrain searching for the next sign that Brady would leave behind.

That sign came within the hour, it was another piece of cloth. This time there were four knots indicating the kidnappers were turning south. "Where do you think these pieces of cloth are coming from?" Ranger Gibson asked.

"Going by the color and the cleanness of the cloth, I would say one, or both, of the girls, are loosing their petticoats a little at a time. When Brady finds them he places them where we can see them very easily."

The sun stayed behind the clouds all day and offered very little heat to compensate for a cold blowing north wind. It forced the men to tie down their hats and pull their coats tight against their body to preserve as much heat as they could. The desert always turned cold at night and now it was turning even colder because it absorbed very little sun all day.

After making camp the men put on a pot of coffee and fried up a skillet full of bacon. Luther tried to keep his mind filled with the things that had happened during the day but he kept thinking of the girls and what they were going through just to stay alive.

The kidnappers in the barn heard another round of shots. They opened their eyes to take a look around the barn. Those two shots came from a distance much closer to them and some of the men felt like they came from just outside the barn. The men in the house started moving away from the window and door in case someone was outside trying to get a shot at them.

The girls had their hands tied behind their backs and had been forced to sit on the floor with their backs against the bedroom wall. Every time they heard the gunshots they would look at each other and grin, they knew they weren't alone. They knew that there was someone out there that was looking out for their safety.

Wade Weston kept trying to sleep, but he would flinch each time he heard the sound of the gun going off in the distance. In his mind he knew it had to be Brady Wells, the half-breed. The gunshots gave the girls hope and it was keeping his men from getting any rest at all. He would deal with Brady when the time came. It would never be to soon for them to end this half-breeds Indian population once and for all.

The sky was fashioning an orange streak across the eastern horizon when the land started showing signs of life. Soon there would be the animals scurrying around searching for their daily supply of food. This thought reminded Wade Weston that he hadn't eaten for a long while. He walked over to the girls who were sleeping on the floor in the bedroom and he used the toe of his boot to wake them.

"The men will be hungry soon and they'll be needing coffee in a little while," Wade said. "Get yourselves busy with the coffee and fix whatever is available for them to eat."

"We can't do all that with our hands tied behind our backs," Abbey said. "By the way, those shots you're hearing, they're warning shots to remind you that you're going to be facing your judgement day quicker then you had planned."

"Shut your mouth," Wade said, as he brought the back of his hand down across Abbey's face again. "The two of you will know enough about judgement day when I turn you over to the men for their amusement."

Brady approached the abandoned cabin with caution, he could smell the coffee odor coming from the house and he could almost taste it. He had crawled up next to the big barn where the bulk of the kidnappers were sleeping. He needed to put a scare into these men until the posse could catch up.

He could see through the cracks in the walls of the barn and it let him know where each man was sleeping. There was a man sitting on the barn floor just to the side of him, his hat was pulled down over his eyes, he was leaning up against the wall, the board he was leaning against had a knothole in it. Brady placed an arrow in his bow and pulled it back to its maximum strength. Placing the tip of the arrow into the knothole he released the bowstring. The arrow hit its target.

The man he shot didn't make a move or a sound, he just slumped over in a sitting position, and his hat still pulled down over his eyes. Brady waited until he was sure there was no other movement in the barn. Then he moved very quietly to another position of the barn. He found a second man with his back exposed to a crack in the barn wall. Brady's next arrow sent the second man to his death. This process was repeated one more time. Then Brady moved back to the crevice that kept him out of sight from the kidnappers. He wanted to stay close enough to watch and hear their reaction when they found that three of their comrades were killed during the night.

There was an old water run off that had formed a small trench in the ground behind the crevice and it was deep enough and far enough away from the barn to let Brady move around while he observed the men's reaction.

He had no sooner got settled into the trench when he heard a man yell, "Charley, there are three dead men lying here in the barn. They've been killed by those red devils that's been trailing us."

The barn came alive with men talking about the three dead men that had been killed during the night while everyone was sleeping. Charley left the barn in a fast trot headed for the main house. “Wade come out here!” Charley yelled.

Wade opened the door and stepped out on the small porch in front of the house. Brady felt Wade Weston was part of this kidnapping bunch but he just wasn’t sure until now. He had a good view of the main house and he could hear their conversation.

“Wade, we were attacked last night while everyone was sleeping,” Charley said. “We got up to three dead men with arrows in their back.”

“It’s that bunch of Indians from the B/A Ranch,” Wade said, as he scanned the horizon with his eyes. “Get the boys to start building a barrier around the house and the barn. If they’re going to attack again we’ll be ready for them.”

Charley ran back to the barn and Wade went back into the house. He walked to the stove and poured himself a cup of coffee without saying a word to any one.

Brady needed to figure out other ways of tilting the scales before they could make any attempt to rescue the girls.

He heard the snap of a twig that brought an immediate reaction from him. He flipped from his hands and knees over to his back. With gun drawn and cocked, he pointed it in the direction of the noise. It took great restraint to keep from pulling the trigger and blowing the head off of Indian Joe and Yakima, who stood there with a silly grin on their face. "You're getting slower in you're old age," Yakima said.

"You two could get yourselves killed coming upon a fellow like that," Brady said. "But I'm sure glad to see you. The girls are in that house and they're very well guarded. There's over fifteen men gathered in the barn."

"Where are their horses?" Yakima asked.

"In the corral behind the barn," Brady said.

"If we could scatter their horses, we would close down one of their means of escape," Yakima said. "That just might cause more confusion for the kidnappers."

"I'll try anything at this point," Brady said. "There are to many men for us to handle head on. We need some other ways to decrease their numbers."

The three men crawled on their bellies to the tree line. The area between the tree line and the corral was open land and a bad place to be if someone spotted them.

"We have the element of surprise on our side," Brady said. "I'll go back to the front of the house and draw the kidnappers attention to me, then you two make your way across that open land to the corral."

"There is another way," Indian Joe said. "We make our way through the tree line until we reach the area behind the corral. Then we move to the corral using the horses for our cover."

"Good idea," Brady said, "Except we use both tactics and that should give you even more protection."

Brady started his crawl back to the front of the house as Indian Joe and Yakima moved deeper into the trees. The time it took for Brady to crawl to his spot in front of the house left the Indians plenty of time to get ready for their charge upon the corral.

"Wade Weston," Brady yelled. "You've really lowered yourself to the standards of a lowlife polecat. Care to crawl out from behind the women's skirts and fight like a man?"

The men inside the house stopped what they were doing and listened to the voice that came from outside. The men in the barn became silent as they tried to hear what was going on at the cabin. It was a short while before they heard the second round of talk.

"Wade, your men are starting to feel that you can't handle yourself in a real fight," Brady said. "You have to have a crowd backing you when the chips are down."

"You can talk all you want Brady," Wade answered, "But the facts are, we have two close friends of yours and we'll kill them if you don't take your Indian friends and leave this part of Texas for good."

There was a loud yell that came from the direction of the barn. That noise was joined with hoof beats and the sound of horses stampeding from the corral in back of the barn. The men in the barn ran outside to see their horses disappearing into the tree line with Indian Joe and Yakima riding the last two horses to safety.

The men from the barn fired shots at the two Indians but their targets were already out of range. The kidnappers never expected to receive fire from outside the barn until two of their men dropped to the ground with bullet holes in their chest.

Brady had set his target on the group of men standing outside the barn and he made both shots count as he fired the third shot that looked like it hit the leg of the last man to return to the barn.

"Wade Weston," Brady yelled. "Now we have your horses. There's no way to get out of here except through us. We know your men don't want to die by the Indian method of torture, so give it up. We'll even let your men ride off without bringing charges against them. Keep resisting and you'll all answer to the law."

"You aren't going to take the chance of getting your women killed," Wade answered. "You'll ride out of here before they have to die."

"Wade, these women aren't cowards like you," Brady said. "They have standards that they live by and if it means they have to die to get you brought to justice, so be it."

There was no answer from the house. Then Brady turned his attention to the barn. "What I just said goes. If you men want to ride off from this situation without charges being brought against you, you had better walk away from the barn now and move to the tree line. Your horse will be waiting for you as long as you leave the area."

There was a long pause before the barn door opened and three men walked out with their arms in the air and then they ran to the tree line. Then five more stepped out and made their way to the tree line and the horses.

As the eight men rode away Brady spoke again. "The rest of you men in the barn have until sunset to make your decision, then you'll have to face the charges of kidnapping and attempted murder."

Yakima crawled up to the spot where Brady lay watching the door of the house, Yakima was wondering what he could do to keep the girls alive.

"We have company," Yakima said. "Marshal Hunter has brought Ranger Gibson, Luther and Boca to give us a hand."

"Stay here and watch the door of the house and barn," Brady said. "Give us warning if there's any change at all."

Brady moved down the crevice and over to the tree line where he met up with the four extra riders. Indian Joe and Yakima had built a tree shelter that covered a fire they had made. The men had gathered around the fire and they waited for Brady to bring them up to date.

"We've been able to cut their forces down some, but they still have enough to keep us at bay for a long time. They have threatened the lives of the girls," Brady said, "But I'm betting that Wade is afraid of us and he wants to keep the girls alive as a bargaining point."

"Do you have any plans for getting the girls out of there?" Marshal Hunter asked.

"I'm going to ask you, marshal, to move to the far right side of the house," Brady said. "Find you a spot where you can fire upon the house and remain safe while you're doing it."

"You trying to make them think we have the cabin surround with just seven men," Marshal Hunter asked. "Good idea if it works."

"Ranger Gibson, you'll take your stand over in the tree line just in front of the barn," Brady said. "You've got to give them the impression that you brought other rangers with you."

"Luther, you'll have the hardest job," Brady said. "You and I are going to make our way over to the gorge. From there we must get as close to the main house as we can. If there is a move to take the girls life I want someone close by to do what they can to save them from getting killed."

"I can do that job," Luther said. "I'll try and keep the girls alive even if it means my life."

"I know you will," Brady said. "You've got to give up the thought that you were somehow responsible for the girls kidnapping."

"Boca, you'll use the fire arrows to set the barn on fire," Brady said. "Indian Joe and Yakima will shoot anyone who tries to escape from the barn."

"That's well and good," Yakima said. "But you haven't said what you'll be doing all the time this is going on."

"I'm going to try and make my way inside the cabin while Luther stands watch from the outside. There has to be someone inside to try and stop an attempt on the girls lives."

Each man went to his position to wait for Boca to start the fire arrows flying into the barn. The wind had died down and the air seemed musty from the sand and dust that seemed to hang in the mist of the fog. Clouds were forming in the south and this could mean trouble if they turned into rain clouds.

Brady felt like it was taking an eternity for Boca to make his move. Then the trail of fire rose above the barn and dropped squarely on top of the roof. The attack had started. Brady moved ahead of Luther as the two men made their way to the cabin.

The second arrow found its target in the backside of the barn. Moving the fire around would keep the men inside from concentrating on just one spot. The third arrow wasn't even necessary because the fire had caught on and was starting to spread throughout the barn. The dry wood was burning like a tinderbox.

All eyes were on the flames that were shooting up from the roof of the barn. Even Wade Weston knew that this was an old Indian tactic that was going to bring his men out of the barn and to their death. Things were looking bad but he felt he still had a chance with the women as a shield.

Brady and Luther had made their way to the main house as the barn started to show signs of collapse. Now it was

Brady's turn to find a way into the house without alerting the kidnappers. He knew all eyes were on the barn so he went to the back door and lifted the latch. The door came open and Brady slipped into the kitchen area unseen.

The door swung opened at the burning barn and two men stepped out with their hands in the air. One was waving a white piece of cloth. The Indians kept their eyes on the men from the barn as the two ran across the open space to the tree line. Then others started making the same move. The plan was working.

Yakima met the men at the tree line and forced them drop their weapons. They were placed in an area where Indian Joe could keep an eye on them. It only took minutes for the frame of the barn to fall and the roof to crumble into ashes.

Wade Weston stood at the window and watched his men as they ran from the barn to the tree line where Brady's men captured them. Things were changing fast and Wade knew he had to make his move soon.

He grabbed Abbey's arm and pulled her in front of him as he placed the barrel of the gun to her temple. "Charley, get the other girl and follow me out the door," Wade said, as he opened the door of the cabin and walked out on the porch. The rest of his men from in the house followed close behind him.

Luther saw what was happening and he moved back behind the side of the house so he couldn't be seen. Then he watched as Wade spoke to the Indians outside.

"These women die if we aren't given our horses and allowed to leave here right now." Wade said, as his men started spreading out across the porch. They were becoming much braver with their human shields in front of them.

"Your horses are over in the tree line," Marshal Hunter said. "It'll take us some time to round them up and get them to you."

"You have no time left before we shoot the tall girl," Wade said. "Those horses had better be on their way here in two minutes or people will start dying."

Ranger Gibson fired a shot in the air to start the horses moving in the direction of the house. At the same time Luther grabbed Charley by the right arm and pulled him and Bernice behind the side of the house. One twist of Luther's big arm caused Charley to drop his gun to the ground. Bernice forced his left arm open as she escaped the grasp that Charley had on her.

Wade turned and let off a shot toward the commotion on the far end of the porch. When he did this he felt a hard blow across his right wrist that broke his grip on his own gun. Brady had already started firing at the other men as he pulled Abbey into the main house to keep her from being hit by a stray bullet.

Then chaos broke out from in front of the cabin. There were arrows and bullets flying all over the place. Among the confusion Charley and Wade Weston grabbed the reins of a running horse and made their get away. It only took seconds but there were five more dead men on the ground as the posse watched Wade and Charley ride off in the direction of town.

"Hold your fire," Brady yelled. "There's time enough for us to round up those two later. Anyone get hurt in this ruckus?"

"Everyone's accounted for," Marshal Hunter said, as he rode down to the main house to check on the women and the dead kidnappers. He thought this operation was planned by a mastermind and carried off in a manor of a military leader. Job well done with no causalities. He knew then that Brady had the makings of being a great federal marshal.

"Brady, did you leave anyone behind to take care of the ranch?" Abbey asked, as she followed Brady's every step. He stopped long enough to try and answer her when he felt her bump into his back.

"Abbey, if we're going to be married, you're going to have to give me credit for something," Brady said.

"We're going to be married?" Abbey asked, as she grabbed Brady's arm to slow him down long enough to get an answer from him.

"Who could I get to watch after my best interest?" Brady said. "You're the only person that I know of that'll work this hard for my measly wages."

"I bet you thought you were going to lose me. That's why you want to marry me. You want to marry me for my inheritance," Abbey said. "You want my third of the ranch."

Brady laughed out loud and said, "Your part and my part together don't mount up to a hill of beans."

"It will because I'm going to make you rich and maybe a cattle baron," Abbey said, as she turned and yelled, "You're all invited to my wedding."

Bernice ran to Abbey hugging her around the neck. "I believe it was worth it to be kidnapped by bandits and rescued by our knights in shinning armor," Bernice said. "Now all I need is to convince one of the knights that he can't get along without me." The group of men started laughing as they watched Luther turn red in the face.

The dead men were identified and buried behind the burnt ashes of the barn. Their names would be turned over to the county register's office and bulletins would be sent to other sheriff's department so they could remove the wanted posters.

It was to late to start the trip back to town so the group settled themselves around the house while the girls made a large pot of cowboy stew.

Sleep came to most of the men as soon as the sun disappeared. The girls sat up and told Brady and Marshal Hunter what they had witnessed during their capture. A lot of talk about how much money they were to receive when the job was done but no names was ever mentioned.

Wade kept his associate's name to himself, he received his orders and money from an unknown colleague. The rescue of the women could cause things to escalate or it could bring the source out in the open.

Ranger Hunter brought up the situation of Brady becoming a federal marshal but that was soon squelched. Brady wanted to spend more time on the ranch and try to make a go of it before he lost the ranch to taxes or some other problem related to money.

The money that he received from Graven, the old prospector, was a great help, it paid off his debt to Thomas

Durham and got him through a couple of winters. With the Indians depending on him, he had to find more ways to get a larger cash flow.

"You have great help from Luther and the Seminole Indians," Marshal Hunter said. "I have no doubt that the ranch will start turning a profit soon."

"We could use a man like yourself around here," Brady said "There's a lot of potential for this ranch and a partnership if you'll take it."
"I'll give it some thought," Marshal Hunter said, as he found himself a spot on the floor of the cabin to lay his head.

The next morning everyone seemed to be ready to start the trip back to town. Luther had already rounded up a couple of horses for the girls and he had them saddled and ready.

After an hour on the trail Brady spotted Captain Keith Benson and his Texas Rangers returning to Abilene with several Indian captives. They were mostly women and children dressed in the same fashion as the Apaches. Dear skin dresses and loincloth covered the captives. Dust covered their moccasins as they trailed along behind the rangers. Their cheeks were sunk in from malnutrition. Their eyes showed no sign of hope as they were herded along behind the rangers.

Captain Benson held up his right arm for the column to halt when he saw Brady and his group coming toward them. There were some greetings as the two groups came together but Brady kept looking at the women and children that stood with their heads down, eyes fixed on the ground.

"What brings you out in this direction?" Captain Benson asked. "I thought you would be tracking down your cattle rustlers."

"We were, in a sense," Brady said. "We just rescued the ladies from Wade Weston and his band of cut throats."

"We're making camp just past that clump of Cottonwoods," the captain said. "Mac Donald said there was a stream of water next to those trees and we felt the women and children needed a good rest before we continued to the fort."

"We'll follow you," Brady said. "Hope you have enough food to go around. Indian Joe and Yakima are out scouting for game as we speak."

"They'll need to come up with something," the captain said, "We ran out of meat two days ago. Been living on biscuits and hardtack. Still got plenty of coffee and we're willing to share what we have."

The two groups moved to the water stream and made camp. The sun was starting to set when one of the rangers reported to the captain, "Indians coming," he said. "Looks like they have a couple of goats thrown across their saddles."

"That's Indian Joe and Yakima," Brady said. "They seem to show up at just the right time."

The fires were built and limbs were cut to push threw the skinned goats so they could be turned over the fire till they were good and done. The smell of fresh cooked meat filled the air as biscuits were prepared to go along with the goat meat.

The captives squatted on the ground showing no emotion, as the food was being prepared. Brady called one of the women captives over and offered her a cup of coffee but she refused. Then she went back to her people and brought the other three women over and they stood there until Brady handed all three a cup of coffee.

When the food was served the Indians waited until they were told to come to the fire and receive their cuts of meat and two biscuits. They fed the four children first but there was nothing left on their plates after the children ate.

Brady refilled the women's plates and offered them more coffee to wash their food down. One of the ladies pulled her beads from around her neck and offered it to Brady. Brady took the beads and placed them over his neck, thanking her for her offering.

All night Brady kept thinking about the Indians and what they were going to do with no men to take care of them. He knew it was too much to ask his people to take in the captives and let them earn their living on the ranch, but it was food for thought.

Chapter 13

"You can't save them all," Yakima said, as he watched Brady give attention to the young Indian children. "We tried that back in the everglades before the trail of tears and it didn't work to our advantage. Our people were driven west and they refused to change their ways and it cost them their lives."

"Will there ever be a day when every man will be judged by his actions and not his skin?" Brady asked.

"Pride is a dangerous thing," Yakima said. "I'm proud to be an Indian. The buffalo soldier is proud to be black. The white man is so proud he forces his ways on everyone. Now you are mixed with Indian and white blood, which blood will you choose to be proud of?"

"There must be a way for us all to live on this earth in harmony," Brady said. "I must take my choice of pride by the part of me that speaks out the loudest."

"Then you'll destroy the pride of one of your ancestors that keeps silent," Yakima said. "That in its self could destroy the man that you were designed to be at birth."

"Is there a true choice for me?" Brady asked. "Will I ever be satisfied with who I am?"

"You'll search your heart like every man does," Yakima said. "There is no satisfaction within a man until he finds out who he is and excepts who he is as his life long goal."

"You're a wise man Yakima," Brady said. "I'm proud to have known you." Then Brady made his way back to the campfire where Bernice and Abbey were combing the tangles out of their hair.

"Getting late girls," Brady said. We have a long ride ahead of us tomorrow," Brady knelt close to the fire and poured himself another cup of coffee.

Bernice stood up and stretched before she left the two alone. She wanted to talk to Luther before she called it a night.

She found Luther leaning up against a popular tree with his hat pulled down over his eyes trying to catch some shut-eye.

"Are you asleep?" Bernice asked.

Luther snatched his hat from his face and jumped to his feet as if lightening had struck him. "Bernice, you startled me. I wasn't expecting you."

"Brady said we would be in Abilene by this time tomorrow," Bernice said, as she sat down on Luther's bedroll and took Luther's hand and pulled him down beside her. "Do you think we'll have a run in with Wade Weston again?"

"Yep," Luther said. "Brady will make Abilene safe for every citizen that walks the street or he'll die trying. Right now Wade Weston is a threat to every hard working person in Abilene."

"You put a lot of faith in Brady Wells don't you? Bernice said. "I hope he's the man that you want him to be."

The fire was dying down and the camp was silent except for a few stragglers that were having a hard time going to sleep. Abbey had returned to her bedroll and had left Brady staring into the glowing embers of the fire. There were many things he had to toss around in his head before he made his final decision on which direction he would take in life.

The sounds of the night blended in with the sounds of sleep that had come over the camp. Brady lay down and closed his eyes with the thought of Yakima's words turning over in his head, who am I? The blood of two civilizations was flowing through him.

The next morning the grass was wet with morning dew. The dampness was causing the morning breeze to cause a cold chill in the air. Shivers run up and down Abbey's body when she crawled from the covers of her bedroll. She sat up rubbing the sleep from her eyes and the loose grass from her hair. She noticed the fire had been stoked. It was burning high enough for her to put on the coffee and to warm enough of the goat meat to fill the bellies of everyone before they started their trip back to Abilene.

The smell of coffee brewing woke Bernice from her sleep and she too climbed from her bedroll and started helping Abbey with the morning meal. The light of the fire was all they had to work with until Captain Benson came to their rescue with a couple of kerosene lamps. He placed one on the chuck wagon tailgate and the other close to the cooking fire to help shed light on the area where the women were working.

Abbey had just pulled a large skillet from the chuck wagon when a figure appeared in the darkness. The figure was standing outside the brightness of the lamp and it startled Abbey until she focused her eyes on the darkness and noticed it was one of the Indian women.

The woman walked closer and stood in front of Abbey with her hands extended palms up. Abbey quickly smiled and turned to the wagon tailgate pushing the flower, eggs and seasoning to one side of the tailgate and offered the makings to the Indian woman.

The men started to rise from their sleep and it was almost impossible for Bernice to keep enough coffee brewed to serve the early risers. Abbey had the meat cooking in the large skillet but the most noticeable addition was the pan-fried biscuit the Indian woman had made with the mixings Abbey had given her to work with. The pan-fried biscuits were very popular among the hungry travelers as they filled their bellies with enough food to last them the rest of the day.

The sun was peaking up over the horizon when the last person was fed. The left over meat was wrapped and placed in a gunnysack and given to the Indian woman. What biscuits were left over went into the pockets of the Indian children.

Captain Benson inspected the group before he gave the orders to move out and the small caravan started moving in the direction of Abilene.

Brady and Ranger Gibson brought Captain Benson up to date on what had happened while he was off hunting for renegades.

Marshal Hunter explained that he had an auditor going over the bank records while they were rescuing the women and his findings would determine if the law would pursue the Thomas Durham allegations any farther.

They all agreed that Wade Weston and his followers would be brought to justice and they would stand trial for what laws they had broken, including kidnapping.

"The rangers hands are tied," Captain Benson said. "We need confirmation from Santa Fe before we can join in with the Wade Weston problem."

"The army will be facing the same problem soon," Marshal Hunter said. "Like myself they can't step in until this is a federal problem. The only way that'll happen is if Thomas Durham is actually skimming money from his stockholders."

"You do know the problem that surrounds Thomas Durham, will cause more problems between you and Hannah, don't you?" Brady said. "She's a good person but she'll always be loyal to her father."

"I have given all that some thought," Marshal Hunter said. "The prospects of loosing Hannah's love makes me want to get out of this business and let the law work out its own problems."

In their travels there had been three watering holes along the way, the last one was only five miles from Fort Abilene. Ranger Gibson and Indian Joe rode on to the fort to give them warning that the rest of the group would be arriving after dark and they didn't want to be fired upon.

The soldiers on watch duty had spotted the caravan through their field glass, just as the sun was setting. They still had a mile or so left to travel before they reached the fort. It was turning dark when the group finally reached the fort and the mess hall workers were ordered to stay late to accommodate the hungry arrivals.

Brady had to bite his lip when he watched a small group of soldiers herding the Indians into a stall just inside the livery barn. They were bunched up in the stall like animals. Two guards were posted just outside the stalls and two more outside the barn. They wanted to make sure that there would be no escape by the old women and young children. Brady asked himself, what have we come to when it takes weapons of war to corral women and children?

The food was welcomed but Brady wondered if the Indian captives would've been fed too if Captain Benson hadn't ordered the cook on duty to see that they received a ration of food for each Indian.

"They'll be taken care of," the fort commander said. "First thing tomorrow morning they'll be put in a covered wagon and transferred to Santa Fe. From there they'll join the other tribes to be sent to the Dakotas where they'll find themselves on a peaceful reservation for the rest of their lives."

"That's where General George Armstrong Custer is assigned, isn't it?" Brady asked. "He doesn't seem to be a great protector of the Indians himself."

"There's rumor that he could be our next president," Captain Benson said. "He's not going to do anything to jeopardize that."

The commander had Captain Benson, Marshal Hunter, Ranger Gibson and Brady brought into his office where he briefed them on some of the things that were going on in town and around the fort.

"Wade Weston has convinced most of the town, that he was attacked by Brady and his Indian friends while he was pursuing the girls for questioning. He has ordered his men to shoot on sight, if they see any of Brady's people in town.

"We're going into town first," Ranger Benson said. "Marshal Hunter can ride with us and question his auditor on what he has discovered from auditing the books in the bank."

"That seems like a plan," Marshal Hunter said. "Give me time to talk with Marshal Frank Faust about his audit and I'll get back with you."

The rangers left the next day for Abilene with Marshal Hunter riding among them just in case Wade Weston and his men wanted to cause him any trouble. Wade understood that Marshal Hunter knew the facts about the girls and he didn't want him to spread these facts among the people of Abilene.

Brady took his group back to the B/A Ranch to wait on the information that would come from Marshal Hunter.

The women and children that had been left behind to take care of the ranch had done a good job of running things, but the daily work of the wranglers had fallen behind. Luther took over the assignments again while Indian Joe, Boca and Yakima went back to gathering longhorns and mustangs for the ranch.

Brady could see how the ranch had progressed and the land had been developed for self-preservation. Storage barns were being built to store feed for the cattle, food from the vegetable gardens, and plenty of fruit for the children. There was winter hay that could feed another hundred head of cattle and the corncribs were stocked full.

"When will you ever be satisfied?" Abbey asked, as she took Brady's arm and leaned her head on his shoulder. "You have accomplished everything you set out to do." "Everything but community acceptance," Brady said. "Our neighbors need to trust us and accept us for who and what we are."

"That'll come later when they find out what you're really made of," Abbey said.

"Abbey I'm going to town," Brady said. "Wade Weston has rode roughshod over Abilene long enough and I need to put a stop to it."

"Benson and Hunter both told you to wait on their signal before you acted," Abbey said. "Give them a chance to get all the facts."

"They had better hurry," Brady said, "I'm getting tired of being pushed around by a side-winder that uses fear to get his way."

The town was quiet when the rangers rode in. They made it a point to ride down Main Street to the ranger station. They wanted Wade Weston and the local people to know the rangers were back to help with the law in Abilene.

Marshal Hunter stopped in front of the bank and watched the rangers move on toward the ranger station before he entered the bank. It was still early for the bank to be servicing customers but the employees were busy getting ready for the morning rush hour to start.

Marshal Hunter went right to Thomas Durham's office and walked in without knocking. There was a startled look on Thomas Durham's face as he stared into the deep gray eyes of Marshal Hunter.

"You couldn't keep your nose out of my business, could you?" Thomas Durham said, as he walked around his desk and stood in front of the marshal. "Your auditor friend found out to much for his own good, he had to be stopped before he spread the word that I was a little short of the money to cover my investments."

"What have you done with Marshal Faust?" Hunter asked. "You have been asking for jail time up to now, but if you have harmed Marshal Faust, you'll hang by the neck until your dead, even if I have to yank the rope myself."

"You'll soon see," Thomas Durham said, as he nodded for Wade Weston and Jake Patterson to enter the room.

They both had their guns drawn and they both kept that smirk on their face. "Hunter you're going to see your friend," Wade said. "Just walk in front of me down the back stairs and remember, I can back shoot you and blame it on an accidental shooting."

"You're a piece of work Wade and I'm going to enjoy watching you hang right beside your partner," Marshal Hunter said, as he made his way out the door and down the back stairs with Wade and Jake following him step for step.

When they got to the livery, Wade had the stable boy to saddle their horses. Then it was a matter of time before they were far enough from town for them to get rid of the marshal without any witnesses. The trail they were taking was fading away because it wasn't used any more, it led to old silver mines that had been abandon for several years.

"Hold up," Wade said. "Get down off that horse and no funny business."

Both men held their guns on Marshal Hunter while he swung down from his horse. "Search him," Wade said, as Jake swung down from his horse and began to pat down the marshal. "Take his badge and anything else he has that could identify him."

Jake pulled a pigging string from his saddle and tied the marshal's hands behind his back. Then Wade tossed his lariat over the marshal's shoulders and began pulling him in the direction of the tree line. There were times when the marshal tripped over dead limbs or under brush and fell to the ground, but Wade kept up the pace and forced the marshal to struggle to his feet the best he could, or be drug to death.

Time seemed to stand still for the marshal while he fought the terrain to keep his balance and not fall on his face where he stood the chance to lose an eye or break a limb. Then the tugging stopped and the marshal dropped to his knees to draw his breath.

"Get up," Wade said, as he got down from his horse and started pulling the marshal toward the entrance of the old abandon mine. Jake took a kerosene lamp that was sitting on a rock next to the entrance and lit it. Wade pushed the marshal in front of him, as all three men entered the dark mine shaft and walked several steps into the tunnel.

Marshal Hunter tried to select his steps as he was pushed forward. The light from the lantern didn't shine more than a few feet in front of him and there was loose rock every where. Then there was what Wade called the pit. It was a drop off where the bottom couldn't be seen.

"Now marshal you get to join your friend just like you asked," Wade said, as he pushed the marshal into what he thought was a bottomless pit.

The Indian wranglers had been putting in long hours at the ranch just trying to keep up with the daily chores. Brady was beginning to feel like he was finally contributing to the ranch and it felt good to see some results at the end of a long workday. The April showers were bringing in much needed rain for the crops and Luther, along with the Indians, were planning a long trail drive to Kansas during the time of the spring branding. Everyone felt they could make the drive to Hays City, Kansas during the three months of summer and the three thousand head of cattle could put them in a better financial fix then they ever were.

Things were starting to come together around the ranch as the men filed in from their day's work to get some food and much-needed rest. It wasn't until they entered the house that they caught sight of Captain Benson. He was sitting at the supper table having coffee with Abbey.

"What brings you out to the ranch?" Brady asked. "We weren't expecting you so soon. Marshal Hunter's auditor must have got some fast results."

"That's why I'm here," the captain said. "We haven't seen Marshal Faust since we've been back in town. Day before yesterday Marshal Hunter went to the bank to check on Faust and now, he has disappeared."

"I believe it's time for someone outside the law to step in," Brady said. "I've had my fill of Wade Weston and his hard-line bunch of coyotes."

"You've got to stay in line with the law," the captain said. "Wade is wanting you to go outside the law so he can get rid of you and the Seminole Indians once and for all."

"Well, he's going to get his chance," Brady said, as he walked out the front door and made his way to the bunkhouse. He strapped on the Peacemaker .45 with a cutaway trigger guard. It was special made for him by the U.S. Armory to save him a split second in reaching the trigger. He stuffed his Starr Double-action Army .44 revolver in his belt, took down his Winchester .44 carbine with its twenty-inch barrel that he kept hanging on the wall over his bed.

Every nerve in his body was telling him to slow down and figure out what was happening, but the Indian in him was itching for a showdown. There was a crowd of wranglers standing outside the bunkhouse as Brady swung the door open and stepped out into the dusk of the evening.

"There's still time for me to wire headquarters for a federal officer to come and take charge here," Captain Benson said.

"The two marshals could be dead by the time we get any action from the federal government," Brady answered, as he moved through the crowd of wranglers that had their rifles in hand and ready to follow Brady into hell if necessary.

"I still represent the law Brady," the captain said. "I'll have to hold you and your men accountable for your actions. Don't take the law into your on hands."

"You have until sunrise tomorrow," Brady said. "In the mean time we're going to do a little investigation of our own."

Captain Benson knew he couldn't control the actions of the B/A riders any longer than sunrise tomorrow. The ride back to town gave Captain Benson time to think over the incidences that had taken place after Wade Weston came to town, but he needed more answers to a lot of questions, a lot more answers.

The bank was closed when he rode into town but he noticed that Thomas Durham's office still had a lamp burning. His office sat back from the entrance of the bank so the captain used the butt of his colt .44 to knock on the bank door. There was a long pause before Thomas Durham looked through the window and came to open the door.

"Working late tonight?" the captain asked, as he pushed his way into the bank. "Need to ask you some questions. Can we use your office?"

"Look here captain, you can't come barging in here at all hours of the night," Thomas Durham said, as he followed the captain back to his office.

The door to the office was open and the captain could see that there was someone else in the office. It was no real surprise that the person in the office was Wade Weston. Then from behind the door stood Ranger Gibson.

"Ranger Burt Gibson, what are you doing with these two scoundrels?" the captain asked. "You're a sworn in official to help protect this town."

"We're taking over Abilene," Gibson said. "We've already taken care of your marshal friends and now you'll be out of the way."

"Shut up Gibson," Thomas Durham said, "We need another couple of days to bring in the Mexican Federation and we can claim Abilene and all its territory for Mexico."

"You're all crazy," the captain said. "The U.S. government won't allow this to happen and even if it comes about, it'll only start another war between the U.S. government and the Federation of Mexico."

"By the time that all takes place we'll be royalty," Thomas Durham said. "We'll have millions for the turn over of this land. Then we'll move to Spain where we'll live like kings."

"You can't do that father," Hannah said, from the doorway of her father's office. "You have destroyed my life and the life of my mother."

"What are you doing here?" Thomas Durham yelled. "You should be with your mother."

"Were you planning on taking your family with you?" Hannah asked, "Or did that ever cross your mind?"

"What now?" Wade asked. "To many people know what's happening and they've got to disappear like our federal marshals."

"You get rid of the captain just like you got rid of the marshals," Thomas Durham said. "I can take care of my own daughter."

"How," Hannah said. "If your going to kill me you might as well do it at the same time you get rid of Captain Benson."

Captain Benson stood next to Ranger Gibson when he felt the blow that came down on his head. There was a sudden flash of bright light, then complete darkness.

When he awoke he was cold, his head hurt like the blazes and he could see nothing but darkness. Then he felt something touch his leg. At first he thought it was a snake or some other animal but then it kept pushing at his leg. The captain rolled over and his body came in contact with another body lying next to him. He turned his back to the body and felt with his tied hands to see if he could make out if the person was still alive. He first felt the head of a person and the head was moving in a position where the captain felt a bandana tied over his mouth. He held on to the bandana while the person beside him pulled it from over his head.

"Thanks captain, I'm Marshal Hunter," the voice said. "We're in a mine shaft. Marshal Faust is down here too but I can't figure if he is alive or dead. I have a knife in my right boot but I can't get to it. You have to help me."

Marshal Hunter turned his body until his feet were at the hands of the captain. He felt the captain grabbing his boot. Then the marshal pulled his leg very hard and he felt his boot slip off his foot.

"Will your hand go in the boot far enough to reach the knife?" the marshal asked. "The handle should be close enough for you to reach it."

There was a sharp stick to Marshal Hunter's leg and the marshal felt a sigh of relief. He turned and backed up to the captain as he held the knife steady until the marshal sawed the ropes loose that were holding his hands behind his back.

The marshal cut the ropes that held his feet together and pulled the bandana from the captain's mouth. "You were an answer to an Indian's prayers."

"Cut me loose from these ropes and we'll check your friend," the captain said. "Both men crawled around the bottom of the shaft until they came across the body of Marshal Faust. He had struck the side of the shaft and it caused his neck to snap. There was no life left in him.

"Any idea how we're going to get out of here?" the captain asked.

Marshal Hunter was taking everything from the pockets of his friend. There were people he had to notify. Hunter knew of a mother and a brother that he had met while visiting Marshal Faust during a trip to San Antonio.

"I figure we're about eight to ten feet from the top of this shaft," Marshal Hunter said, as he pulled his boot back on to his foot.

"How much do you weigh captain?" the marshal asked.

"Somewhere in the area of a hundred and sixty-five pounds," the captain said. "I'm sure you have an idea of tossing me out of this shaft but you can forget that. No one can toss a hundred and sixty-five pounds that high."

"I'm going to put my back to the wall," the marshal said. "I'll make a stirrup with my hands. You place your foot into the stirrup and we'll count to three. Then you push hard with your legs as I bring my arms up as hard as I can. You'll be able to move a lot higher than either of us could by jumping."

"Sounds good, but we don't know how high the ledge is," the captain said.

"We'll know in just a few minutes," the marshal said. "Put your foot in my hands. Are you ready? When I count to three you push with all your might. I'll do the same, okay?"

"Ready when you are" the captain said.

"One, two, three, push" the marshal said, as he put all his strength to the upward force of Captain Benson's foot.

There was some sand and rock that fell from above but the captain was on the ledge or hanging on to the ledge. "What's going on up there?" the marshal yelled.

"I'm on top and I'm looking for the lamp," the captain said.

Marshal Hunter waited until he saw a reflection from the light of the lamp coming from above the mineshaft. "What a wonderful sight that light is," the marshal said.

"There's no rope up here so I'll have to find a tree limb to put in the shaft for you to climb up on," the captain said. "I'll leave the lamp here until I get back. It'll keep me from falling into the shaft again."

The excitement of getting out of the mineshaft was keeping Marshal Hunter from thinking about his friend Frank Faust. The time went slower than he thought it would. When he heard the captain yell he was going to lower the tree limb into the shaft, he felt excited again.

The limb worked, just as they thought it would, but Marshal Hunter felt bad about having to leave his friend in the mineshaft until they could bring back help.

"Do you know where we are?" the captain asked. "I was unconscious when they brought me to this place.

"We can follow the old mine trail back to town," Marshal Hunter said, "But that could take us all night."

"We could cut across the arroyo and be at the B/A Ranch in about three hours," Captain Benson said.

"That's our best chance of getting some help. We need help with that bunch of Mexicans that's coming our way and we haven't much time," Marshal Hunter said.

The terrain slowed the two men to a walk as they slid down one side of the embankment and practically crawled up the other side. They could see the light from the window of the bunkhouse when they climbed up from the arroyo but they knew that the light was farther away from them than it looked.

When the two men reached the bunkhouse the men inside were surprised when the door opened and they walked in. The two men looked exhausted. Marshal Hunter asked for water to quench his thirst and cool his parched throat. A canteen was hanging on a peg that extended from the cabin wall. Marshal Hunter's dirty, bleeding hands rapped around the canteen but it was empty.

One of the Indians pulled his canteen from under his bunk and handed it to the marshal as he raised it to his lips with shaking hands. "Slowly," the Indian said. "Drink slowly or you'll get sick."

Captain Benson finished drinking then he poured the remaining water over his head and face. “Where is Brady?” the captain asked.

“Behind you,” Brady said. “Seems like an odd time for you boys to be out on a stroll. What’s happening?”

“We were captured by Wade Weston and Thomas Durham,” Marshal Hunter said. “They tossed us in a mineshaft at the Old Spanish Mine. Marshal Faust is dead, the fall broke his neck, he’s still lying at the bottom of the mineshaft.”

“Ranger Gibson, Thomas Durham and Wade Weston have a plan to take over the control of Abilene and then they want to turn it over to the Mexican government for a price,” Captain Benson said. “The Mexican government has sent men to help with the take over. They could already be in Texas and marching toward Abilene.”

“How many men or soldiers are you talking about?” Brady asked.

“Don’t know,” the captain said. “We need to get to town and take control before the Mexicans arrive.”

“Boca, you’ve got to get to the fort and warn the army,” Brady said. “Tell them we’ll try and hold off the take over as long as we can, but they must hurry.”

Boca had been gone for the best part of an hour when the captain and Marshal Hunter had finished eating their fill of food. The Indian wranglers were mounted and ready to ride when Abbey pulled up in front of the main house with a wagon filled with guns and ammunition.

"Where do you think you're going?" Brady asked, as he rode in front of her wagon. "You're not placing your life in danger over this mess. No disrespect intended."

"Until you place that ring on my finger and say I do," Abbey said, "I make my on decisions. By the way, no disrespect intended there either."

Anger showed in Brady's eyes, but deep down he respected Abbey more for standing up for her beliefs. He felt she would make a man a good wife one day.

"Luther, take them to Abilene," Brady said.

Chapter 14

"You've stolen the investors money," Hannah said. "You've always had the intention of leaving your family behind while you made your escape to Spain or where ever."

"You don't understand," Thomas Durham said. "You and your mother have always been weak. You have always held me back from making something great of myself. Now I'll be able to travel and enjoy myself without the nagging of you and your mother."

"I'll kill you first," Hannah said, as she pulled a small derringer from her purse. "You have destroyed to many lives to remain alive."

A shot was fired and Thomas Durham flinched as he waited for the bullet to strike him. Instead he stood motionless and watched as his daughter dropped the derringer and slumped to the office floor.

"What have you done?" Thomas Durham screamed, as he ran to his daughter's side. "Hannah, Hannah, why didn't you stay out of this?"

"Get up old man," Wade Weston said. "We need to get out of here and join the revolt before we're left behind."

Thomas Durham grabbed the two money satchels and followed Wade Weston out of the bank. There were several mounted riders waiting in the street outside the bank. There was a buggy already harnessed and tied to the hitching rail as Thomas Durham threw the money satchels on the floorboard of the buggy before he climbed in.

The ride out of town was uncontested by anyone or anything, there were too many lives at risk for anyone to take a gamble and start shooting. The dust of the riders was all that could be seen by the town's people, as the robbers made their getaway.

The town's people ran to the bank where they found Hannah lying in a pool of her own blood. She was quickly picked up and transported to Dr. Dewberry's office, while the rest of the crowd formed in front of the ranger's office.

"Where's Captain Benson and Ranger Gibson?" the crowd yelled. "Why haven't they done something about these robberies and killings?"

"They've killed my daughter," Sara Durham said. "Isn't anyone going to do something about all this? If Brady Wells was still the town marshal he would take care of these problem."

"Yea," the crowd yelled. "We need a man of action not a weasel that jumps every time Thomas Durham tells him to."

One of the rangers walked out on the veranda and held up his hands for quiet. "Captain Benson is with Brady Wells as we talk," the ranger said. "He also has Marshal Hunter and the B/A wranglers helping him to round up these men that robbed the bank and shot Hannah."

"We can help too," one of the men said. "Lets form us a posse and help track down these killers ourselves."

Go home men. We'll meet here in a half-hour with our saddlebags packed for a long stay on the trail."

The streets of Abilene were empty and the silence gave the town an eerie sense of anger. Things were changing fast. The people were ready to take back their town from these so-called speculators.

Fort Abilene had been contacted and told of the revolt from the Mexican border. Lieutenant Josh Davis was ordered to form a squad of men and follow Boca to where ever he felt the Mexican soldiers would be by the time Brady and his men confronted them. They took a small howitzer and a wagonload of ammunition with them.

Yakima and Indian Joe had positioned themselves a good mile in front of the B/A riders to furnish them with the eyes and ears necessary to surprise the band of outlaws that had been trying to take over the control of Abilene.

The Indians hadn't been an hour on the trail when Yakima pointed out a dust cloud that was being made by a group of riders. It was coming from a buggy and riders that were headed out of town very fast. There was a second dust cloud rising far behind the first riders and that could only mean that another group of riders were following close behind the first group.

Yakima pulled his spyglass and focused it on the buggy. Thomas Durham was driving the buggy, followed closely by Wade Weston and his band of cattle thieves. They were all headed south as fast as they could ride.

The two Indians waited until they could get a good look at the riders following behind them before Yakima made his decision. "You stay on the trail of the first riders," Yakima said. "I'll see that Brady knows what's going on."

Yakima headed back west to meet up with the B/A riders while Indian Joe kept his eyes on the riders that were so anxious to get away from the men trailing them.

In the southern direction there was more dust swirling toward the sky. Indian Joe felt like it was going to be a meeting of three forces, but who was the third force? Then it dawned on him, that it could be the Mexican revolutionist on their way to Abilene.

Indian Joe kicked his horse in the flanks and made a run toward the dust coming from the south. He had to find out the strength of the on coming force.

The ride back to the B/A riders was cut in half as Yakima made fast tracks across the barren land separating him from the B/A riders. Brady had already put the B/A crew into a trot as they rode forward to meet with Yakima.

Brady held his left hand in the air for the riders to stop and dismount while Yakima started explaining the situation that lay ahead of them. The men waited until Yakima had finished, as they stood in silence trying to figure out what was happening.

Brady gave the order for them to mount up and he turned the men southward, in the direction of the unknown riders.

The unscheduled meeting came at the fork of the Rio Grande River, north of Fort Stockton. The Mexican revolutionaries were riding north to meet the riders from Abilene. The soldiers from Fort Abilene were riding west to meet with the B/A riders. The time of retribution was at hand.

"Marshal Hunter, try using your mirror to alert the army," Brady said. "When they're close enough to the Mexicans they need to fire a warning shot in front of them."

The flashes of light gave an instant message across the area separating the two groups and ended with messages noted. Now it became a waiting game. Brady watched as the two groups near the river advanced toward each other.

Suddenly, a puff of smoke went into the air, then a loud boom, as the warning shot fell very close to the forward guard that was riding in front of the Mexican revolutionaries, so close it knocked the scout off his horse.

There were several minutes when the frightened animals and Mexican revolutionaries became a mixture of overwhelming fear. A trio of riders, carrying a white flag, rode from the columns of Mexicans toward their right flank to try and talk with the army that had fired on them.

As the two armies were discussing the situation, Boca kept flashing his mirror in the direction of the B/A riders.

The riders of the Thomas Durham's crowd was coming nearer to the revolutionaries when the three scouts returned to their commander with what information they had received.

Brady had already been informed of the same information. The Mexicans were going to give Thomas

Durham, Wade Weston and his gang of thieves a safe passage back to Mexico. The Army's answer was "Not without the loss of many Mexican lives."

Brady motioned his B/A riders closer to the action as the town posse halted their advancement just within rifle range of the fleeing robbers.

"You men with longbows, you can start tying the sticks of dynamite to your arrows," Brady said, "Then wait for the army to take the first shot."

Brady watched, as the Mexican revolutionaries talked with Thomas Durham and guided him and Wade Weston to the center of their columns. Brady grinned as he moved his spyglass over to the wagon marked with skull and cross bones. Their ammunition wagon.

"You with the longbows," Brady said, "I want you to concentrate on the wagon with the skull and cross bones on it."

The Mexican revolutionaries started making their turn back to the south when the U.S. Army placed a shot from their cannon into the middle of their column.

"Fire," Brady yelled, as his longbow warriors cut loose with their exploding arrows. They landed with accuracy. The ammunition wagon exploded and there was Mexican revolutionaries lying all over the ground.

Everyone advanced on the Mexicans firing at anyone standing. There was complete chaos among the revolutionaries as they tried to regain their composure. The onslaught kept on coming with fast action and accurate shooting, until the white flag was seen again waving among the living Mexicans.

Brady had Marshal Hunter to flash the army with his mirror and ask them to stop firing. The posse seemed to catch on to the situation because they followed the army's lead and stopped their firing.

Brady rode in the direction of the Mexican revolutionaries with Captain Benson and Marshal Hunter riding close behind him.

A rider broke from the column and started high-tailing it south. Brady figured out very quickly that the rider was Wade Weston. He told the marshal to take over the command, as he kicked his horse in the flanks and headed after the rider.

The sun was high above their heads beating down with fiery and intensity as the two riders raced across the barren land of south Texas. It was going to be a battle of horseflesh and Brady was riding the Appaloosa Boca gave him as a sign of their friendship.

A mile passed and the Appaloosa was in his stride and gaining on the rider that was out front. Brady felt it would only be a matter of time before the Appaloosa would break the spirit of the horse in front of him and the range between them would quickly diminish.

Then Wade Weston started firing shots to keep Brady from gaining to much ground. There were other shots fired as Brady counted the rounds. When Wade Weston's gun was empty, Brady gave the Appaloosa his head. Soon he was riding side beside Wade. It was then that he jumped from his saddle and pulled Wade Weston from his horse.

The two men landed on the soft sand and it kept them both from suffering heavy injuries. Wade did pick up a few thorns from a prickly pear cacti and was trying to pull them from his side and arm when Brady gathered up the front of his shirt and held him as he landed a brutal punch to the man's jaw. Wade hit the sand and lay there with his arms over his face. "You can't hit a man when he's down," Wade said, as he pulled himself up to one knee. "I'll come peacefully."

Brady took Wade by the back of his collar and lifted him from the ground. It was then that Wade turned, bringing his knee up between Brady's legs. The sharp pain caught

Brady by surprise and he tried to cover himself from the attack that followed.

There was a burning sensation in his side as he looked down and saw the blade that came out of his body. It was covered with blood.

Wade Weston stood in front of Brady with a grin on his face and a bloody knife in his hand. "You've given me trouble for the last time half-breed," Wade said, as he twisted Brady's head back by pulling on his hair so he could make the death cut.

The sound of an eagle came from over their heads causing Wade Weston to pause and look up. The flapping of wings and the dive of the bird towards Wade Weston's head gave Brady time to remove his own knife from its sheath and plunge it into the heart of Wade Weston.

Darkness came to Brady's eyes as his mind started recognizing visions in his head. There was a great chief with a beautiful headdress of golden eagle feathers. He was riding a great white horse across the sky. He came in front of a white man and that was riding a large black horse. The two men stopped their horses and climbed down from the horse's back. They stood in front of each other for a long time before each one reached out and took the other's arm.

There was a large streak of lighting that flashed across the sky and the sky went dark.

Brady woke up in the back of the supply wagon with Abbey wiping his forehead with a cool wet rag. The pain in his side was burning like fire. He couldn't move any part of his body except his eyes, because the pain in his side increased with every movement of the wagon.

"Hi cowboy," Abbey said. "Thought I lost you for a while. I don't want you to say a word, just listen. Wade Weston is dead. Most of his men are dead. Thomas Durham is alive and he'll be able to stand trial. We recovered the money and it has been returned to the towns people, they were very pleased."

Brady smiled and shook his head as if he was pleased. Then he closed his eyes and felt the warmth of Abbey's arms as she cradled him close to her body.

The ride back to town was a long one because they drove slowly to try and not disturb the wound in Brady's side.

When they arrived back in town, the news that Hannah Durham was still alive made Marshal Hunter very happy. He went to her house to explain what happened with Wade Weston and his gang along with her father's situation. He knew she was going to be mixed up with the thought of what happened to her family. Her life had been changed forever.

The news couldn't have helped Hannah's recovery but it did bring a close to thoughts of what was going to happen to her father. He was to be tried for embezzlement and charged with murder.

When the B/A riders returned to the ranch, Brady had been put in one of the upstairs bedrooms to recover from his wound.

Five weeks later Brady stood looking out of his bedroom window. He saw the rain starting to fall and he watched the wranglers as they returned to the bunkhouse to get out of the weather. It had been over a month since the Mexican incident and Brady was starting to get around a lot better. Yet the trial judge wouldn't be in town for yet another month.

Brady had sat back down at the desk in his bedroom. He was finishing up on some of his clerical work, when he looked up and saw Tad Hunter standing inside the room. "Abbey let me in," Tad said.

"I had some thought that you might have gone back to Washington," Brady said. "Then it came to mind that you would surely say goodbye to your little sister before you left town."

"That's not why I'm here," Tad said. "I know it's not your place to listen to other people's problems but I feel you're the best person to make a statement on this subject."

"Tad, I'll do all I can to be of any help to you," Brady said, as he stood up and walked around the desk He sat down on the desk's edge as Tad Hunter sat in the big overstuffed chair.

"Hannah has connected me to the reason why her father was arrested," Tad said. "I've grown very found of her and I feel that she blames me for what has happened to her father."

"Understandable," Brady said. "Don't get me wrong but she was my choice before Abbey came into my life and I'll always have feelings for her."

"Understood," Tad said. "No hard feelings. This all took place before my time. Now I have a choice of going back to Washington and losing Hannah forever, or I can stay here in Texas. But it means losing my federal marshal's job."

"Abbey doesn't know this yet," Brady said, "But I have plans to buy Pete Ralston's place. It can bring us enough land to cover the army's beef supplies along with mounts for every fort in this area."

"What's that got to do with me?" Tad asked.

"I'll need another ramrod for the Ralston place," Brady said. "You're the best man for that job and maybe in time I can pay you enough wages to match your pay now."

"I couldn't take a job out of charity," Tad said, "But I've saved up enough money that I might could buy my way in on about a fourth of that new ranch."

Brady laughed out loud while Tad stood wide eyed wondering what he said that was so funny. About that time Abbey walked into the room and stood in front of Brady until he caught his breath from laughing.

"What's so funny?" Abbey asked. "You haven't laughed like this since I've known you."

"It's something Tad said," Brady replied. "He wants to buy a quarter share of the Ralston Ranch."

"What's so funny about that?" Abbey asked.

"Well, it just struck me funny," Brady said. "I was going to buy the ranch and start the B/A Cattle Company."

"That doesn't sound to funny to me either," Abbey said.

"When Tad buys in," Brady said, "We'll have to add a T and call it the B.A.T. Cattle Company."

Everyone got a laugh out of that, then the supper bell started ringing. The three of them went into the dining room still laughing.

Brady used supper as a meeting time to explain what he was going to do and that Tad was going to be a new partner. "I'm going in to town tomorrow to close the deal on the new ranch. Abbey will draw up all the papers for the purchase of the ranch and while she's at it, maybe I can get her to draw up the papers for us a marriage license."

Abbey dropped the bowl of mashed potatoes she was carrying. She stood very straight and stared into the eyes of Brady Wells, her mouth and eyes wide open. Then the tears came and she ran from the kitchen.

"What did I do this time?" Brady asked, as he stood up and followed Abbey out of the room.

"That's one happy girl," Aunt Martha said. "That's been a dream of hers ever since she met Brady."

"Abbey," Brady yelled, as he ran after the woman he loved. "Abbey Simpson, stop acting like a spoiled brat."

"You have treated me like a sister," Abbey said. "You turned me into a secretary, a financial advisor, a ranch coordinator and now you say you want me to get a marriage license finally, so you can add another job to my long list of duties."

"I love you Abbey," Brady said. "I don't know any pretty speeches or fancy words, I jut know how I feel."

"Why have you waited so long to tell me how you feel?" Abby asked. "I don't know whether to hug your neck or dish you up a plate of vittles."

Brady smiled and put his arms around Abbey and reminded her that she would make a beautiful mother for his children.

"Go back to the table and let me make myself presentable," Abbey said. "Behave yourself until I get in there to keep you straight."

Supper went well even though they were short one bowl of mashed potatoes. The crew was expecting a change in the weather and by the time supper was over the wind had died down. It seemed to be a lull before the storm.

Abbey watched as a flash of lightening blinked way off in the south. She had opened the front door and walked out on the porch. "We may have some bad weather blowing in tonight," Abbey said, as she pulled her shawl around her shoulders.

The men had followed her out on the porch. "We need to tie things down in the barn," Luther said. "I'll turn the horses out of the corral."

"I got the barn," Tad said, as he walked across the distance between the house and the barn. "Need to close the shutters over the windows if a Texas twister is going to show its claws tonight."

"I've got the windows in the house," Abbey said, as a cold chill ran down her back. She tightened the shawl around her shoulders and went into the house.

Brady watched as the rest of the crew started putting action into motion. There was a colder chill in the air that had built up since supper. The lighting was getting closer and lingering longer. There was a deep rumble of thunder in the distance and Brady knew they were in for a blow tonight.

Before Luther and Tad returned to the ranch house the rain had became a downpour. Indian Joe ran upon the porch shaking the rain from his hat. "Boca and Yakima are watching the herd tonight," Indian Joe said. "I'm going to take the chuck wagon out to the pasture and let them use it for shelter from the weather tonight."

"You do that," Brady said. "Don't take any chances if the weather turns real bad. Find cover and keep yourselves alive."

A lighting flash lit up the southern skies and it ran from the heavens all the way to the ground striking a large blackjack tree that had already been split by lighting once before. The thunder that followed rattled the glass in the window frames. The lighting was flashing more often and the winds blew so hard that section of the roof came off the barn.

Brady remembered that Indian Joe was in the barn hooking up the chuck wagon. When the next flash of lightening lit up the skies, Brady made a run for the barn. He tried to open the barn door but the wind kept such pressure on the door that Brady couldn't swing it open.

Hail started beating down on him striking him with bullet like force. The wind kept increasing until the side of the barn started to separate into small segments of wood. Then suddenly there was no barn insight. Brady tried to yell for Indian Joe but the sound of the wind and thunder drowned out his voice.

Brady could feel something behind him. When he turned, the flatbed wagon was on its side and moving in his direction. He reached for the hitching rail that was in front of the barn and when his hands circled the post he hung on for dear life.

The flatbed wagon lifted up in the air and it too separated into smaller pieces. Brady kept watching for the house to separate but for some reason it was holding together.

Then as quickly as it started, the storm ended. When the wind stopped blowing it left an eerie feeling that made the hair on your neck stand on end. There were no signs of rain or hail, just complete calm. The quiet was enough to drive you crazy. Brady turned his glance back toward the barn and he realized it was gone.

The front door of the house opened and the women started running out into the open area where the barn once stood.

"Brady," Abbey yelled, "Are you alright? Was anyone hurt?"

"Indian Joe is missing," Brady said, as he stood staring at the empty spot where the barn once stood.

When Luther and Tad walked up to explain the damages that had been done to the ranch, Brady held up his right hand for silence. "Indian Joe is missing," Brady said, "I want everyone saddled and on the hunt until we find some trace of him."

"No need boss," Luther said. "He's in the pasture with Boca and Yakima. They turned that chuck wagon over and used it for shelter from flying rubble."

Brady grinned as he mumbled, "Them Indians are going to out live us all." Then he held up both hands as he heard the chirping sounds of crickets. In his mind he knew the storm was really over, but it left a lot of work to be done. It was Mother Nature's way of separating the weak from the strong.

After a good nights rest the crew woke up to many jobs that had been created by the storm. Some of the wranglers checked on the cattle. Some started picking up the rubble left behind. There was a barn to be built and they could use a storm cellar instead of a root cellar if and when a Texas twister blew in again. None of the work could be done in a day, but unless they got started now, it would never get done.

After breakfast, Brady took Abbey and Tad into town with him. They would be checking on the new land that they were to purchase. Tad wanted to see how Hannah was taking the news of her father being tried for embezzlement and maybe murder. Yet when they arrived in town there were more problems.

There were signs of last night's storm all along the road. Trees down, streams flooded, debris lying everywhere. There were spots where the road was washed out. This had to be fixed soon if the judge was going to make it to town for the trial.

There had been a lot of damage done to the town. There were folks working hard to restore this damage as soon as possible. There was one building that suffered no damage, the huge Durham Bank. It stood along with the brick jail and the Texas Ranger Station. The rest of the buildings seemed to have suffered from either wind or rain damage. The debris was mostly tree limbs, sagebrush and wood from the rooftops.

The mud in the streets made it hard to travel through town. Wagons were stuck and people were trying to get around with their boots full of red clay that was formed when the water washed away the topsoil that had been covering it.

Bernice Pickings stood in front of the diner waving her arms in the air hoping that Brady, Tad or Abbey, one of them would see her signal. When they did see her, she motioned for them to ride over to the diner.

The three riders noticed that there was acavalry horse in front of the diner but none of them could make out a reason for them to be there.

When the three interred the diner, Captain William Moss stood at one of the tables motioning them over.

There were greetings exchanged but the captain got down to business right a way. "Brady, the army feel we have a problem brewing up north. On November 27th, 1868 on the upper Washita River Black Kettle was killed. Custer's Osage scouts scalped him."

"This is bad," Brady said. "Especially after the Sand Creek Massacre."

The captain went on to say, "Over forty Indian women and children were killed that day. Black Kettle died alongside his wife. There is already rumor that the white man would strike hard at any tribe that showed the slightest resistance to them and that they would be forced to survive on reservations. Now the Indians are on the move north, looks like they're headed for Canada."

"The Sioux, Comanches, and Kiowa may be moving north," Brady said, "But you can bet your life they have a plan for the one they call Long Hair."

"You feel that there is enough resentment among all these tribes that they'll draw themselves together against the white man?" the captain asked.

"You can bet on it," Brady said. "The Plains Indian gains honor in battle and they'll fight harder for vengeance than any other reason."

"Brady, the commander has requested that you be assigned to his company for one year," the captain said. "He'll give you a commission to captain and reassign you to the U.S. 7th Cavalry, under the command of General George Armstrong Custer."

"A year with the army could last a life time if the Indians decide to take on Long Hair and his 7th Cavalry, one on one." Brady said. "I'll talk with my friends and family and let you know tomorrow."

The captain called Bernice over and asked her to feed these people on his expense. Then he clicked his heels and gave Brady a salute before he departed the diner.

"The answer is no," Abbey said. "You have responsibilities to many people at the ranch. They depend on you for there livelihood and I depend on you for my on selfish reasons."

"I've seen that look in men's eyes before," Tad Hunter said. "The look of determination and wonderment. If you go, I'll go with you to make sure you return unharmed."

"I'm going to need you and Luther here to run the ranch and see that Abbey keeps the home light burning until I get back," Brady said. "A year will go by fast and the Indians aren't as strong as they used to be."

"Remember the sign you saw just before you passed out from that knife wound?" Abbey asked. "You saw the coming together of the Indian and the solder."

Brady's mind went back to the meeting of the big black horse and the large white horse. Each horse carries a great chief. One was a white man and the other was a red man and as their arms went out in friendship, the clouds came and covered the sun. There were sparks of lighting that looked like gun flashes and the thunder rumbled across the sky leaving visions of bodies laying around for miles. Brady couldn't make out what the vision meant but he did know he had to follow his destiny.

The ride back to the ranch was very silent as each person mulled over the thought that Brady would be involved with the peace between the 7th Cavalry and the Plains Indian.

Chapter 15

The sun breaking through the eastern skies brought the old red rooster to the fence railing to do his honorable duty. The sky was dark blue and filled with large fluffy clouds that seemed to form visions of animals or faces across the heavens. Abbey stood on the porch with her shawl wrapped around her shoulders, only because of habit not because of the weather, she was watching the rooster as it fluffed its feathers and stretched it's neck to let out its wake-up call. Abbey was looking for Brady to come to the house for his breakfast like he did every morning when he spent time on the ranch.

"Warriors leave unnoticed," Yakima said. "Brady is a great warrior and he'll ride with the Gods one day."

"Where is Brady?" Abbey asked. "I want to see that he gets a big breakfast this morning."

"A warrior cannot say goodbye," Yakima said. "Brady will follow the wings of the eagle from this day on. He rides to the Black Hills of the Dakotas to join with Long Hair, who is of his mother's blood or he rides to join with Sitting Bull who has his father's blood."

"Has he already left?" Abbey asked, as the tears trickled down her cheeks. "You know more than you're telling me, Yakima. Why are you hiding your secrets from me?"

"In my vision last night I saw the fox attack the bull elk," Yakima said. "The one with the long hair reminded me of the bull elk. The fox was the mixture of our people fighting for survival. There were many foxes that killed the bull elk, but the red man's greatest victory will go down in the white man's history as a massacre."

"What will happen to Brady?" Abbey screamed, "Will he come back to us safe and sound?"

Yakima turned and walked toward the barn. "I must ride after my blood brother and watch to see that he takes the fork of the road that will bring him back to us safely."

Abbey stood and watched Yakima as he rode from the barn and disappeared from sight down the long road leading away from the ranch. The clouds had turned black over head and the wind blew her shawl from her shoulders. Cold chills ran down her spine as she looked up into the clouds and saw the eyes of a Seminole Indian medicine man. The eyes showed sadness.

Tad Hunter had become foreman of the new B/A Ranch. He worked well with Luther and between the two men the

B/A Ranch began to grow into one of the largest working ranches in Texas.

Thomas Durham was tried and found guilty of embezzlement and murder and was sent to prison for the rest of his life. Hannah Durham took over the Durham Nation Bank and swore she would pay back every penny that her father had embezzled from the town's people. There weren't many customers that would trust her with their money after the trial was over, but the B/A Ranch kept their money in her bank and that in its self was a help to her. The B/A Ranch invested enough money into the Durham National Bank to keep Hannah going at least until she got back on her feet. They were all hoping that the people would forgive her in time for her to save the bank from going under.

Many months had passed and rumors were going around that the plains Indians were gathering at a place that the Indians called the Greasy Grass River.

Sitting Bull had come through the ranks as a medicine man but now was the Chief of the Oglala Sioux. The rumors were he was looking for vengeance for the death of his sister at the hands of the long yellow haired soldier.

Sitting Bull called on his favorite tactician, Crazy Horse, to come up with an idea that would place Indian glory in the eyes of every tribe in the nations. Crazy Horse's knowledge of the terrain and his skill in tracking made him the Indians choice to organize this great battle.

Crazy Horse rode into the Bighorn Mountains where his head joined the thin clouds that moved slowly through the sky. The valley below was partially covered with dark shadows on this early summer morning. Crazy Horse could see the Greasy Grass River as it wounded itself along the east side of the valley floor. There were places where the river was so narrow a person could throw a stone across it. The river was belly deep to a horse and surrounded on one side by high bluffs.

Crazy Horse sat on the mountain edge where he could look down and see the many teepees of all the tribes that had gathered and were waiting for him to make the final decision to what the Indians next move would be. The Indian campsites spread for three miles down the Greasy Grass River. The young warriors were ready for a fight and they relied on their leaders and their own bravery to led them to a great victory.

The Indian camps were too large to stay together for a long period of time. The army made routine patrols and the grass for the ponies would soon wear down. There had to be a decision made and Crazy Horse was troubled over that decision.

Crazy Horse rode a yellow pinto, which was one of his two best war ponies. It was always close to his side in these days of war. Now the pony showed nervous tensions as he raised up on his hind legs and let out a whiney that brought Crazy Horse back to his senses. When he turned he faced an unusual warrior that was holding a Sioux warrior's bow and it was pointed at Crazy Horse's heart.

Crazy Horse showed no sign of fear and he made no movement to get away from this strange warrior that had his sights on killing him. It was now the choice of the great God of battle to decide his fate.

"I'm Seminole," Yakima said. "I come from far away to the east, they call my land Florida. My name is Yakima. I've traveled to your side to show you that I could take your life. Instead I want to ask for a life."

"Your bravery is unquestionable," Crazy Horse said, as he stood and faced the great warrior. "You would make a great Sioux. I would name you, Quiet Man Walking."

A mist shrouds the Big Horn Mountain as Yakima lowers his bow and asks, "Crazy Horse, can you spare the life of one man? One that is half white and the other is half Indian."

"If he rides with the solder called Long Hair he is dead already," Crazy horse said. "I cannot tell you one thing and do another."

"I give you your life," Yakima said. "You must turn your attention back to the valley below and may your horse be swift and your judgement wise."

Crazy Horse turned and sat back down on the ground and looked upon the mist that was slowly taking away the view from below. There was no noise, but when Crazy Horse turned back around he was again alone with his war pony. Then the thought came to him. Divide and conquer, split the soldier's forces and weaken their strength. He raised his arms to the skies and said, "The Gods have spoken."

Crazy Horse returned to his large camp circle and tied his horse to a small willow tree next to his lodge. He ducked through the entrance of the teepee and yelled for Gall, a leader of the Hunkpapas Indians. "Make ready for war!" Crazy Horse yelled.

Brady Wells had camped near the headwaters of Rosebud Creek overnight. The next morning he saw a large army at a stand still down stream, they seemed to be waiting for their long column to catch up.

He also noticed that the army was out in the open unprepared. Before he could issue them a warning an Indian scout rode into the column shouting, “Sioux, many Sioux!” As shots rang out. The Indians were upon the army riding charging horses.

The army tried to form picket lines but the Indians, riding low alongside of their horses, kept the solders busy while another group of warriors charged from the hills to the west.

Brady took noticed that the second group of Indians met head on with the Shoshones and Crows that were riding with the army. After ferocious fighting the Sioux warriors fell back, regrouped and charged again. Soldiers and Indians died violently fighting the battle from horseback and on foot. The gun smoke, was nauseating as soldiers, Indians and horses were trampled into the ground. The Sioux gave up ground until the army felt they were beaten back.

Then the army disengaged its cavalry companies and rode up Rosebud Hill after what they thought was fleeing Indians. This left a weak spot for the remaining Sioux and they took advantage of it. The army’s weakness was so weak the cavalry had to break off the chase and return to their position at the battlefront.

The Sioux fought until they found themselves in a pincer movement that took them by surprise. The Sioux made one more pass at the soldiers and escaped with the loss of thirteen warriors. They left behind twenty-eight dead troopers, fifty-six severely wounded, not counting the dead or wounded Shoshones and Crow scouts.

It was later learned by Brady, that General George Crook was leading the army at the battle of the Rosebud. The Sioux warriors gave General Crook a strategic defeat that day. So big was the defeat that it prevented him from continuing his search for the main body of Indians that he knew was hiding in the Black Hills.

Brady also learned that with this defeat and the fact that the army couldn't pursue the attacking Indians gave Crazy Horse and his warriors the freedom to fight another day. Little did anyone know that this was only eight days from Sitting Bull's greatest battle.

Lieutenant Colonel Custer was under orders to circle about and try to drive the Indians between General Alfred Terry and Colonel John Gibbon's army, but Custer threw strategy to the wind. He was uninterested in sharing any glory with any other ranking officers.

A broad Indian trail led toward the Little Big Horn River, it was there that Custer committed his first error of judgement. He split his forces not knowing he was facing a far superior enemy in numbers alone. He wanted Major Marcus Reno to take a fourth of the army and create a diversion, while he took the rest of his army to strike the Sioux camp.

Major Reno did manage to surprise a small portion of the Hunkpapa Indians but it didn't take the Indians long to regroup and fight off Major Reno's forces, causing them to withdraw. Suddenly Major Reno's troops were facing a thousand warriors. Major Reno's army was disorganized and before they could escape back across the river they had lost half of their troopers. Over one hundred and fifty men lay dead or wounded.

Sitting Bull looked to the heavens and knew that the Indian's fulfillment of vengeance had started. Crazy Horse would complete this vengeance by mounting a reckless attack that would leave Yellow Hair and his soldiers lying in the dust and blood of defeat.

Colonel Custer took his troops north to the Sioux encampment. There was confusion among the women and children as they watched Custer's troopers lining up along the crest, across the river.

Brady Wells had found the same spot where Crazy Horse sat and planned his war against the yellow haired leader of the soldiers. He could see the Indians that were hidden in the crooks and crevasses of the Big Horn Mountains. The

Indians had Custer pinned down as they flanked both sides of his cavalry.

Suddenly Custer felt he had been out maneuvered by a bunch of savages that shouldn't be allowed to roam this great country. He felt that if he was going to die, then he must take as many savages as he could, to their happy hunting ground.

Instead of charging, Custer gave the order to dismount while Sitting Bull and Brady Wells looked on from a far distance.

The deadly outcome would be buried under a large cloud of dust but both Sitting Bull and Brady Wells had seen the out come in many of their visions.

Crazy Horse was a formidable fighting man and he made sure that the Seventh Cavalry's two hundred and fifteen men were completely wiped out before he called off the young warriors.

The battle area was turned into a looting contest for the Indian women of every tribe. The warriors filled their booty with cavalry saddles, uniforms, weapons and ammunitions and then there was the scalping and mutilation of the solder's bodies.

Brady knew that Sitting Bull would gain greatness among the Indians nations but he also knew that the looting of Custer's men would bring grief to the Sioux nation in the future.

Brady saw the coming together of his two spirits, the white man and the red man. He felt there would always be differences between the two worlds but he also felt that he would always be tormented between the same differences within himself.

Then a sound came from within the tree line behind him. There was a moment of silence and then a second sound of groaning. When Brady turned he saw Yakima stumbling out of the wooded area holding his chest.

Brady ran to Yakima's side. "Old man," Brady said. "Why have you come to this place of death and destruction?"

"It is my time to meet the Gods," Yakima said. "The spiritual power came in my vision. I was on a large mountain and the spirit came to me in the form of a great bird."

"You hang on and I'll get you to the fort, there's an army doctor there," Brady said, as he started to lift Yakima from the ground.

"No" Yakima said. "Take the pouch from my neck. Go to the bluff and spread its contents to the four winds."

Brady let the tears flow as he watched the spirit slip from the eyes of his trusted friend. Then he removed the deerskin pouch from around Yakima's neck. The day was clear and when Brady stood up a great bald eagle swooped down and landed on Yakima's left shoulder. The eyes of the eagle looked through Brady and a vision came to Brady. Then like the wind the eagle was gone.

Brady took the bedroll from Yakima's horse and wrapped Yakima's body in it. He tied both ends and the middle with rope. Securing a rope to the middle tie, he lowered the body of Yakima to a ledge below the bluff. Dropping the rope to the same ledge, Brady felt Yakima would be able to over see the valley below and help to keep the red man's blood and the white man's blood from mixing again through anger and war.

Brady sat down on the edge of the bluff and tossed the contents of the deerskin bag to the four winds. He prayed to the Indian Gods to make Yakima's journey a happy one. He prayed to the white man's God to join with the other Gods and make the relationships between himself and his spirit become one that could be settled by searching his soul. He wanted spiritual aid in this time of need.

Several days had passed before Brady felt the urge to leave his position on top of the Big Horn Mountain. The visions came and went and they all seemed to point to the one person that made him the happiest.

Abbey Simpson had made her rounds in town and she stopped at the bank to say hello to Hannah Durham and to check and see how the bank was doing. Tad Hunter was in Hannah's office and when Abbey walked in she caught them embracing.

"What a wonderful sight," Abbey said. "You two are made for each other."

Hannah pulled away from Tad brushing her dress as if it was going to leave a tell-tell sign of what they were doing.

"Abbey," Hannah said, "Tad and I are going to be married."

"That's why I'm in town today," Abbey said, "I'm going to make arrangements for Luther and Bernice. They too have intentions of tying the knot. Maybe we can have a double wedding?"

"That would be perfect if you and Brady could join us," Hannah said. "Have you gotten any word from him at all?"

"Indian Joe talked with a Sioux chief called Red Horse," Abbey said. These words brought tears to Abbey's eyes. "The story is that the Sioux destroyed Major Reno's forces early. They drove Custer's troops to the fork of the Little Big Horn and then they charged the troopers with wave after wave of young warriors. By the time the infantry showed up, it was all over. The Seventh Cavalry was completely destroyed to the last man. Major Reno lost over three fourths of his command. The Indians suffered one hundred and thirty six dead and one hundred and sixty wounded. Too many losses on both sides."

"The last word we got came from a letter you received from Brady," Tad said. "He had joined up with Custer to help seek out the Sioux warriors."

"Abbey I'm sorry," Hannah said. "Brady had always struggled with the fact that he was a half-breed and I'm sure he made the right choice before he made any kind of a move."

"How is the bank coming along?" Abbey asked. "Are you getting your head above water?" She asked these questions, with tears in her eyes. She would never be able to get Brady out of her mind.

"These last three years have been a blessing to me," Hannah said, as she handed Abbey a handkerchief. "With you and the B/A Ranch helping me and Tad letting me cry on his shoulders ever so often, I believe I'm going to pull myself out of this horrible mess."

"Well, I hope not," Abbey said with a look of discuss on her face.

"That's cruel of you to say that Abbey," Hannah said.

"Cruel, yes, but if you do well there's a chance I might loose one of my best partners," Abbey said, as she put her arms around Hannah and gave her a kiss on the cheek. "You see I always have a selfish motive. I'm so self-centered."

The weddings went well and Abbey was as happy as she could've been under the circumstances. Bernice came to the ranch to make her home with Luther and let her family run the diner. She was a great help around the ranch and Abbey wished that Hannah would join them also, but she knew that Hannah was a proud woman and she wouldn't give up the bank until she met her father's obligations.

The spring rains had brought out the buds of the new plants and it looked like the land would furnish plenty of wheat and hay for the following winter. Abbey had storage barns built for storing the animals feed. Root cellars dug for can goods. Salt beef hung from the cellar roof as some of the women carved it up and made beef jerky. The wranglers were working on a grain storage bin at this very moment for winter storage while Abbey kept the women cooking and carrying water for the men.

Abbey was so busy she didn't notice the three soldiers that rode up to the farmhouse and dismounted. By the time Abbey noticed the soldiers a terrible thought came to her mind. She had always wondered what happened to Brady and she knew she needed closure, but she wasn't sure if she was ready for this kind of information, not at this time.

"Major Josh Davis?" Abbey said. "Sergeant Patrick McKinley and now, Colonel William Moss. What fine solders you've both turned out to be."

"We didn't know if you would remember us," Colonel Moss said. "We've all grown up a lot and our promotions make us seem like old timers but its really only been five years since we rode and fought with your husband, Brady Wells."

"Brady and I never had the chance to get married," Abbey said, as she looked off into the distance as if she was recalling her past. "Another one of those acts that we chalk up to coincidence. Come to the porch and catch me up with the past five years."

When the four walked upon the porch Abbey asked the men to be seated while she brought out some refreshments. The soldiers stood for a while looking over the large ranch, watching the workers moving around like bees in a beehive. Then they removed their sabers and made themselves at home. The cool breeze kept a pleasant feeling in the air as the clouds kept the sun hidden from their eyes.

Abbey returned with a large pot of coffee while a young Indian girl carried a platter of cookies. The second girl had a pitcher of lemonade and several glasses.

"Hope you gentlemen don't mind some of my family joining us for refreshments?" Abbey said. "We'll be loosing them this summer to join a young ladies school back east."

The soldiers stood up and removed their hats as they exchanged introductions. The drinks were poured and the cookies started disappearing very fast as the women smiled and lifted their drinks for a toast.

"You are going to complement us with your presents at our dinner table?" Abbey asked. "The girls could use your information about what's going on with the fashions in town. Things like styles and color. What's the latest look for the young ladies?"

The soldiers laughed and Sergeant McKinley stood up and did a pirouette around the porch. "This is as close as we can come to the styles and fashions that's going around our part of the world."

Everyone got a laugh out of Sergeant McKinley's performance. Abbey knew that time was passing fast and the bad news had to come sooner or later. She wanted to relieve her mind of all these unknown images about Brady as soon as possible. She really wanted to crawl back in a corner and bawl her eyes out.

"Miss Abbey," Colonel Moss said. "We've come here for a very important mission. We've been close friends with Brady Wells for many years and we felt it was our duty to bring you the latest news."

Abbey stood up and walked to the porch railing wrapping her arms around one of the bracing post. Tears filled her eyes, as she looked down the empty roadway that brought every kind of information to the ranch. "You can tell me the truth," Abbey said. "My heart has hardened to the point that closure might help me cope with it."

"We were sent ahead of the column to warn you what you should be expecting anything and not to let the news place you in an unusual situation," Colonal Moss said.

Then the long line of blue uniforms came into sight. The riders were in columns of two and the parade of soldiers was slowly making their way toward the farmhouse. The flag was flying above the column causing Abbey to take a deep breath. All the workers had stopped their work and gathered around Abbey. The women had come from the house and they filled the porch with their presents. Silence filled the air and Abbey couldn't hold back her tears.

Abbey had heard how the army brought their dead soldiers home in a magnificent ceremony but this was enough to take here breath away. She couldn't take it any more, her heart was about to burst when she sat down in a chair with the help of Colonel Moss.

The columns split open as a rider rode to the front of the advancing soldiers. Then the rider kicked his horse in the flanks and the horse jumped to a run. The crowd finally got a look at the rider and cheers rose from the crowd.

"Abbey," Martha Sigils said. "It's him, it's Mr. Wells."

Abbey stood up and wiped the tears from her eyes as she tried to focus her stare on the faceless rider. Then her faded sight suddenly focused on the face of Brady Wells.

There was no strength left in her legs as she dropped to the wooden boards of the porch. The darkness seemed to last for only a minute when she opened her eyes and looked into the eyes of her greatest love, Brady Wells.

About the Author

While serving with the U.S. Air Force I was able to travel throughout the western states collecting as much data as I could on the western movement. While teaching U. S. History, I was able to combine the knowledge of my travels with the knowledge of my studies to create my version of the wild and exciting west.

I hope I have come up with the right combination that will give my readers many hours of enjoyment. I have tried to relay my feelings of what I believe it would have been like moving west during the high times of the American cowboy. Their dazzling exploits lasted for only one generation but made an impression that will last for an eternity.

The true life of the cowboy has been handed down in written form since the mid-1800s and I only hope I do the cowboy justice when I put them on paper and bring them to life in the glamorous style that I believed they played to bringing this country together.

Don Wingfield